Love on a Midsummer NIGHT

CHRISTY ENGLISH

sourcebooks
casablanca

Published by Sourcebooks Casablanca, an imprint of Sourcebooks, Inc.
P.O. Box 4410, Naperville, Illinois 60567-4410
(630) 961-3900
Fax: (630) 961-2168
www.sourcebooks.com

Printed and bound in the United States of America
VP 10 9 8 7 6 5 4 3 2 1

For my brother, Barry English,
who makes me laugh
And for my godmother, Vena Miller,
who loves my books

ACT I

"The course of true love never did run smooth…"

A Midsummer Night's Dream
Act 1, Scene 1

One

ARABELLA DARLINGTON, DUCHESS OF HAWTHORNE, stood beside her husband's coffin. As she left a small spray of white roses on the lid, she looked up to find the only man she had ever loved staring at her from the second pew.

Raymond Olivier, Earl of Pembroke, watched her from a distance, his dark blue eyes devouring her. His shoulders were broader than when she had seen him last, his hair longer, the blond waves falling into his eyes the way they had ten years before. The day she had left him to marry another, she had told herself to forget him. During the numb, lifeless years of her marriage, she had almost succeeded.

There was a worldliness about him now that seemed to have nothing to do with the boy she had known. He sat beside his acknowledged mistress, some actress dressed in vibrant emerald green that set off the deep red of her hair. Arabella could not believe that the man she had once loved had brought his doxy to her husband's funeral. But in spite of lines on his face and the dissipation that seemed to roll off his body in waves, he was still so beautiful that the sight of him stole her breath.

The Archbishop of Canterbury intoned another blessing, the eulogy complete. She stepped back as William Darlington, the new Duke of Hawthorne, placed his hand on her arm, the chill of his touch making her shiver. She shrank from her husband's nephew, but his gloved hand did not drop from her elbow.

She still felt Raymond's eyes on her, but she could not meet his gaze. She could not acknowledge his presence with that woman at his side. She felt her legs tremble, and she straightened her knees in an effort to shore them up.

She moved to leave the church, Hawthorne still shadowing her. The funeral was over, and there would be no condolences after the service. Her husband's heir had made it clear to all that the duchess would grieve alone. The London *ton* seemed ready to agree to this stricture, but Raymond Olivier, Lord Pembroke, ignored it.

"Arabella."

Raymond stood directly in her path, blocking her way to the door. He had left his doxy behind in the pew when he stepped into the aisle. She felt Hawthorne tense beside her.

"Raymond."

His name slipped from her unguarded lips before she could catch it and hold it back. He seemed to stand too close, though he was actually a decorous distance from her. It was as if time stood still, and the beat of her heart with it. She could take in the scent of cinnamon on his skin, and the heat of his body seemed to engulf her. She took an involuntary step back, but she knew that there was no place for her to go, no way to run from Raymond Olivier.

"I am sorry for your loss."

His words were strangled, inadequate, but they moved her to tears. She blinked hard and swallowed the lump that lodged in her throat. Her love for him was a phantom she thought she had conquered, a shadow that rose to life again as she looked at him.

"Thank you."

She searched his face for pity, for some trace of all they had been to each other. His eyes were bloodshot, their lids reddened as if with weeping. She knew well, better than most, that he had no cause to mourn her husband. No doubt his eyes were red from drink. His clothing was immaculate, his cravat well tied, his bottle-green coat smooth across his shoulders. But there was an air of hopelessness about him that had nothing to do with death and everything to do with the way he chose to live. He had turned from all decent society years ago and ran with a fast set, drinking and indulging himself both in London and on the Continent. The old biddies who had come to console her upon her husband's death had spoken of little else, of how a great name had fallen into disrepute, of how Pembroke's father had been a drunken lout, and now his son followed him.

But that day, as Arabella looked past the bloodshot veins, all she could see in Raymond's eyes was sorrow and an unspoken longing that reminded her of her own pain. No doubt her mourning veil was obscuring her vision. The pain she thought she saw on his face might only be a trick of the dim light.

"Arabella, I must speak with you."

His voice had taken on a strange note of urgency. Arabella almost raised her veil so that she might see him better. Before she could move or speak again, she felt Hawthorne's heavy hand on her arm.

"Her Grace is unavailable for private speech, Lord Pembroke. If you wish, you may write a letter of condolence. My man will see that she receives it."

Pembroke's gaze hardened like granite, as the sympathy of the moment before vanished like so much smoke. For one heady moment, she thought that Raymond might be jealous of Hawthorne's hand on her arm. But then she realized that what she saw in his eyes was not jealousy of the duke, but contempt for her.

Raymond stepped back and gave an exaggerated bow, including the new Duke of Hawthorne in the gesture with an air of negligence, as if telling them both to go to the devil. She opened her mouth to speak, not knowing when, if ever, she might see Raymond again, but her nephew's hand was beneath her elbow, propelling her forward. She almost tripped on her skirts as he drew her down the long nave of the church. No one else moved to speak, but all watched her pass as if she were an exotic animal in a menagerie, as if, now that her illustrious husband was dead, she was no longer worth acknowledging.

Her husband's nephew half carried her down the

stairs that led from the cathedral's great door and raised her into his black lacquered coach without waiting for a footman to assist her.

She craned her neck and looked back as the carriage pulled away from St. Paul's, but all she could see were pigeons that had come to roost on the steps. No one had followed them out into the sun, not even Raymond.

❧

Arabella entered the house on Grosvenor's Square, Hawthorne trailing behind her. She was not sure why he had decided to come inside. Perhaps he meant to demonstrate his power over her yet again. Or perhaps he had simply come to Hawthorne House to look over all he would be getting.

She thought of Raymond and felt a hint of something like hope. She pushed aside the thought of his contempt and focused only on the feeling that rose within her, like a sleeping dove that just now began to stir. The ache of the loss of him woke with it. It had been so long since she had felt anything but numbness that she savored the pain and the hope together. All was not lost if she could feel something, anything, again. Then she looked at Hawthorne and pushed both hope and pain aside. There was room in her life only for survival.

"You were very kind to escort me home, Your Grace," she said, her voice even, her tone empty. "With your permission, I will retire. I find that my head aches. It has been a long day." As she curtsied, Arabella kept her eyes downcast so she would not have to look at him.

Hawthorne laid his silver-tipped walking stick on a table by the door, along with a small bouquet of flowers. He straightened his morning coat, smoothing away nonexistent wrinkles. He ignored her words as if she had not spoken. "It was a decent service, I thought. Though the archbishop droned on too long for my taste."

Arabella felt a splinter of fire in her breast. The archbishop had been kind to her. He had been the only one at the service to weep.

"The archbishop is a good man," Arabella said.

"Yes. It is surprising that he has prospered."

Arabella raised her eyes to find Hawthorne staring at her, his cold gray gaze weighing her, judging her. She wondered for a moment if something about her appearance was amiss. Under his heavy scrutiny, she wanted to reach up and cover her face again with the crepe veil of her mourning bonnet.

Through an extreme force of will, she stayed still and silent. She could not bear the sight of him. Soon she would not have to bear the sight of him ever again. His solicitor would deal with her finances, allotting an income from her dower portion, and she would go home to Derbyshire. She could not get away from this accursed place soon enough.

Hawthorne crossed the room until he was standing in front of her.

Arabella held her breath. It was the second time in the same day that he had stood so near. His presence was oppressive. She felt as if he had drawn the air out of the room. She took as deep a breath as she might, her stays clutching her ribs like a vise. As Hawthorne drew close to her again, Arabella had to suppress the need to run.

His long-fingered hand reached for her chin and tilted her face up so that she was forced to look at him.

"How lovely your eyes are," he said.

Arabella jumped as if he had struck her, but his fingers gripped her jaw. He did not let her go.

"You are still quite young. Twenty-five, are you not?"

"Twenty-seven," she said.

"Ah, well. No matter. When there is money to recommend a match, then trifles like age can be overlooked."

She felt her nausea rise, though she had eaten nothing that day. Surely she had heard him wrong. She swallowed hard and forced herself to speak.

"But I have no money, Your Grace."

"I beg to differ, Arabella. May I call you Arabella? Of course I may, as we are to be betrothed. You have my uncle's money, Arabella. One third of the income of the Duchy of Hawthorne, and the dower lands in Shropshire, along the Severn. Do you know how much income a third of the revenues from the Duchy of Hawthorne constitutes, Arabella?"

His fingers were like claws on her jaw, close to her throat. The cold gray of his eyes had begun to burn with the fire of anger. She had never seen an emotion in his face before.

Arabella wondered how she might get away from him, if she might calmly walk to the door as if it were any other spring day and she was going out to sit in her garden. The bellpull was ten feet away. Her small sitting room had never looked too large before. But today, for the first time, she wished it were smaller.

She kept her voice calm and even, hoping that her gaze was as bland. She had survived her childhood because she had been able to lie to her father and make him believe it. She would lie to this man now, until she could escape that room.

"No, Your Grace. I know nothing of money."

"You may rely on my word when I tell you it is a very great sum indeed."

He released her jaw then, and Arabella stayed where she was. She did not step back from him, nor did she rub the sore place where his fingers had dug into her flesh. She forced herself to breathe and to wait. If this man was anything like her father, she would have one moment in which she could move. She would have to wait for it and be ready.

The menace in his gaze and in his touch was now palpable, as if his malice stood beside her, a third person in the room to flank her, to keep her from escape.

"An engagement would not be proper, Your Grace, for another year at least," she said.

He smiled then, and she shuddered. There was something predatory behind his eyes that seemed to flare and warm as he looked at her. This time, he did not keep his gaze on the contours of her face, but let it rove over her body, as if he could see the curves of her flesh beneath the layers of bombazine and crepe. She felt as if a noxious odor had slipped into the room and realized that the look on his face held some blighted form of desire. For the first time since her father died, she felt real fear.

Arabella couldn't stop herself from taking a step

back. She bumped against the mahogany table, sloshing the pitcher of orange water set out for her.

"We will be secretly engaged for a few months only. I will not wait out a tedious year of mourning without even a taste of you," Hawthorne said. "During our engagement, you will retire to my house in Yorkshire where you will consider your future and be grateful for the opportunity to please me. We will wed, we will bed, and you will bear the next heir as you should have done ten years ago."

"And you will have my money," she said.

He smiled, and his smile chilled her more than his anger had done. "No, my dear. I will have all of *my* money. You will bear me sons. And all will be as it should."

He reached for her cheek, brushing it gently with one fingertip. She stood frozen under it, a rabbit in a snare, unable to move forward or back, or even to take a breath. "Uncle could not get sons on you," Hawthorne said, his voice heavy with lust. "He was too old, I fear, but you will find that I am not. There will be a son in your belly by next Christmas."

Hawthorne recalled himself then and stepped away from her, lowering his hand. He took up his hat and walking stick from where he had laid them on a table near the door as calmly as if the last few moments had never happened. He smoothed his already immaculate sleeves before setting his tall hat once more upon his head. He drew on his gloves, the silver ball on the end of his walking stick gleaming in his hand.

"I give you tonight to pack your things for the move to Yorkshire. It is a pleasant place, if rather rustic. I will come to see you at the Christmas holidays, and then to collect you next spring. I thought we might honeymoon in Scotland. Another lovely, if somewhat rustic, place. I think you will enjoy it."

"And if I refuse your suit?" She raised her voice, trying to inject a strength she did not feel.

Hawthorne's smile turned cool. "That would be unfortunate. Yorkshire is a world apart, you know. Quite wild. So many accidents happen on the roadways in these troubled times. Highwaymen. Robberies. Sometimes ladies run afoul of such creatures. If such an accident were to occur, I would not be responsible for the consequences."

The chill that shook her now had nothing to do with cold and everything to do with fear. Still, her years in her father's house had taught her to reveal nothing, to hold her ground in the face of danger, no matter how horrible. Her voice was still steady when she spoke the unthinkable.

"And if a fatal accident befalls me while I am in mourning, you will have my money anyway."

Hawthorne's smile warmed, a lick of flame behind the gray of his eyes. "Indeed. Your money, as you call it, would then be mine. But I would not be able to touch you. I think my solution is far more elegant. Do you not agree?"

Arabella stood in silence, trying to take in the fact that her husband's last living relative had threatened her life so that he might get his hands on her widow's portion. And yet, he seemed to want her, as no man had wanted her in years. She thought back over the few times she had seen him in her husband's house, the few times he had reached for her hand when he need not have done so. She thought of the cool touch of his lips through the soft kid of her gloves. Her bile rose.

"I will come for you on the morrow and see you off in my own coach. Sadly, I cannot make the journey with you. I must stay in London and see to estate affairs. There is much to be done."

He left Arabella then, closing the door quietly behind him. The room around her was unchanged, her own quiet haven on the first floor of her husband's house. The rose-colored settee was still drawn close to the fire, her mother's antique lace still graced the sideboard.

She remembered the flowers he had left lying on the table by the door. She approached the cluster of blossoms slowly as if they were an adder that might rise to strike. No soft irises lay waiting for her, but deep purple belladonna, deadly nightshade—flowers that brought nothing but death.

Though it was May, it was cold in her husband's house. A small fire burned in the grate. Arabella lifted the spray of poisonous flowers and cast them into the flames. The fire flared and then continued to burn as if nothing had happened, as if the new Duke of Hawthorne had never been there at all.

Arabella carefully drew off her black cotton gloves and tossed them into the fire. She poured the last of the orange water over her hands, then dried her fingers with her handkerchief. Her husband's initials were embroidered on the linen, along with her own.

Gerald had been sixty when they wed, seventy

when he died. He had not loved her or she him, but he had protected her from the evils of the world. She saw now that she would have to learn to protect herself.

She felt a jolt of unaccustomed longing as Raymond's face rose before her. She wished she might return to him and right the wrongs that had come between them. But too many years had passed. It was already too late.

She stared at her reflection in the looking glass above the sideboard. Her honey-colored hair was tucked away beneath her widow's bonnet, the black dyed straw leeching every hint of color from her face. The ice blue of her eyes was the only color left to her, the color she had been born with. Duchess for ten years, she would take little else with her when she left this place.

Two

ARABELLA GAVE HER MAID STRICT INSTRUCTIONS TO throw out the remaining orange water at once, not into the garden, but down the privy. Maude's soft blue eyes looked surprised, but she promised faithfully to do as her mistress said. The girl had not managed to close the door behind her when Stevens appeared.

"Forgive me, Your Grace, but there is a visitor."

Raymond Olivier burst into the room behind her husband's butler. His eyes pierced her like a blade, and for a moment she lost her breath. She thought of the woman he had brought to her husband's funeral. She tried to force her anger to rise, but instead, she felt an unexpected joy at the sight of him.

Stevens stood in the doorway, frowning like thunder. Raymond brought the scent of the outdoors with him, but the clean smell of spring was almost covered over by the scent of brandy.

"Thank you, Stevens. You may leave us."

Her husband's butler hesitated. He no doubt feared to cross the orders left by Hawthorne. But she would never turn Raymond Olivier away.

"I will ring if I have need of you," Arabella said.

Stevens bowed low, giving Lord Pembroke an evil look as he closed the door behind him.

"Stevens is very strict," Arabella said. "And I am not supposed to receive anyone. The duke felt it inappropriate for me to entertain company while I am in mourning."

"And your lover? Will he be turned away?"

"I beg your pardon?"

"Who is he?"

Raymond stepped close, but she did not feel threatened as she had with Hawthorne. She took in the scent of cinnamon on his skin, the sweet flavor that had not changed, mingling with the scent of brandy on his breath. She trembled and took one step back.

"I have no lover, my lord."

"Don't toy with me, Arabella. Tell me who he is. Or is there more than one?"

His eyes were even redder than they had been hours before. Brandy seemed to leach from his pores as if he had not just drunk it, but bathed in it. She should feel repulsed. The scent of the brandy reminded her of her father in his cups. But Arabella did not feel revulsion. All she felt was sorrow, and the certain knowledge that she could do nothing to help him. She had thrown away her rights to his good graces long ago. She had written to him, not long after her marriage, explaining all that had happened, but she had never received a reply. He had disowned her and no doubt had wished her to the devil. No doubt he still did. She could see no evidence of the boy she had loved in this man's face, save for the dark blue of his eyes.

"They speak of you at my club as if you are a common whore."

Arabella flinched as if he had struck her. She thought of the few *ton* parties she had attended, the darting eyes of all she had seen there, their false smiles and malicious whispers. Those people fed on rumors and innuendo. Could it be that now that her husband was dead, they had turned to feed on her? She sat down before her knees gave way.

Raymond pushed his dark blond hair out of his eyes. He stood over her, his gaze roving across her body, just as Hawthorne's had not half an hour before. But this time, in spite of the madness of his words, she felt a warm flush rise over her cheeks, heat flooding her throat and the tops of her breasts beneath her gown. He sat down beside her, taking her hand in his.

His hand was so much larger than her own that his palm engulfed hers. That at least had not changed. Nor had his warmth or the strength of his touch. Drink had not taken that from him. Arabella almost lost herself in that moment, in spite of the brandy on his clothes, in spite of the insults he had just moments before offered her. No matter what he said, this man was Raymond Olivier. Before he had inherited his title, when he had been a castoff of his father's, he had been her one refuge in a hostile world. She could not bring herself to forget.

"I've come to offer you my protection," Pembroke said. "You look as if you need it."

Arabella could not understand him. But then he raised her bare hand to his lips and pressed his tongue into the center of her palm.

Pleasure shot through her until she almost shook with it. She had not been touched so intimately in years, if ever. Her breath caught in her throat, any words of protest lodged behind it. She could not speak or move, but sat still, bound as tight as a coney in a snare.

"I know you're Hawthorne's now. I'm no duke, but I think I can offer you more pleasure than he can."

Arabella watched his fingers as they played over hers. His hand was gentle on hers, his touch soothing even as it enflamed. She had never felt such desire before, not even when she was seventeen. She had always thought desire and all that came with it the province of men. She wondered now if she had been wrong.

"If you're looking to change lovers, I will take you up. You'll need new clothes, and you'll have to leave off your mourning, but that can't be any worse than sleeping with Hawthorne."

"Get out." Her voice was hoarse, and she swallowed hard. She felt as if her mouth had gone dry, as if her tongue would not work properly. All she could take in was the scent of his skin and the heat of his hand on hers. She tried to pull away.

Lord Pembroke looked at her as if she were a morsel of marzipan that he might take upon his tongue. He let go of her hand, slowly, as if to say he knew he did not have to relinquish it but did so only because it pleased him. He did not rise to leave, but lounged back against her settee as if the room and all in it belonged to him.

"You won't even offer me a drop of sherry before I go?"

"You've had quite enough to drink already."

Pembroke laughed at that, and for a moment it was as if the years had dropped away. It seemed to her that she heard a hint of the boy he had been in the depths of that laughter, rusty and dissipated as it was. The sounds drew her toward him on the settee, but he was already on his feet, moving toward the door.

He turned to look back at her, his hand on the knob. "When you tire of Hawthorne's bed, come to me."

She felt a frisson of heat pass between them across the length of her sitting room. He was gone then, and she sat alone staring into the dying fire. The heat on her skin vanished as soon as he was gone.

For a long moment there was no sound in the room but the ticking of the Dresden clock on the mantel. Shepherdesses frolicked with their lambs, frozen in porcelain as they danced around the clock's face for eternity. She got to her feet and picked up that hideous piece of china and dropped it into the fireplace, where it shattered on the stone tiles.

She shook with anger and leftover desire. She had no business feeling lust for any man, much less Pembroke. Whatever he had once been, whatever they had once been to each other, he was a different man now, and she was a different woman.

She blinked back tears of frustration. She was sick of tears. She had spent her entire life weeping in helplessness. No longer. She was her own woman now, and neither Pembroke nor Hawthorne nor the entire *ton* would keep her from living her life as she saw fit. Let them spread evil tidings all around her. She was going home. They would never find her there.

Her father's money had come from the slave trade. To be a tradesman was bad enough in the eyes of the nobility, but to trade in human flesh and misery was the lowest a man could stoop. Her father had stooped that low, and gladly. Her mother had been the youngest daughter of an earl caught up in debts. Her father had bought her mother, paying the earl's gambling debts. Her mother had not lived long, but even her gentle breeding had not afforded Mr. Swanson the entrée into Society that he had hoped for, and he had never let her forget it.

The thought of her mother brought real tears to her eyes. Sometimes she still woke with the touch of her mother's hand on her hair in her dreams, the phantom woman whose face she could no longer remember. No one in the *ton* knew of her father's house in Derbyshire, save Pembroke and Angelique, and they would never tell. She would go to her father's estate and hide herself away, and forget that London Society had ever existed.

As she wiped her tears and blew her nose with her black-edged handkerchief, Angelique Beauchamp, Countess of Devereaux, burst into the room in a swirl of royal blue silk.

"You've been weeping."

Angelique moved with the same graceful elegance wherever she was, in a ballroom, in her own house, and now as she stepped into Arabella's sitting room. Her dark curls brushed her shoulders as she tossed her cloak onto a nearby chair.

"Don't tell me that you're crying for the old man? I would not have thought it possible."

Arabella laughed in spite of herself, the humor in her friend's eyes warming her like a good fire in winter. No one ever looked past Angelique's beauty to see the woman who lived beneath it. The countess was the loneliest woman Arabella knew, save for herself.

"You must take some tea," Angelique said, ringing for the maid. She wrapped one slender arm around Arabella's waist and led her back to the settee. "I saw that vulture Hawthorne leave. I drove around the square and waited until he had gone to knock on your door."

Maude brought in a tray of tea and biscuits, then knelt to throw coal on the fire. Angelique drew a cushion from another chair to place behind Arabella's back, then poured a cup as Arabella liked it, with a touch of milk and no sugar. She tucked a biscuit onto the saucer, iced gingerbread still warm from the oven.

"I can eat nothing," Arabella said.

"You will eat that," Angelique answered. "You need more sweetness in your life."

Angelique watched with the eyes of a hawk as Arabella took a bite of the biscuit and a fortifying sip of tea. The warmth and sweetness suffused her with a sense of well-being.

Satisfied with watching Arabella eat, Angelique poured her own tea, adding no sugar and no milk. She did not touch the gingerbread herself, but set another biscuit on her friend's saucer.

"I have bad news," Angelique said. "I came at once, because you need to hear it."

"More bad news?" Arabella asked. She thought of the rumors, and of the bizarre sight of lust in Hawthorne's cold gray eyes. It was almost as if she could smell the poisoned flowers he had left for her, and she shuddered.

"'Trouble comes not in single spies, but in battalions,'" Angelique quipped.

Arabella smiled. "*Hamlet*. Your favorite."

"*Macbeth* is my favorite and you know it. But to come to the point, Hawthorne is putting it about that you are a loose woman who played your husband false. That all the years of your marriage, you pretended to be a quiet, biddable wife when all along you have been the whore of Babylon."

Hawthorne was hemming her in, closing off all means of escape, leaving nothing to chance.

"He wants to make sure you stay isolated. He has put it about that you are leaving for Yorkshire in the morning in disgrace, that he has discovered your affairs and has taken a firm hand."

"Affairs? I have never touched another man but Gerald."

"I know that. And you know that. But a quiet wife who in secret has been a whore for years makes a much better story than a virtuous widow."

Arabella's tea had grown cold in her hands. She set the cup aside. "He is forcing me to marry him."

"He'll keep your widow's portion."

"Yes. And he wants me." Arabella shuddered.

Angelique could not mask her disgust. She was on her feet then, circling like a caged tigress who could find no way out of her prison. "You cannot marry that man. You need a protector. Before, I would have gone to Anthony. He would know what to do."

No one else would have heard a change in the melodious tones of her friend's voice when she spoke her old lover's name, but Arabella could. Her friend's heart had been broken, and it would not mend.

"You cannot go to Anthony Carrington."

"I would, for you. But he is in Shropshire with his wife. They left yesterday, after the christening of their son."

"I could contact Gerald's solicitor. He might help me."

"Mr. Brooks is not Gerald's solicitor; he is the solicitor for the Duke of Hawthorne."

Arabella knew what that meant, and she knew that Angelique was right. She had no money and no recourse under the law. She had five pounds left from her quarter allowance, barely enough to trim a new bonnet, much less to start a new life.

Gerald had protected her widow's portion. He had kept her as safe as he knew how, but she had no way of protecting herself from his heir.

"Pembroke is in the city," Angelique said.

"I know. He was here just before you were."

"Pembroke would protect you," Angelique said.

"No," Arabella said. "He offered to make me his mistress…"

"Perfect!"

Arabella laughed at the outlandishness of it, her friend pushing her into the arms of any man. She set her empty cup down and took up another biscuit. "I will be no man's mistress," she said. "Nor will I marry again."

"What will you do?" Angelique said. "I've got a bit

of cash on hand, but not enough to hide you until my ship comes into port. You might come to Shropshire with me."

"I am going to hire a carriage and go home to Derbyshire."

Angelique sat down as if her knees had given way. "Won't Hawthorne follow you?"

"My father's house has been all but abandoned. No sane person would go there. And Hawthorne doesn't know it exists."

"He knows you didn't spring fully formed from under a rock."

Arabella laughed again. "True enough. But my father has never been mentioned among the *ton*. It was my mother Gerald always spoke of, and her connection with the Earl of Amesbury. Swanson House might as well have never existed."

"I'd rather you came to Shropshire. Hawthorne might know more than you think."

Arabella wondered if he had spent years watching her, waiting for her husband to die before he closed in. The thought made her nauseous. "I am sure there are a few retainers left at my father's house. I could never live there again, but I remember where he hid his gold. He would never list that money in his will, or anywhere else, so Gerald may not have found it. It won't be much, but it will be enough to start my own life."

"Where, for God's sake?"

"Anywhere but here."

"Anywhere but Yorkshire, with the duke," Angelique said.

"Yes."

"Whatever I can do, you have only to ask."

Arabella reached for her friend's hand. Angelique's tapered, manicured fingers were cold, and Arabella warmed them between her own.

"You have been my friend all these years, when I had no one else."

"And you've been mine," Angelique said. "My only friend, I think."

Arabella kissed her on the cheek very gently, a glancing touch, like a hummingbird's wing. Angelique Beauchamp did not startle or flinch away as she would have done if anyone else had tried to touch her.

Angelique tried to break the moment, for sentimentality was something she could not tolerate, in herself or anyone. "So you will not accept Pembroke's offer?"

There was a glint of laughter in the other woman's eyes, but beneath that, a real concern for her. Angelique was the only woman alive who could guess what Pembroke meant to her, even after all these years.

Arabella laughed in spite of the ache beneath her heart, feigning a lightness she did not feel. "No indeed. I'll leave at first light for Derbyshire. Lord Pembroke will have to content himself with the doxies and actresses of London, for I will have none of him."

"Never say never," Angelique said, her lips beginning to curve in the mysterious smile she was famous for.

"I did not say 'never,'" Arabella answered. "If I have learned anything in my life, it is not to tempt the Fates."

✥

Before Arabella rose to go to her room to sleep her last night in her husband's house, she thought of all the things she must take with her when she left, all the things she could not live without. Her mother's locket and gold chain. Her mother's lace. Pembroke's ruby ring. She stepped over to the sideboard and took the lace up, folding it carefully.

Her heart was thundering in her chest, so loud that she almost could hear nothing else. She had never stepped out on her own before. If Hawthorne had not forced her hand, she would not have had to do so now. She would pack a small bag and leave at dawn, hiring an unmarked carriage to take her on the North Road. With the money Angelique had given her, she would travel slowly until she came to Derbyshire, and home. She would not think beyond the journey. Too much freedom and too much hope warred in her breast. She could not contain them, so she pushed them aside.

She did not know what she would do if Hawthorne followed her. She prayed as she lay down to sleep that night that as soon as she disappeared from the capital, he would forget her. Surely, for once, the Fates would smile on her.

In spite of her need to wake before dawn, she slept deep. She would have slept all night had not the sound of her husband's bedroom door woke her.

She had not heard the door between their rooms open in years, but Arabella remembered well the first hideous year of their marriage, those nights when she never knew when Gerald would come until she heard that door. He would lie on top of her, his skeletal hands on her body, lifting her nightgown. She did not shudder at the memory, but lay still between the soft sheets of her bed, listening.

Hawthorne stood over her in the dim light of the lamp.

Arabella tried not to show the fear that instantly flooded her. "Your Grace, I fear you have lost your way."

"No, Arabella. I have found it."

Hawthorne made his way through the shadows closer to her bed. He was dressed in evening clothes, but his cravat was askew and his black coat thrown open. Arabella wondered idly why he always dressed like an undertaker. It was then that she saw the glint of the knife in his hand.

Her heart was pounding and her throat was dry with fear. She swallowed convulsively and forced herself to sit up, bringing the bedclothes with her to shield her body from his eyes. She thought frantically for what she might use to hold him off, what words might persuade him to lay that weapon down. Her death was like a shadow, a phantom in the room come to claim her. Her terror rose to choke her, or she would have screamed.

Hawthorne stopped within a foot of the bed, laying his lamp down. He reached for her with the hand that did not hold the knife. She flinched, but his fingers only took up her honey-colored braid where it fell across her shoulder. He hefted the weight of her hair, fingering the end of it as if testing a bolt of fine silk. Arabella felt her nausea rise, bile coating her throat and mouth. She swallowed again, moving closer to her bedside table. Would any of the household staff help her if she screamed? She swallowed again, desperate to find her voice.

He reached out with the knife then, and with one expert flick of his wrist cut away the top three buttons of her nightgown. She felt the cool night air on her throat and on the tops of her breasts. His eyes gleamed at the sight of her exposed flesh, as if she were a feast he were about to devour.

She would not die here. She did not know how she would live, but she was damned if this man would be her doom. Death could come back another night, for she was going nowhere.

"I would have you now," Hawthorne said, "before I take you to Yorkshire. I find a year is too long to wait."

"Never is not long enough, my lord."

Arabella took up the first thing her fingertips touched on her bedside table, an unlit lamp recently filled with oil.

As Hawthorne bent as if to kiss her, the knife still in his hand, Arabella raised the heavy lamp and brought it down on the back of his head.

The porcelain base shattered against his skull, coating his head, her nightgown, and the bedclothes in a layer of flammable oil. He fell against her, and for one horrible moment she thought she had failed. But when he did not move, she pushed him off her, drawing her legs from beneath him, climbing over him to get off the bed.

His knife fell from his fingers, but not before it sliced into the skin of her wrist. She gasped in pain, her blood staining the sheets, for the blade was razor sharp. Had he slit her throat, at least it would have been quick.

She pushed this thought from her mind, slicing away a piece of the bedclothes and hastily, clumsily binding her wrist. She wrapped the bloody knife in another bit of linen before she turned back to the duke.

For a moment, she hoped he was dead. But when she saw him breathing in spite of his bloody head wound, she knew it was for the best. Never leave an enemy alive behind you, some Persian had written. She felt the weight of the duke's blade in her hand. Well, the long-dead Persian might be right, but she was no murderer. She could not kill a man, now or ever.

She stood in the center of the room. No way now but forward. She had struck down one of the most powerful men in the kingdom, an intimate of the Prince Regent. No one would care that he had tried to rape her in the dark, or that he perhaps might have killed her after.

Well, Angelique would care. She would be incensed, but at one word from the duke, her interests in the West Indies would be reduced to nothing, her livelihood cut off. In spite of what many thought, all Angelique's wealth came from trade. Arabella would not repay ten years of loyalty by ruining the finances of the only friend she had ever had.

She quickly dressed in a plain gown of black wool, drawing the long sleeve down to cover the wound on her wrist, her thoughts turning frantically. No time even to wash it, or bind it properly. She would deal with it later.

She had belonged to her father, then her husband. No matter how many dukes came at her with a knife in the dark, she was free now, and she would stay free. She would never belong to a man again. But there was no way to survive completely alone.

There was only one place she could go, only one man powerful enough who might take the trouble to hide her from Hawthorne until she could get away. No matter how she had betrayed him in the past, Pembroke would help her. She had to believe that. For if he turned her away, both his soul and her life were utterly lost.

Three

PEMBROKE LEFT TITANIA PRETENDING TO SLEEP ON HIS bed. His mistress had insatiable appetites, but she also had the courtesy to allow him to brood in peace.

The Hellfire Club was meeting in Mayfair, and Pembroke was not in attendance. On any other day there was nothing he liked better than to join his more raucous friends to sample their chosen courtesans away from the prying eyes of the London *ton*. But after seeing Arabella, he could not face a crowd.

Tonight the new Duke of Hawthorne was throwing an impromptu fete with the Club, a celebration of his elevation to the dukedom. He would drink and whore and enjoy himself, while rumors circulated throughout London, ruining Arabella's life.

Pembroke sat smoking his cheroot, trying without success to calm his temper. The lazy spirals of tobacco smoke circled his head, rising until they dissipated into the darkness. A fire burned in the grate. His favorite brandy sat by his elbow, poured by his butler, Codington, who followed him everywhere, from one house to another, from the country into town.

Codington had done more to raise Pembroke when he was a child than his father ever had. Only Codington's firm hand had kept Pembroke in any sort of acquaintance with the straight and narrow; only Codington's compassion had tempered Pembroke's fury as a boy. His father had beaten him, and Codington had dressed the wounds. Until the summer Pembroke turned eighteen, when he had run away to join the army.

Pembroke could not think of that summer. He thought of that summer only when drink no longer blunted his wits, when the women no longer distracted him. As the ormolu clock on the mantel struck two, Pembroke took up his drink and downed it.

Arabella. He had not seen her in years but remembered the exact color of her ice blue eyes. Those eyes were cold, aloof, as if she had never felt any emotion other than quiet calm. But years ago, Pembroke had held her in his arms. He had kissed her delicate lips until the roses came into her pale cheeks, until those eyes glowed like blue flame, warming him as no other fire ever had, nor ever would again.

Pembroke cast his empty glass into the hearth where the fine crystal splintered into shards. He sighed and cursed himself. No doubt as soon as he went back to bed, Codington would have a maid down on her knees, cleaning up the mess he had made. One of the realities of being an earl was that other people were obligated to clean up the messes he left behind.

A scratching at the door made Pembroke jump.

"There is a lady to see you, my lord," Codington

announced. "She gives the name of the Duchess of Hawthorne."

Hope pierced him, and he felt his lust rise out of nowhere, as if her name had conjured it. He told himself not to be a fool, that she had left him without a backward glance and had betrayed him for a duchess's coronet.

But he wanted her anyway, in spite of that, because of it. With Arabella in his bed at last, he could finally conquer his demons, his old illusions of her. He could have her and move on.

Codington bowed, and without another moment passing, she was there, the woman he had spent his adult life running away from, the memory of whom would never leave him, not even ten years later, not even when he slept.

"Arabella."

He had no right to use her given name, but he could not seem to help it.

"Lord Pembroke. You are kind to receive me without warning, so late at night."

She spoke as if he had not seen her that afternoon, as if he had not propositioned her in her own sitting room. Her voice was still like honey, its sweetness rich and resonant, the one thing about her that had not changed.

She was smaller than he remembered. In spite of the layers of silk and black bombazine, she looked as if she might blow away with the next strong wind. Her face was covered by the thick crepe of her mourning veil.

Codington withdrew, closing the door to the library with an emphatic click. Pembroke would have smiled at his butler's censure, but he could not look away from Arabella.

He wanted her, and now she had come. His heart began to race, his breath to come short. He felt suddenly like a boy of eighteen, an untried youth. He shook his head to clear it, but his heart kept pounding.

She carried a heavy leather bag, a satchel too large for her to hold. She hefted it awkwardly, trying to find purchase, struggling to be graceful and failing. Pembroke fought to control his breathing as he crossed the room and took it from her. It was heavy in his hand and should have been completely unwieldy in hers. He laid the bag aside then stepped back, gesturing to an armchair by the fire.

She did not sit but stood before him still in silence. Only then did she lift her veil. Only then did he see her eyes.

Pembroke turned his back on her. To cover his shaking hands, he poured himself a brandy. He poured two glasses, one for her, and one for him. His voice sounded properly sardonic in his own ears when he finally broke the silence.

"You honor me, Your Grace. So you've changed your mind? You've decided to take me up on my offer?"

Arabella stared at him as if he were the interloper, as if he had intruded in her home in the small hours of the morning and not the other way around.

"I have not, and you know it."

Pembroke tried to shore up his defenses against her. But her voice was a soft as he knew her body must be. He had wanted this woman all his life simply because she was the one woman he could not have. The one woman who did not want him.

He felt the knife of her old betrayal slide into his heart, a smooth, unexpected caress of pain. His breath was gone as he stood in front of her, two useless glasses warming in his hands.

He thought he saw pain in her eyes, a pain that mirrored his own. But in the next moment, that pain was gone, and he was left alone in his.

"If you are not here to become my mistress, why do you trouble me?"

"Hawthorne came to my house."

"Indeed. It is his house now."

She raised one hand and waved his words away. "No. He came at night. While I was sleeping."

Pembroke felt the floor beneath his feet tilt as if he stood on the deck of a ship. The room righted itself but not before his long-buried jealous fury rose to blind him. He thought he had killed that anger, but here it was again, rising to consume him. He could not bear the thought of another man touching her.

"Hawthorne is your lover. I assume he is often there at night and stays on into the morning."

If it was possible, Arabella grew even paler. She must have become a consummate actress in the years since he had last seen her to affect such ladylike horror. But then he remembered. He had once thought she loved him. No doubt she had been playacting then, too.

"He forced himself on me."

Pembroke shook with rage, with the sudden desire to take his cavalry sword and run the duke through.

He breathed hard, fighting for control. Then he remembered that this woman was Hawthorne's lover, come to draw him into their quarrel. Why she would foist herself on him after all these years did not bear examining. She had been a liar then, and no doubt she was a liar now. "Why should I believe a word you say?"

Arabella met his eyes, and he saw that there were tears in hers. He cursed himself and turned away but not before his rage began to give way a little. No doubt she was a liar, and yet she still had the power to move him.

She drew a package of linen from the pocket of her cloak. She unwound the ragged cloth to reveal a knife with a wicked blade. "The duke brought this with him," she said.

She raised her sleeve next. A wound had bled through the hasty bandage, coloring the white with dark blood. Pembroke was on his feet in an instant, taking her arm in his hand, forcing himself to touch with a tenderness that belied the anger coursing through him. He feared for the first time in many years that he would fall into a rage from which he could not find his way back out. With great difficulty, he released her and pulled on the bell to ring for Codington.

Pembroke had fought many battles and had learned to control his anger so that it would not control him. A cool head in the midst of fury had saved his life more than once in Belgium, in Italy, in Spain. But now he stood in his own library, fighting his temper as if he were a boy again.

Arabella looked frail standing before his fireplace,

almost as if she might faint. No matter his own emotions, he was not a man who could watch a woman suffer and do nothing. He took his temper in hand, making certain that the black well of his rage was closed behind its wall of stone before he crossed the room to her and steeled himself, taking her arm gently.

Arabella jumped at his touch, and he knew that she had taken no lover. There had been talk at White's in the last few days of her wanton wildness, that a depth of fire was hidden beneath her widow's weeds.

Pembroke knew women well, and this was a woman who had been touched very little in the last ten years, and then not with tenderness or with passion. At least no touch had kindled passion in her. She was brittle, dried up, as if she might break between his hands.

Pembroke felt his heart bleed at the loss of her pliant sweetness, a sweetness that had no doubt been killed by the callous indifference of her husband. He pushed his pity aside. Whatever her husband had been, however the old duke had treated her, she had chosen him.

Arabella relaxed under his hand, and he felt as if he had been given a great gift: her trust. She moved obediently with him as he drew her toward the armchair next to the fire. Her small hands twisted together in their cotton gloves. He pressed her hands with both of his own, chafing them as if to warm them, gently so as not to disturb her bandage.

Startled, she met his eyes again, and he thought he saw a glimmer of the girl he once had known peek out at him from behind the veil of the past. He knew that girl was an illusion, but still he looked for her. He needed to get away from this woman, or he would keep searching her face for traces of the girl who had once loved him, the girl who had never existed.

Pembroke stepped back and handed her the glass of brandy he had placed at her elbow. He stood close by until she took the first sip. The brandy and the fire began to bring color back into her cheeks, so Pembroke withdrew to his own corner, where his brandy and cigarillo waited for him.

Codington came in and Pembroke asked for bandages and warm water. The butler did not raise an eyebrow but left as silently as he had entered.

"I can dress my wound myself," Arabella said. "I have no need of water."

"You have a great need of it," he answered. "And soap. I've seen too many wounds turn putrid on the battle field not to treat that one."

No matter what happened between him and Arabella in the next few moments, he knew that if he ever laid eyes on the duke again, he would kill him.

"How did you get away?"

"I struck him over the head with a lamp."

Pembroke laughed, a loud guffaw that shattered the quiet of the room. In spite of the dire circumstances, Arabella smiled. Codington brought the soap and water then, along with fresh bandages. Pembroke nodded his dismissal, though the butler's eyes lingered on her wound.

Once they were alone again, Pembroke knelt before her, gently peeling away the bloody linen. The blood had dried and had begun to stick to the flesh beneath. Pembroke soaked the bandage with water until it fell away. Arabella flinched at first under his hands, but as he worked, as she saw that he would not hurt her, she sat still under his ministrations, as trusting as a child.

Pembroke's heart was throbbing along the line where she had broken it, but he bit down on his pain and dressed her wound. He forced himself to speak lightly, as if he felt nothing. "I can't believe that little Arabella Swanson of Derbyshire brained the Duke of Hawthorne. But I admire your humor. I never would have thought you capable of making me laugh."

"I only tell the truth."

"And I am only the King of Lapland."

She stiffened, and he finished dressing her wound in silence. He rose to his feet then and crossed to his brandy, drinking the rest of it in one gulp. He was not sure he was strong enough to look at her again, so pale and vulnerable in his great armchair, but he knew that he must.

As he turned back, he saw that she was on her feet as well. "Thank you for your help, my lord. But I should not have come."

Pembroke mirrored her movements, keeping himself between her and the door. "Damn right you shouldn't have. You should keep your lovers' quarrels behind closed doors or find some other fool to dress your wounds. But we both know why you're really here."

Four

ARABELLA TOOK ONE STEP BACK AS PEMBROKE MOVED toward her, but her knees hit the chair behind her, blocking escape. Her arm throbbed, but she forgot her pain as he stepped close to her. All she could think of then was the scent of brandy on his breath, and all she could see were the red lines around the blue of his eyes.

Though he was the second man to approach her that night, she was not afraid of him. She wondered why that was as she stood and stared at the fury on his face. She had run from men's anger all her life, and when she could not run, she had hidden within herself. But now, standing with Pembroke, she did not feel threatened. Some secret part of her soul was certain that he would never hurt her. That knowledge more than anything held her where she was as his hands reached for her, as his great paws cupped her elbows and drew her toward him.

Pembroke seemed to take up all the air in the room. His black evening clothes were the height of elegance, his gold waistcoat gleaming against the black superfine of his trousers. But his cravat was gone and his coat with it. He stood in his shirtsleeves, the heat of his body radiating from him as from a small sun. Arabella lost her breath as his mouth came down on hers.

He did not devour her or press her too hard, as she thought he might. Instead, his lips were gentle, teasing her as they lightly moved across her mouth, imparting feather kisses to each corner, his breath warming her cheek as he pulled away.

"You taste like a sweetmeat," he said.

"All I ate today were ginger biscuits."

Arabella's voice was hoarse in her own ears. She did not sound like herself. She swallowed hard, staring up at him just as he stared down at her.

"You didn't come here to become my lover," Pembroke said.

"No. I did not."

He cast an errant lock of hair back so that it fell across his forehead, ready to obscure his vision again in the next moment. She wondered that he had never changed his hairstyle, not in all his years in the army. He had always cut it short, but the waves of his straw-blond hair fell into his eyes just as they always had.

During the summer they had spent together, she had wiled away one long afternoon, pressing her hand into those waves, smoothing them back, seeing if she might make them lie still through the force of her will and patience alone. She had failed at that and at so much else. Pembroke was irrepressible. It was one of the things she had always loved about him.

He stepped back suddenly and let her go. She straightened her sleeve over the new bandage and drew down the crepe veil of her bonnet until it covered her face. She crossed the room and lifted her heavy satchel, the bag that held the wreckage of her life. She had been a fool to come. This man did not even know her anymore. She did not know him. To ask for his help, to impose upon him in this manner was foolhardy.

She was safe from Hawthorne by now, surely. In a city as large as London, he would not be able to trace her when she had vanished in the dark of night. She would hire a carriage and drive to Derbyshire to collect her husband's money. And then she would disappear from all polite society. She would hide somewhere safe, somewhere no one would ever find her.

For the first time in her life, she would be free.

"I am sorry to impose on you. When the duke surprised me in my room, I panicked. I was foolish to come here."

"I invited you," Pembroke said.

Arabella laughed then and heard his own warm laughter answering her.

"You did indeed. But as I said before, I must decline your invitation. I am no man's mistress, nor will I ever be."

"Please sit, Arabella. I am bored. Help me spend the hours of this night that would usually be wasted on drink. Tell me your tale. I promise this time I will listen."

"There is no need, my lord. I will solve my own problems. I thank you for your time, and I bid you a good evening."

Arabella turned to the door, her vision obscured by

her cursed veil. She did not get far, for Pembroke was at her side in an instant, taking hold of her good arm.

"Damn it, woman. Sit down."

"I will not. You are neither my husband nor my father. You are nothing to me. You may not swear in my presence or use that tone of voice with me."

"I am not nothing to you. Or why else are you here?"

"I thought to ask for your help, but I see now that I was mistaken."

Pembroke swore again, this time under his breath. He raised her veil, pushing it back from her eyes. He took her bag from her and tossed it out of reach. He held her upper arms so that she was caught between his hands.

She felt for a moment as if she stood in the shelter of a wall, while the winds of the world swirled around her. She fought the urge to huddle against him, to give in and let him protect her. But a feeling of safety crept into her body through the warmth of his hands. Whatever would happen tomorrow, this was why she had come. So that she might feel safe like this again, if only for one night.

"Sit down, Arabella. You need to eat if all you've had all day are ginger biscuits."

She did feel light-headed, though she was certain it was from his nearness and little else. She should already be gone, taking the North Road to Derbyshire. But even though she had been wrong to come, she was glad she had. She would never see him again after this night. As she faced that truth, she also realized that she could never have disappeared into exile without looking on his face one last time.

So though she was losing hours she needed on the road, she sat down and shrugged her cloak from her shoulders, letting it pool on the sofa around her. Her fingers did not shake as she untied the ribbons of her bonnet, the black-dyed straw left beside her on the settee. She picked up her brandy and took a sip. The fiery liquid burned her mouth first and then her throat, but it warmed her stomach.

Pembroke rang for Codington again, and within minutes the porcelain bowl of bloody water was whisked away and thick sandwiches of beef and bread were brought as well as slices of cake on delicate plates, along with a large pot of strong black tea. Arabella took on the role of hostess, pouring tea for him, adding two sugars and milk before she thought twice.

As she handed him the cup, her arm froze in midmotion. His sky blue eyes did not leave her face. He knew, as she did, that she should not have remembered how he took his tea, not after an absence of ten years. He accepted the cup, his eyes searching her face. "You remember," he said.

"It would seem so."

An awkward silence descended as she ate her sandwich.

"So what is this wild tale you bear of Hawthorne? For all I know, you cut your wrist yourself to gain my sympathy."

In spite of his mocking words, he listened close as she spoke. Arabella's voice was calm, almost detached, for she had learned survival in her father's house at the hands of a harsh master. But when she mentioned Hawthorne's threats of highway robbery and of her death brought by an accident along the road, her voice wavered. She took a sip of tea, which had already cooled. As she watched him from the corner of her eye, she saw that Pembroke's hand had formed a fist upon his knee.

"And after threatening your life and attempting to rape you in the dark of night, he hopes to carry you to York in the morning?"

The anger in his voice was barely hidden and might actually have been hidden from anyone but her. She looked at him, but he would not face her. He stared into the fire as if it held the answer to his question.

"Yes," she said.

Before she could speak again, Pembroke exploded in violence, his arm drawn back, throwing the cut crystal glass into the grate. The brandy caught fire and burned hotter, the flames rising. Pembroke stood in the center of the room, shaking with the effort to control himself while Arabella sat motionless until his fit of temper passed.

Though she knew in her heart that this man would never hurt her, would never raise his hand to her, she flinched at the sound of shattering glass, at the ragged edges of his breathing. The scars along her back ached anew at the sight of violence, and she felt her bile rise to mingle with the taste of beef in her mouth. She swallowed hard and fought her nausea down.

Pembroke seemed to remember her presence then, and he made a concerted effort to push his fury behind the iron wall of his control. As her fear began to dissipate and her heart to slow its rapid beat, Arabella found herself strangely moved by his anger, that he felt such strong emotion on her behalf. Her husband had been kind but absentminded. He had never displayed an emotion other than calm reserve even in their marriage bed.

Pembroke turned to her, and she felt for a moment as if she had indeed found a haven in an uncertain world. She knew that this was an illusion, but she wanted very much to believe in it.

"I am sorry, Arabella. That is the second glass I have broken tonight. Codington will be displeased."

Arabella smiled. The old butler had often helped them in their exploits the summer they had been engaged, making sure that the picnics they took by the riverside were kept a secret from Pembroke's father.

"It is no matter. You are kind to be so angry. I would be angry myself if I were not so afraid."

Pembroke moved to sit beside her, tossing her widow's bonnet onto an armchair. He did not draw her into his arms this time but held her hand. At his touch, she was catapulted back into the past as if the last ten years had never happened. For the first time in many years, she wished herself back there, to the time when she was safe, to the time when all was well, those days when Pembroke loved her.

"Well, this is a charming scene."

The tall, red-haired woman Pembroke had brought to the funeral that morning stood in the doorway, smiling down on them. She wore a dark green wrapper of silk, and even Arabella's inexperienced eyes could tell that she wore nothing beneath it.

"You make a pretty picture with your lady friend, my lord. May I ask her name?"

Arabella tried to draw her hand from his, but he clutched it reflexively for a moment before he let her go. His mask of cool indifference descended then, and he stood, moving away from her.

"Names are unwieldy, Titania. You do not need to know it."

Arabella drew herself up straight under the other woman's scrutiny. She felt those green eyes on her skin like the edge of a knife, running along the surface, searching for weakness. Arabella could not tell if she found one, for the woman smiled.

"Welcome to Pembroke House, my lady."

"I am Arabella."

The red-haired woman's smile turned more genuine and less barbed. "I am Titania, as Lord Pembroke said. A lady of the stage."

"A woman of independence," Arabella said.

"As independent as I can be," Titania agreed.

"I wish to be a woman like that."

"As a duchess, you're well on your way."

Arabella fell silent then. The woman had stopped pretending not to know her.

"I must go," Arabella said. "Thank you for the sandwich."

Pembroke spoke, his voice cool. "Titania, would you leave us a moment? I must speak with Her Grace alone."

Titania sized him up with her eyes, almost as if she might refuse him. It seemed something in his face changed her mind, for she shrugged one shoulder and smiled.

"Come up, my lord, when you're done here. I'll be waiting."

The beautiful redhead's hips swayed as she walked away. Arabella felt her heart contract with what could only be jealousy.

The gentle man she had seen just moments before was gone as if he had never been. Pembroke's glib tongue threw coal on the fire of her emotions, so that she felt his words burn just above her heart.

"You aren't going anywhere, Arabella. Codington has instructed my people to keep you here for the night. Not that there's much of the night left."

Arabella opened her mouth to protest, but he raised one hand. She saw the stubborn set of his jaw and knew that in this mood, he could not be reasoned with.

"You are welcome to the guest room Codington has arranged for you. Or..." His blue eyes gleamed with wicked thoughts. "You could always join us."

Arabella blinked, wondering at first what he meant. Slowly it dawned on her that he was offering to share his bed with her and his mistress both. She felt a flash of quicksilver anger, the first in years, and she almost spat at him.

"I regretfully decline," she said, drawing on all the years of haughtiness she had ever witnessed in the *ton*.

Pembroke laughed as he crossed the room to leave her alone. "I always try to live without regrets."

❦

Arabella surprised herself by falling asleep almost at once in the soft, bland confines of Pembroke's guest room. She thought she might start at every sound or think of Pembroke with his mistress, but her exhaustion claimed her as soon as her head hit the pillow, drawing her down into dreams.

She dreamed of her father's house, the old, dark place that held her childhood, a place that had haunted her for years after. The familiar menace of the dream changed as she escaped into the sunshine of the kitchen garden only to find the new Duke of Hawthorne standing among Mrs. Fielding's plants, waiting for her.

Arabella could smell the dust on his clothes, though his immaculate coat was well brushed and fit him fashionably tight. Despite the starched white confection of his cravat, in his black coat and breeches, Hawthorne still looked like an undertaker. The knife he had brought into her bedroom gleamed in his hand.

In the dream, Arabella had more presence of mind than when she was awake, or perhaps she simply felt less like holding to false dictates of Society that kept her tied down and obedient. She said not a word to him but dodged through the garden, lifting her skirts to her knees as she ran. As soon as she decided to run, the terrain changed, and she was standing in her childhood haven, the Forest of Arden.

The wooded land that divided her father's estate from Pembroke's did not officially possess such a fanciful name. It had no name at all. But she and Pembroke had christened it the Forest of Arden the summer they had been so close, calling it after the fairy haven of Shakespeare's *A Midsummer Night's Dream*. They had both needed a haven from the world, he from the cruelty of his father and she from the cruelty of hers. Those woods took on a sense of enchantment for both of them, and for the first time in years, she stepped into them again.

Hawthorne was gone. Perhaps he could not follow her into that enchanted place. She did not question her good fortune but breathed deeply of the soft green scent of the leaves, watching as the sunlight shone through the branches of the oaks overhead, the canopy covering her, separating her from the world. Bluebells grew along the edges of the path she walked on, and she followed it down to the riverbank where she and Pembroke had spent so many happy hours, simply sitting side by side, not talking, just watching the river as it slid quietly past them, her small hand in his great one.

In the dream, Pembroke was waiting for her there. He was not the boy she had known but the man she had just met again. He smiled at her openly as he once had done, as if he were free to love her, as if the pain that had passed between them had never been.

He reached into his coat pocket and drew out his mother's ruby ring, the ring he had given her on the day he had asked her to marry him. Arabella at first felt a moment of fear, that she had lost it, that it was not tucked away in her small jewel case as it had always been. Then she stepped forward and took the ring into her hand. The ruby gleamed in the sunlight by the river, the depths of its red facets throwing hints of the sun back to her. She clutched the ring in her fist but did not put it on.

She woke then, before she could speak to him, before she could tell him how sorry she was. She clutched the ruby ring and the soft sheet of her borrowed bed.

Arabella lay still for a long moment, trying to calm the frantic beating of her heart.

She was not sure how the ring had come to be in her hand. She had packed it in her case when she fled, the leather satchel that now sat on a chair across the room. She must have taken it up before she slept, but she did not remember. Even as she held it, the round, rough cut of the ruby digging into her palm, she felt as if she were still in a dream.

She returned the ring to its place in her box. She buried that box once more at the bottom of her baggage, beneath simple gowns and linen petticoats, so that she would not have to look at it again.

Five

PEMBROKE TRIED TO MAKE LOVE TO TITANIA WITH Arabella asleep down the hall, but his body failed him. He could not remember the last time a beautiful woman had lain naked beneath him and he had been left unable even to feel desire.

He was grateful that Titania was a friend as well as a professional, for she made a joke of the whole thing, telling him of the illustrious men she had slept with in the past who had not always been able to bring themselves to the sticking place. She had even managed to make him laugh before she fell asleep.

She did not leave him as she usually did but spent the night beside him, as if she might protect him from his divided soul. Of course, she could not. Still, Pembroke was grateful not to be alone. If he had been, the temptation to go to Arabella's room would have been too great, and he would have behaved little better than Hawthorne.

In the morning, Pembroke waited for Arabella in the breakfast room, his coffee cooling in front of him, trying to read *The Times* and failing. He read the same paragraph three times over before he finally gave up. As he cast the papers aside in disgust, Arabella stopped in the doorway as if the breakfast room was a den of iniquity and she had no wish to join the damned.

Pembroke rose to his feet, as he always did when a lady entered the room. He did not move again but watched as a footman drew out her chair, so that she might sit a little way down the table from him. Her simple dark blue gown showed the slender figure beneath it, the curve of her small breasts beneath the demure bodice making his mouth go dry. Every clever quip, every dismissive comment he had ever known seemed to vanish as he looked at her.

"You did not come to me last night," Pembroke said, his voice sounding rusty in his own ears.

Arabella looked up at him, as calm as a bishop as a footman brought her tea. "Did you expect me to?"

"I had hoped you might."

Arabella smiled then, and he caught a glimpse of the girl she had been. "Hope springs eternal, my lord, but I would not expect miracles."

"Would it take a miracle for you to come to me?"

"Perhaps that is the wrong choice of words. I am no light skirt, and you…"

"I am a rake."

"Yes."

"You think to marry me then?"

Arabella laughed, the sound sweet in the sunlit room. Her laughter was always surprising, for it was not delicate and quiet as she was. There was nothing ladylike or demure about it. Arabella laughed from her belly and shook with her whole body as tears of mirth came into her eyes. Pembroke felt as if he had been catapulted into the past, long before they had been separated, long before she had married another. She had laughed like that during their picnic by the river when her bonnet had blown into the water and he had been forced to wade into the current to retrieve it.

"You have made it abundantly clear that you are not the marrying kind," she said.

He took in the scent of cornflowers on her hair, and he felt the perfume like a fist in his sternum, a blow he had to take a moment to recover from. She had worn that same scent as a girl, and for a moment he was taken back to the forest in Derbyshire, eating the last of the summer berries, watching the river slide by.

"People change," he said.

Her eyes turned to him, the same light blue as they were in his dreams, and he felt himself caught as if in amber.

"No," she answered. "They do not."

He forced himself to sit down, and a silence stretched between them. He heard the ticking of the clock in the hall and swallowed hard to clear his throat.

"You should not tease me, Pembroke. There is too much afoot for you to do nothing but make jokes."

"I was not joking."

Arabella smiled. "You think me the same simple girl I once was. I am no woman of the world, but I am old enough to understand a joke when I hear one."

When had he last felt such longing for a woman? He wanted to bend down and kiss her soft pink lips, to run his hands over her shoulders, down to cup her breasts.

Every woman he knew threw herself at him. Countesses and baronesses pursued him relentlessly. Each wanted to sample his favors so that they might confirm for their friends whether or not his reputation for skill in bed was earned. The whores he dallied with were more honorable, giving and receiving pleasure for a fee and leaving afterward without a fuss. But none of those women, baronesses or courtesans, made him catch his breath as Arabella did.

"Thank you for taking me in last night, Pembroke," she said. A light blush rose in her cheeks, and once more he felt the need to reach for her. "I suppose I should call you my lord earl."

"You used to call me Raymond," he said without thinking. He watched her face and thought he saw her flinch before she lowered her eyes, her brown lashes hiding any hint of her thoughts. A long silence stretched between them, and he cursed himself for a fool.

"You may call me anything you wish," he said.

He took a sip from his coffee, which had long since gone cold. Pembroke set his cup down and gestured to the footman who stood behind him. His coffee was replaced in a moment and fresh bread set down at his elbow. "There is no need to thank me. No honorable man would turn his back on a woman in need."

She looked at her empty plate. "No, I suppose not." She raised her head, and he felt as if the cornflower blue of her eyes had pierced him. "But I have never before known an honorable man."

He drank from his cup, swirling cream in it first, depositing a lump of sugar, though he always took his coffee black. He made another gesture, and a full plate was brought to her, heaped with stewed tomatoes, kidneys, eggs, and bacon. She stared down at it as if she had never seen food before, and for a moment he thought that she would have none of it. But Arabella remembered her manners, for she had always been refined, even as a girl. She lifted the heavy silver fork by her china plate and began delicately to eat the eggs. Pembroke offered her the basket of fresh rolls, and she took one of those and began to butter it.

"No toast?" she asked. He almost laughed at the inanity of the question. After ten years apart, they sat on opposite sides of his breakfast table. After spending a chaste night in the same house, she had little more to say to him than to ask for bread. A footman brought a plate of toast to her elbow.

"An affectation I brought home from the Continent," Pembroke said. "I found that I cannot start the morning without a brioche."

She stared at him without blinking, uncomprehending. He gestured to the basket between them. "*Brioche* means fancy French roll, Arabella."

For a moment he thought he had embarrassed her, but as a delicate pink suffused her cheeks, Arabella dropped the roll she had been buttering onto her plate and began to laugh.

She wiped her eyes with her napkin, and Pembroke simply sat and stared at her, trying desperately to ignore the knife lodged in his chest. She had set that knife there ten years before. It was still there, just where she had placed it, cutting his heart in two.

She turned her bright blue eyes on him, all traces

of diffidence and fear gone as if they had never been. She looked for a moment as free and happy as she had been as a girl. He had dreamed of that girl for many years, and here she sat at his breakfast table. He was grateful to whatever god might be that he had caught a glimpse of her.

"Arabella…"

He was not sure what he would have said, but whatever tender words he might have uttered, whatever mad declaration of undying passion he might have made died on his lips, unspoken. For the door to his breakfast room was flung open in the next moment, as if before a great wind. Arabella turned away from him, her eyes wide, to stare into the hazel green eyes of his mistress.

❧

"Pembroke, for the love of God, since when do you take breakfast?"

The beautiful woman standing in the doorway stared at Pembroke imperiously, waiting for an answer. Her brassy red hair was a shade that could only come from a chemist. She was dressed this morning in a dark green gown of satin and pearls, cut low over her enormous cleavage. Her shoulders were thrown back, her cloak cast behind her, as if she had popped into the breakfast room on her way to better things. The woman looked like a carving that might adorn the prow of a ship. Arabella forced herself to take a sip of the black tea in her china cup.

"You didn't go to Hawthorne's party last night, and no doubt he is furious. When I see him, I'll tell him that you found far prettier company than any he had on offer."

The woman eyed her shrewdly, but Arabella didn't sense any jealousy or spite in her assessment.

"I did not think to ask last night, but where have you been hiding this ravishing creature?" the woman asked. "She must be the reason why you've been so gloomy of late."

"Titania." Pembroke shot his mistress a look of warning, which she ignored.

"But of course she is!" Titania said, laughter rising. "I never knew you had a taste for the schoolroom, but there she sits."

"I am not from the schoolroom, madame, I assure you," Arabella said, rising to her feet. "Forgive me for not properly introducing myself last night. I am the Duchess of Hawthorne, and I must cast myself on your mercy."

Titania sat down when she heard that, waving one hand as she shrugged off her cloak. Not one but two footmen jumped to do her silent bidding, bringing her a plate piled high with victuals as well as her own cup of tea. Clearly, she was a frequent visitor.

"At my mercy? Well, there's a phrase I don't often hear. Pembroke, sit down and stop gaping at us. The women are talking now, and you're making me nervous."

Lord Pembroke, landowner and cavalryman, sat down at his mistress's bidding. Arabella smiled in spite of the jealousy that bloomed in her breast.

She had never had cause to speak to a woman of the *demimonde* before, and she doubted that she ever would again. Titania seemed to have more sense and kindness than any of the so-called ladies Arabella had met among the *ton*. There was a warmth and charm about Titania that made Arabella relax almost against her will. As they sat across the table from each another, Arabella tried to forget how often Pembroke took this magnificent creature into his bed. She failed.

The needs of men made her sick. She sometimes still woke in the night cringing away from the touch of her elderly husband in her dreams. The memory of his clammy touch and grunting in the night still made bile rise in her throat. And now thoughts of Hawthorne cutting the buttons off her nightgown would plague her. She shuddered.

That this woman took men into her bed for money was distasteful, but no more distasteful than being forced to marry an elderly man for a title. She and Titania had a great deal in common. Like all women, both lived their lives at the whims of men.

"What's this talk of mercy then?" Titania took a huge bite of bacon and eggs, following it shortly with a forkful of kidney. Arabella sipped her cooling tea and forced herself to meet the woman's eyes. For some reason Titania's steady gaze made her feel safe.

"I am fleeing from the Duke of Hawthorne."

"But he's dead, Your Grace."

"Not my husband, Madame Titania, but the new duke."

"Oh… I see. You've gotten on his bad side already, have you?" Titania took another huge bite of kippers and tomatoes, her eyes never leaving Arabella's face.

"He's bent on marrying me."

"And you'd rather be dead."

Arabella blinked in surprise but answered steadily. "Yes."

"Well, that is a pretty mess. That one is a black-guard, dark and dismal. Not fit company for a lady like yourself. Not fit company for me, though he pays quite well."

Pembroke made a strangled noise of protest, which Titania dismissed with a wave of her fork. She chewed thoughtfully then made a pronouncement. "I wouldn't see a dog go into that man's hands for life, much less a woman. Whatever help you need from me, you've got. Pembroke has always been good to me, though I see his whoring days are over."

Pembroke did not let that sally pass. "Titania, mind your tongue. There is a lady present."

Titania did not look at all chastised but stared at Pembroke as if seeing him for the first time. "You poor bastard. God help you."

He opened his mouth to shout again, but she simply waved him into silence with her tea cup. "Well enough. The Duchess of Hawthorne is a fine lady, so I'll try to keep a civil tongue in my head. But if you've made an enemy of the new duke, you need to leave the city before your tea's gone cold."

"You will tell no one that you saw me here?" Arabella asked.

"I give you my word, I will not. No one thinks to ask actresses and whores much. If someone asks, I've never seen or heard of you."

Titania stood to leave, drawing her cloak over one arm. Arabella stood when she did and came around the table to offer her hand. "Thank you, Madame Titania. I am in your debt."

"You may call me Molly, Your Grace, if we meet again."

"I am honored, Molly. And you must call me Arabella."

Titania laughed, her booming warmth filling the room again. "Oh no. Too rich for my blood. Your Grace will do until you marry again."

"I have no intention of ever marrying. Once was enough."

Titania cast an eye on Pembroke, who sat glaring at her from behind his coffee cup. "Well, time will tell. God speed, Your Grace. I'll leave by the back gate. Wear my cloak when you climb into Pembroke's carriage. It will throw Hawthorne off your scent. And get out of town before another hour has passed."

Arabella did not tell her that she had no intention of going anywhere with Pembroke, that he had done too much for her already. She simply said, "I will."

"You need not trouble yourself on the duchess's account, Titania. I will look after her," Pembroke said.

Titania shot a sardonic smile his way before she crossed the room to stand beside him. "So I see, my lord. So I see." She leaned down and kissed him then as if he was a clear running river and she had the need of a drink. Arabella blinked in surprise and horror, not knowing where to look, unable to look away.

Pembroke kissed Titania back as if Arabella were not there, his mouth opening over hers. She surprised herself by not feeling repulsed by the open sensuality of the moment. All she felt was pain, sharp and clear, a pain she had earned. She had given him up, and now every woman in the world had more right to him than she did.

Without another word, the actress turned to leave. Codington closed the door behind Titania with an emphatic click. Pembroke sighed, and Arabella sat down once more to finish her brioche.

"Colorful company you keep," she said. She swallowed her pain and jealousy but found that they would not dissipate. The soft bread was like sawdust in her mouth, but she forced herself to finish it. She needed to be on the road soon, and it would be hours before she stopped to eat again.

A scratching at the door broke through her pain, and Codington entered the room without being called. He brought a letter on a silver tray, not to Pembroke but to her. She broke the seal that bore Angelique's crest, a phoenix rising from the ashes.

"Hawthorne has left my husband's house. He's searching the city for me."

Arabella's hands shook as she stood and cast the heavy paper into the fire.

"I must go."

Pembroke stood as she did. "You aren't going anywhere without me."

"You have enough to amuse yourself in town. I will go, and you will stay, and all will be as it should."

He did not argue but silenced her by placing one great finger over her lips. The warmth of his touch made her tongue seize. Pembroke smelled of cloves and cinnamon, as if he had been baking. She could not catch even a hint of brandy on his breath from the night before, only dark coffee with cream.

"We will go to Derbyshire, to my father's house," he said. "I will not leave you to Hawthorne's tender mercies. Nor will I let you gallivant across the countryside alone. You came to me for help, and now you have it, madame, whether you want it or not."

Arabella could not catch her breath. She simply stared into the blue of Raymond Olivier's eyes. In spite of all that had happened between them, she remembered one simple truth. Every promise Pembroke had ever made to her, he kept.

ACT II

"Thy lips, those kissing cherries, tempting grow…"

A Midsummer Night's Dream
Act 3, Scene 2

Six

THE DAY ARABELLA FLED FROM LONDON WAS THE longest of her life. Even the day her husband died, with its crush of physicians and vultures come to pick the bones clean, could not compare.

On the journey out of town, Arabella sat in the traveling chaise with the crest of the Earl of Pembroke emblazoned on its side. She kept the hood of Titania's cloak up, hiding her face whenever they stopped to water the horses. They took their luncheon in a private room in an inn along the North Road, and she wore the dark green cape even then, drawing all eyes. If Hawthorne chanced to look for her here, he would hear only of Pembroke and his doxy, nothing of the Duchess of Hawthorne.

Angelique had left for her estate in Shropshire, traveling with a maid dressed in a fine black gown. She had sent word to her acquaintances in the city that she had retired to the country for some much-needed rest. Arabella hoped that the simple duplicity would be enough, that Hawthorne would head toward Shropshire first.

Arabella knew that she would not be able to hide for long. Hawthorne was a man of keen intelligence. She could only hope that his search for her would take him to her mother's family in Devon after his aborted attempt to find her in Shropshire. No one had ever acknowledged her father's birthplace. The duke would have to dig hard to find it. She was betting her life on it.

She had only a week or two at most to find the money she looked for, the money that would help her escape the rule of men for the rest of her life. Then she would have to disappear in earnest.

She tried not to think of Hawthorne and his gray eyes, the glint of the knife in his hand. She tried not to think of Pembroke, though he sat across from her in the carriage, swilling brandy from a flask.

Instead, she cast her mind not on what her life was but what it might become. When she thought of the future, it was of a year hence, when she might be tucked away by her own fire, making lace for a new dress, a kettle on the hob and roses beginning to bloom in the garden. The sight of this mythical cottage was the only ease she could find as she fled north under Pembroke's protection.

Even now, as darkness began to rise from the land around them, Pembroke looked slightly dangerous, his blue eyes hooded, his blond hair falling across his forehead to further obscure her view of him. He wore all black, save for his silver embroidered waistcoat. He did not look at her but kept his eyes firmly on the countryside beyond the window, his silver flask in his hand.

His servants in town had thought nothing of loading an unknown woman into his carriage and spiriting her off to the country for a tryst. No doubt he did such things all the time. No doubt he often did much worse.

The setting sun cast its fading light over the deep green country, throwing the interior of the already darkened traveling chaise deeper into shadow. Arabella shrugged the hated green cloak from her shoulders to reveal a dark blue pelisse and matching bonnet. The dark blue of her clothes, while not strictly appropriate for a widow in the first month of mourning, was certainly more appropriate than a harlot's satin. Not that anything was appropriate under the circumstances. Arabella had never been schooled in the proper etiquette of running for her life.

Titania had been kind to shield her, another woman in her lover's keeping. Arabella felt a surge of jealousy at the thought of the beautiful actress, Pembroke's mistress. She wondered, had their positions been reversed, if she would have been as generous.

No doubt the ruse of Titania's cloak had bought Arabella more time out from under Hawthorne's boot, but the actress's choice of perfume left a great deal to be desired. The sickening sweetness of heavy lilac had surrounded Arabella all day, choking the air in the carriage. When the traveling chaise finally came to a stop at the Unicorn Inn outside of Oxford, Arabella did not wait for Pembroke to hand her down but leaped out of the carriage on her own, taking deep breaths of fresh evening air, leaving her borrowed cloak behind.

Pembroke raised a sardonic eyebrow as he pocketed his flask. He offered his arm and steered her into the inn, which was clean and well lit. The tavern keeper greeted them with a bow, asking no questions and giving her no sideways glances. The staff soon had them settled in a private parlor with a fire lit and cider on the hob.

Arabella drank her cider gratefully, the pewter mug warm in her hands, savoring the tart taste mixed with sweetness. She wondered if the innkeeper's wife might part with her recipe. She opened her mouth to ask, but the staff withdrew as soon as Pembroke had dismissed them, handing coin all around. She assumed it was to keep their silence.

Alone once more, she and Pembroke simply stared at each other, the only sound in the room the quiet crackling of the fire in the hearth.

"I've taken one room," Pembroke said at last. "I stay here a great deal, and it would look odd for me to take a separate room for..."

"Your mistress," Arabella said.

"For the lady in my company," Pembroke answered.

She nodded but did not speak again. She looked past his shoulder to the bedroom beyond, where the coverlet had already been turned down.

"I will sleep in the parlor on this settle," Pembroke said. "It will place me between you and the door."

She could feel his gaze heavy on her, and Arabella found that she could not look away. She searched his eyes for the boy she had known but could not find him. There was only the man he had become, his dark blond hair falling over his forehead, his deep blue eyes staring into hers, taking her breath.

Pembroke did not smile or speak, did not soften the moment with some flip remark. Instead, his gaze drifted down, as Hawthorne's had the day before, to take in the small, soft curves of her breasts, the line of her throat. He looked hungry, his eyes hot, as if she were a package of sweetmeats, a gift left on his doorstep.

Her skin flushed as heat rose within her. She felt suddenly as if she stood too close to the fire. She took a step back and drew out her handkerchief to blot her temple, but the smell of lavender did little to soothe her. He did not turn away.

She moved suddenly to the window set above the courtyard. Even with her back to him, she could feel the weight of his gaze. The heat on her skin did not dissipate. She struggled with the latch, which would not budge. She settled for pressing her palm to the glass in the hope of cooling herself, but it had been a warm day, and she could feel the heat of the sun still caught in the pane.

Pembroke was beside her then, his hand over hers. His palm pressed hers down, trapping her fingers against the glass. He held her prisoner there, his breath on her hair, the scent of cinnamon surrounding her. For one mindless moment, she wanted to lean back and feel the strength of his body against hers.

It was madness, and she knew it. Nothing good could come of it. But she wanted it. She wanted him.

Pembroke reached past her with his other hand. The casement swung open for him easily.

Arabella knew that she should move away, but he stood between her and the rest of the room, shutting out the world. She tried to talk of something, anything: Derbyshire, the state of the roads, her gratitude for his kindness. But she could not find the words. She simply stood like a rabbit caught in a snare, trapped by the heat of his hand on hers.

It was Pembroke who broke the spell. He cleared his throat and took his hand away. She turned to watch as he moved away from her, as if the touch of her skin was a pot that had scalded him. He pushed his great paw through his unruly hair, and the golden heft of it fell back against his forehead again and into his eyes. He searched the pocket of his coat and took out his flask, but he found no solace there. It must have been empty, for he tucked it away again, his eyes never leaving her face.

"I will see about dinner," he said before he fled, closing the door of the parlor behind him.

Arabella sat down on the hard wooden settle, the thin cushions doing nothing to soften the oak. There was a little breeze from the window now, but her skin was still flushed. She thought to move the fire screen to block the blaze, but she did nothing. She only stared into the flames, her fingertips touching her lips.

Had she ever felt such overwhelming desire? It had been many years since she and Pembroke had loved one another, since they had stood together by the river in their Forest of Arden, but she did not think she had ever felt such overwhelming lust when she was a girl.

She would have remembered.

Arabella could not become a slave of the past or to

her own fancy. She could not moon after Pembroke as a grown woman. Once she reached Derbyshire, they would part—he to return to town and his mistress and his drink, she to start a life of her own. He already had a life of his own, and he was living it. He had not wasted his youth, locked away as she had been. He had gone abroad and fought wars on the Continent. No doubt Pembroke had long ago forgotten all that had once passed between them.

Of course, that did not mean that he would be averse to making her his mistress now.

She could not let him touch her again. She could never become his mistress, no matter how much heat rose in her at the touch of his hand.

Arabella knew enough of marital relations to be certain that she wanted no part of it, now or ever. She had survived the first year of her marriage. She had lain in bed, night after night, waiting for Gerald to come to her, thanking God when he did not. The humiliation, the physical pain of those couplings was still with her. She needed no such pain in her life again. She was free, and she meant to stay that way.

❧

All Pembroke knew was that he had to get out of the room. He slammed the door behind him as if sealing in the hounds of hell. He stood in the corridor outside, the sounds and smells of the taproom below rising up the narrow staircase. He stood with his back pressed against the wall, breathing heavily as if he had run a fast mile. He forced himself to regain control, reaching for his lost courage. He could not seem to find it.

He had been confined all day in a closed carriage with the woman he still wanted more than any other. The acrid, too-sweet scent of Titania's perfume had soon worn away, and all he could take in was the soft hint of cornflowers and cream on Arabella's skin, the scent warmed by the confines of the carriage they sat in.

There was something about Arabella, just as there had been all those years ago. Her soft vulnerability called to his better instincts and made him swear once again to protect her, to shield her from the world. He could barely remember the boy who had first made that promise, but somehow, seeing her again, Pembroke began to be curious about that boy. Why had he loved her? Why had he been so moved by a slip of a girl? How could he still be so filled with lust at the sight of such a delicate, ladylike creature when all the women of the world were at his fingertips, waiting for him only to beckon to them?

He would take Arabella to Derbyshire, as he had promised. And then he would let her go.

Pembroke stood in the hallway outside the sitting room, a sharp pain lodged in his lungs just above his heart. He should hate her. Pembroke told himself this, but his lust went nowhere. He would not touch her again, no matter how much he wanted to.

His man, Reynolds, stepped forward out of the shadows. "My lord, are you quite well? Is there anything I might fetch you?"

Pembroke forced his pain down and drew out the smile he always wore unless he sat alone or with his friend Anthony. "No, Reynolds, though I thank you.

An elixir to help me forget the past if you have one about your person."

Reynolds had served him as valet for the last two years, since Pembroke had come home from the war. He must have been used to his lord's strange turns of phrase for he did not even pause in his answer. "No, my lord, I fear not."

Pembroke laughed, clapping his man on the shoulder. Reynolds winced at the impact of the friendly blow, and Pembroke laughed harder. "Just dinner, and then you may see to your own comfort."

"You will be staying the night in these rooms, my lord?"

Reynolds never judged Pembroke for any of the women with whom he kept company, nor his gambling, nor his drinking. He turned a blind eye to all of Pembroke's vices. But clearly something about Arabella had caught his valet's eye, making even his man feel a certain protectiveness toward her.

"Indeed I will, Reynolds. But I'll be sleeping on the settle."

Reynolds bowed. "Excellent, my lord. I will have more pillows sent up."

"No need. I don't want the rest of the inn to know that I sleep on hard wood instead of the decent feather bed I'm paying for."

A ghost of a smile flitted across Reynolds's face, but it was gone before Pembroke could fully take it in. "Indeed, my lord, as you wish. Dinner will be served in twenty minutes."

"Thank you, Reynolds."

Pembroke was glad for once to keep country hours.

The sooner he and Arabella ate, the sooner she would disappear behind her bedroom door. He would have a few hours' reprieve while she wrapped herself in the coverlet of the warm feather bed.

Before going back into their rooms, Pembroke went downstairs and washed his face and hands in cold water in the inn yard, making his linen damp. Reynolds would be annoyed when he saw the evidence of Pembroke's carelessness, but no matter. Cold water was called for, so cold water was what he doused himself in. It would be a long night.

Seven

With no lady's maid to attend her, Arabella rang for hot water, recalling her youth when her father thought such expenses as personal servants a needless extravagance.

The bedroom Pembroke had taken for her was comfortable, with dark wood beams between swathes of whitewashed plaster. The air was scented with thyme and rosemary. As she washed her face, Arabella could smell chicken roasting in the kitchen below and hear the faint clamor of copper pots being set down on the stove.

The kitchen had been her haven in her father's house during the dark years of her childhood after her mother's death. She would sneak away during her governess's nap each afternoon and spend an hour with her father's cook, Mrs. Fielding, who spoiled her, feeding her pastry fresh from the oven. Mrs. Fielding had always proclaimed that Arabella was far too small for a healthy girl and that she needed fattening up. Arabella had eaten every morsel her benefactress bestowed upon her, setting the cook high in the pantheon of her heart, worshiping her as she worshiped her long-dead mother.

Arabella did not change her dress, for she had brought only a few more suitable gowns with her. Her bag was heavy with the flotsam and jetsam of her life. She had not pressed many gowns into it. She had only the boots on her feet and the ugly black-dyed bonnet trimmed in blue ribbon that now rested on her vanity table. Perhaps she might find time to sew a new dress while in the country. In her father's house, a few of her old dresses might still lie in the clothespress, gowns she had worn as a girl, all of which had been deemed too shoddy to bring into her new life as the Duchess of Hawthorne.

She heard Pembroke come back into the sitting room. Arabella met her own eyes in the looking glass and breathed deeply, shoring up her courage before she stepped into the parlor.

He stood by the door as if afraid to come in. She could not remember seeing him so uncertain of his welcome even when he was a boy. Her heart seized, and without thinking she extended her hand to him and offered him a chair by the fire across from her own.

"Dinner will be served in a moment," Arabella said. "Come and sit. May I offer you a brandy? I had the staff bring up their best bottle. I hope it will suit."

Pembroke pushed his dark blond hair out of his eyes and simply stared at her. He blinked as if waking from a deep sleep. "There is no need. I have brought my own."

Arabella sat and he followed her example, watching as she drew her chair close to the table. Pembroke's sensuous lips quirked in another smile, and her heart paused in its beating.

She told herself that she must not stare at him, but she found that she could not bring herself to drop her gaze. They sat for a long moment in silence, the expanse of their empty dinner table and the cheerful crackle of the fire between them.

Their dinner of roasted lamb and new potatoes, creamed spinach, and carrots in wine sauce was brought in, and they turned their attention to it as if they might not ever see another meal again. They ate together in companionable silence until Pembroke asked her a question over pears in brandied sauce.

"When you are free, what will you do?"

Arabella froze, her dessert fork halfway to her lips. She set the fork down again, the pear speared on it forgotten. Her hand trembled, and she forced it to be still, pressing it hard against the white cloth on the table between them.

She was afraid to voice her desires, lest they be taken from her. But the fact that he had thought to ask the right question, when no one else on Earth, save perhaps Angelique, ever would, made her heart catch in her throat.

"I would like to live quietly somewhere," she said. "If Hawthorne stays away, I would take a cottage in the village near the old manor house where I grew up. I would grow roses and plant an herb garden."

"You won't live in your father's house?" Pembroke asked.

She could not help from shuddering. "Dear God, no."

Pembroke took a swig of his brandy and reached for her hand. He toyed with her fingers almost absently.

She felt as if she had swallowed her tongue. She tried to pull away, to get up from the table, but he held her still. He spoke as if he did not feel her struggle, his eyes on her fingertips. "Why not live there? The house is yours as a part of your dower lands."

"No," she said, forcing herself to speak. She stopped trying to take her hand back. "I love Derbyshire. It is home. But I will never live in that house again."

Even with Pembroke's hand on hers, distracting her, she found her mind going back to those days in her father's house, the care she had to take every day not be noticed, not to cause him to turn his rage on her. No matter how careful she had been, no matter how hard she had tried to please him, his temper would snap, and she always caught the brunt of it. Whether a slap on her face or a more formal beating with his riding crop, she bore the scars of her father's attacks on her back and on her soul. She knew that she would never be rid of them.

If Pembroke saw the pain that the mention of her father's house caused her, he was kind enough not to speak of it. But he did not let go of her hand. He took another drink from his brandy glass.

"When did your father die?" she asked.

He took his hand away then, as she had intended. His face closed off, like a gate being drawn against invaders. He had hated his father, who had beaten him, too, until Pembroke was too old for it. His father had been a wastrel and a drunkard. Arabella watched as Pembroke pushed his brandy glass away.

"He died five years ago."

"And yet you did not come home."

"There was a war to be won," he said.

"They might have won it without you."

"I would not leave my friend."

"Anthony Carrington," Arabella said.

"Yes. I stayed on the Continent until the war was over."

Arabella leaned back in her hard oak chair. She saw a hint of the pain in his eyes that he meant to hide, but she pressed on, heedless of it.

"You drink as he once did."

Pembroke's eyes were sharp on hers, twin blades that pinned her to her chair. They both knew that she was no longer speaking of Anthony. She took a shallow breath, for the air had suddenly become heavy, hard to breathe.

"I drink to please myself."

"And gamble and visit ladies of ill repute? For your own amusement? Or to get back at him?"

"He would not have cared, had he known. My father never loved me, as you well know."

"My father did not love me either," she said.

"It is best that they are both dead then."

She did not answer. A bit of coal fell in the grate, but Pembroke did not rise to stir the fire up again.

Arabella wondered if she should tell him what had really happened on her wedding day. She wondered what had happened to the letter she had sent. Had he received it? Had he simply ignored it or cast it into the fire? If she could speak of his father, if she could speak of his drinking, she could speak of anything. But she sat frozen, as if she had suddenly fallen mute.

Pembroke reached for the cut glass filled with brandy, but instead of drinking it, he tossed the liquor onto the fire.

The coals flared for a moment, then died down again. All Arabella could hear was the ticking of the clock in the hall and the sound of her own heart beating.

"It doesn't matter what you say, Arabella. I will never strike you. You know that, don't you?"

She watched him closely, as a snake might watch its charmer. She stared at him, at the hard contours of his face, at the sky blue of his eyes. "I know that," she said. "I don't know why I tried to tempt you."

He smiled then, and a little of his old light came back into his eyes, if only for a moment. "You meant to test me, before we go any further down the road to Derbyshire. Know this, Arabella, because you no longer know me. I am not my father. I am not yours."

"I know you, Raymond. Sometimes I think I am the only one who does."

He laughed at that, and the derision in his voice was worse than a beating, like acid on her skin. "You know nothing about me but the rumors you've heard. I am just the fool you left for a rich duke, a boy you never thought of again."

She wanted to say, *I did think of you. I do think of you.* But she said nothing, she did not speak of the letters she had sent, swallowing her words as she might swallow poison. It was many years too late to try to make amends now. She saw in the hard planes of his face, all light fled from his eyes, that he would not listen to an apology, even if she knew how to give him one.

He rose to his feet, and she did the same. The fire was beginning to go out.

"It has been a long day, and we have a long day of travel ahead of us tomorrow," was all he said.

Arabella tried to offer a smile and failed. She spoke some polite nonsense, as she sometimes had as a girl, when she thought to diffuse a bad situation, when she thought to deflect her father's wrath. "The bed is very fine. A thick quilt and a deep feather mattress. I will be a sight more comfortable than you will be here on this settle."

Pembroke must have heard the fear beneath her foolish words. He attempted a smile, and though it did not reach his eyes, his attempt was better than hers. "I have slept on worse. You need not concern yourself about me."

She had reached the end of her strength. She needed the deep peace that only sleep could bring, the one fortress that her father, her husband, even Hawthorne had not been able to breach.

"I bid you good night," she said. She crossed the room, but something made her turn back at the door. Pembroke was watching her with no hint of lust or anger on his face, without even a hint of old pain. He simply looked tired to the bone, as she was.

"You are safe, Arabella. No matter what we have lost, no matter what once passed between us, you will always be safe with me."

Eight

IN SPITE OF THE TENSION OF THE DAY JUST PAST, Arabella fell at once into a deep sleep. That night, just as she had the night before, she dreamed.

Moonlight filtered in from an unseen window, covering the bedclothes with soft, creamy light. In the dream, she lay in bed in her husband's house. She knew in the dream that her husband was dead, but in the sleep of night, this was not foul news. She was widowed and free with no specter of Hawthorne looming over her. But as she lay on the feather bed in her husband's house, she knew that she was not alone.

Pembroke stepped out of the shadows dressed in the same clothes he had worn the night she had first come to him. His black evening clothes blended with the darkness of the room as the moonlight picked up the bright white of his cravat and the gold embroidery on his waistcoat.

He said nothing but moved to stand beside the bed where she lay unmoving, as if caught under a spell. She was not afraid, but the rational part of her mind knew that she must send him away. If she asked him to, Pembroke would go. No matter how dissipated he had become, he would never force himself on any woman.

Though the moonlight was dim, in the dream she could see the deep blue of his eyes. They had always reminded her of a clear summer sky, the color of the sky the summer she fell in love with him. There was no pain between them, no awkwardness. It was as if all of that had been washed away. Pembroke sat beside her on the bed. The feather mattress shifted under his weight so that she was forced to sit up and catch herself or else roll into him.

He did not move to touch her even then.

Arabella leaned close, reaching for him. He caught her hand in his, his great paw closing around her fingers and palm so that they disappeared. Surrounded by his warmth, her hand began to tingle. She leaned closer to him still and took in the scent of cinnamon, the inexplicable sweetness his skin always seemed to bear. Arabella would never have had the courage to do such a thing in waking life, but she knew even as she drew closer to Pembroke that she still dreamed.

She pressed her free hand against his cheek. Beneath her fingertips, his skin was rough where his fair beard had begun to grow back in. She could not see the flush of color come into his face, but she could feel the warmth of it. She scooted closer still and pressed her lips to that same cheek.

His arms came around her then, very carefully, as if she were made of spun glass. He did not jostle or startle her but drew her against his chest, so that she could hear the soft beating of his heart. The heavy feel of his arms around her, of his weight against her, was nothing like her elderly husband's thin arms and spindly frame. Though she was no longer a maid and had not been a maid for ten years, she felt as if she were a virgin once more, sitting tucked safe in Pembroke's arms on those soft white sheets.

Though she felt lost and at sea, she was not afraid as she had been on her real wedding night. She was safe, and she knew it, for Pembroke was with her.

"I would like to kiss you, if you will permit me."

Arabella laughed a little under her breath. He had never sounded so formal in her life, but this was a dream, and she did not want to wake. She savored the feel of his body against hers, warmth beginning to rise between her thighs.

She had never felt such a thing before, not even when she was a girl and happy. Pembroke had only kissed her once that summer, the same afternoon he had given her his mother's ring. She had been transported by the feel of his lips on hers. It had been so long ago that she could not now remember what it felt like to be kissed by a man she loved, by a man she had chosen.

"Yes," she said.

Pembroke leaned down then, holding her effortlessly, his strength cradling her as if she were an egg that might crack. His bright blue eyes were on hers, watching her face steadily, in case she might change her mind. She did not move to touch him but waited quietly as his lips descended on hers.

She closed her eyes and felt their feather touch, as light as down, and as soft. She sighed, opening her mouth beneath his, and he pressed his lips against hers, harder this time, as if he might devour her. She gasped at the onslaught, and he drew back a little, as if afraid that he had offended her.

"No," she said. She took hold of his shoulders and drew him down to her once more. This time it was her lips on his, her mouth that moved beneath him, clumsily but with enthusiasm. Her husband had kissed her only rarely and never well. She had never truly learned for she and Pembroke had been engaged only for one night.

He smiled against her mouth and leaned down again to kiss her in earnest. Pembroke was still careful to draw her out slowly, but his lips moved over hers with such lazy experience, with such sensuous skill that she found almost at once that she had lost her breath.

He instructed her with the motion of his lips until she followed suit and kissed him as he had been kissing her. Then he ran his tongue along the edge of her mouth, sucking on her lower lip until she opened up to him. He plundered her mouth then, and for the first time she felt the ragged edge of his control. The sense of it did not frighten her but made the warmth in her body tighten, its languid heat turning into hunger. She was not certain what she was hungry for, but she knew that Pembroke would sate it.

Arabella gasped, coming fully awake as she heard the maid dropping coal into the grate. She listened as the woman moved about beyond the curtains of her bed, her hand pressed against her chest as if she might stop the erratic beating of her heart.

The dream lived with her, its vivid contours

making her blush even as she lay alone, unseen by anyone. Never in her life had she felt such liquid warmth, such seductive heat. She wondered if such a thing was real or if she might find such sensations only in a dream. She shivered as the maid opened the curtains of her bed.

"Good morning, m'am. The gentleman is up already. Do you need help dressing?"

"No, thank you. Just some tea and breakfast brought into the parlor. We will be on the road early this morning."

"Yes, m'am." The girl curtseyed, showing no sign of judgment or censure, though no doubt she thought that Pembroke had spent the night in that same bed. Very likely the staff of that inn had seen a great deal where Pembroke was concerned. She wondered if he had ever brought Titania there, if he had ever brought the actress to his home in the country. Jealousy prodded her spleen, and she pushed it away.

She dressed quickly in the gown from the day before, straightening its dark blue muslin into some semblance of order. She drew her hair from its night braid and brushed it out quickly before drawing it into a bun at the nape of her neck. A few stray wisps escaped her pins, but she liked the way they framed her face, so she let them be. She had never been a beauty, not even in the full flush of her youth, but that day, with the heightened color in her cheeks and the hint of freedom on the road before her, Arabella smiled at her reflection and was satisfied.

Before she allowed her traveling bag to be taken downstairs, she reached into the bottom for the box hidden there and took out a small velvet bag. She drew it out carefully, almost reverently. She untied the ribbons that bound it closed and opened her palm to catch the only piece of jewelry inside it.

Though she had been a duchess for ten years, her husband had given her few jewels. Her wedding band still rested on her finger, but the other pieces he had given her, a strand of pearls, a brooch of jet, had all been left behind in London. She did not feel as if they truly belonged to her.

Arabella stared down at the ring that rested in her palm. It was the only piece of jewelry she had ever loved.

The ring Pembroke had given her gleamed gold in the light of the fire. She kept it well polished, so it looked as new as the day he had placed it on her hand.

On her wedding day, she had hidden it away so that her father and her husband would not see it. She drew it out only rarely, for it was a piece of her past that never failed to pierce her heart.

She slipped the ring onto her hand, and its ruby caught the light. She kissed it once, furtively, before drawing it off again. Instead of hiding it in the velvet bag, she drew a ribbon from her hair box, a thin ribbon of light pink silk, a color she had always loved but had never worn. She slipped that ribbon through the ring and tied it fast before drawing it around her neck. The ring lay against her heart, between her small breasts. She pressed it once between her palm and her heartbeat, then slipped it inside her bodice where it would be hidden from all eyes, even her own. The high collar of her gown concealed the ribbon completely.

She knew she must in all honor give the ring back. It had been his mother's, and no doubt, in spite of his wild ways, Pembroke would marry one day. He would want to give that ring to the bride he had chosen. She could not in good conscience keep it. Once they were at Pembroke House, safe in Derbyshire, she would give it back to him.

Nine

THE JOURNEY INTO DERBYSHIRE TOOK ANOTHER TWO days. Pembroke sat across from Arabella in his traveling chaise, taking the occasional sip from his brandy flask.

He found that he needed less and less of the stuff to keep his hands from trembling. He wondered if his dependence on the alcohol lived in his mind as much as his body. The first night alone in the sitting room at the inn had been the hardest.

He knew his own weakness and despised it. He had given up brandy once before while on campaign. He had done so to stay alive long enough to watch Anthony Carrington's back when they were at war. Life without brandy had not been worth living. He wondered if he would be able to give it up now.

He held the flask where Arabella could see it because it irritated her to watch him drink. She eyed him from beneath her hideous bonnet, moving her gaze between the scenery beyond the window and him.

Pembroke wondered where she had acquired her distaste for alcohol. Her father had not been much of a drinker. Old Mr. Swanson had come straight into his fortune from the slave trade in the West Indies and had never needed the liquor to make him a violent man. His reputation for striking servants had covered the county. Pembroke wondered how often he had raised his hand to his daughter.

Arabella sat as calm and still as a church mouse, the black crepe of her veil pushed back over the brim so that he could see her face. Since he did not want to look her in the eye, instead he watched the curve of her throat, the fall of her hands in her lap, where they lay encased in black cotton gloves. She had not completely left off her mourning, though if he had his way, she would give up her hideous black before the week was out.

Of course, he had never gotten his way where she was concerned. Why he thought that he might now was a mystery to him.

He spoke without thinking. He knew only that he could not endure another moment of the silence.

"So you will give up your mourning?" he asked.

Arabella turned to him, the wings of her bonnet making her face him straight on. "I beg your pardon?"

"You didn't love your husband. You aren't sorry he's dead. So why wear black when you look so terrible in it?"

He almost wished his words back. For one hideous moment, he thought she might cry. But then he saw that the gleam in her eyes was not tears but barely repressed fury.

"You have no right to speak to me in such a manner."

"I'm the one saving you from a fate worse than death. I think that gives me plenty of rights where you're concerned."

"I beg to differ, my lord."

"I have always wanted to hear you beg. Somehow, I thought it would sound sweeter."

She was almost spitting in her rage. She breathed deeply, her beautiful breasts rising and falling beneath the blue gown she wore and the hideous black bombazine of her cloak. He wanted to peel the crepe and silk away and touch her as he had always longed to touch her, to feel her beneath him as he never had.

Pembroke raised his flask and found that his hand was shaking. He knew this time it was not for need of drink, but he took a swig anyway.

"You are a perfidious bastard."

The words seemed to slip from between her lips of their own accord, so incongruous and unladylike. Pembroke stared at her in shock, his flask forgotten. And then he laughed.

"I absolutely agree with you. I can only hope for my mother's sake that I am not my father's son, though I fear on that count you are mistaken. More's the pity."

She had shocked herself with her own words. He could see that in the sudden flush in her cheeks, in the quickness of her breath. If she were any other woman, he would have drawn her across his lap and let his hands and lips feast on her body. But she was a lady. And he was a blackguard and a cad, but he would never touch a woman against her will. He wondered if he could put his years of experience to the test, if he might seduce even her. Part of him wanted to reach for her and damn the consequences.

Arabella stared at him. If looks could kill, he would

lie bleeding across the velvet squabs of his coach. She reached up then with trembling fingers and untied the ribbons of her hideous black bonnet. She lowered the window beside her very deliberately. The glass tried to stick at first, but she was determined, and the window finally gave way to her wrath. She took the black-dyed straw in one hand, crumpling it, forcing it through the window beside her.

The chaise was traveling at a good clip, for his matched blacks were some of the best horses in the country. The wind of their passing took her bonnet, and it flew out of her black-gloved hands. He stared at her, wondering if he had lost his mind and was dreaming the entire thing, but then, her eyes snapping fire, she drew her gloves off and tossed them after her hat.

Pembroke closed his flask and slipped it back into the pocket of his coat. He thought for a moment that he had swallowed his tongue with lust, but he found it still functional.

"Might I help you with the rest of your gown? I'm not certain it will fit through that window."

He thought she might strike him then. He was sure her hand itched to slap the smug smile from his face. He could not take his gaze away from the cornflower blue of her eyes that seemed to flash silver in her ire. Her cheeks were pink, and he imagined that if he moved to sit beside her, if he pressed his fingertips to those cheeks, they would be warm beneath his touch.

She reached for the top button of her gown and loosened it. She undid the second one, and then the third, until he could see the swell of her breasts beneath. She extended her hand to him, and he almost took it. But he did not, for she did not want him.

"Your flask," she said. "I would have a sip."

He drew it from his pocket and handed it to her, careful not to touch her bare fingers with his own. She took a swig as she had no doubt seen him do, the same practiced flair, the same smile after. Either she drank on the quiet, or she had been watching him very closely over the last two days.

She offered the flask to him. "Thank you. You are rude and you are a thorn in my side, but you are right. I do not mourn my husband. I hate these clothes. I need new ones."

Pembroke swallowed hard. "I will be happy to pay for a new wardrobe, Your Grace."

She laughed at that. "No doubt you would, my lord. But I am not your mistress, nor will I ever be. I'll make my own clothes, and I'll pay my own way."

"With what money?"

"With my father's money."

"Ah." Pembroke did not argue with her inanity, for he was too distracted by the hint of creamy skin above her bodice. He had seen many beautiful women in various states of undress, but none were as erotic as the sight of Arabella with the first buttons of her gown undone.

She did not speak again but leaned back against the squabs of his coach, settling against the velvet as against the pillows of a feather bed. As he watched, she closed her eyes, finally able to lean comfortably now that the hideous bonnet was gone. She slept in the next moment, and he was left watching the rise and fall of her breasts beneath the loosened silk of her gown.

He shifted on his bench, uncomfortable in spite of the cushions beneath him. They were only two hours from Pembroke House, but he knew that they would be two of the longest hours of his life. Still, he did not close his eyes. He let his gaze roam over the curves of her body. He breathed in the cornflower scent of her skin and hair, wishing himself back in time, to the Forest of Arden, where they had both been young, when he once might have touched her.

⤝⤞

Arabella tried to sleep, but with Pembroke's eyes devouring her, she could not. She managed to keep her breathing even, and her eyes closed, but that was as far as her deception went. She was almost glad that she did not sleep, for at least then she did not dream.

Every night since she had left London, she had dreamed of Pembroke coming to her bed. Her sudden obsession with this fantasy was a mystery to her. She hated the marriage bed and all that went with it. But somehow, when Pembroke touched her, it was different. All the world seemed different when she was with him.

She hoped to put her fascination with the carnal aspect of her own mind behind her, but it seemed that her body had different ideas.

In spite of the layers of her gown, shift, and pelisse, she could feel the heat of his body radiating from across the expanse of the coach. She did not know what had possessed her to throw her hated bonnet out of the window, to unbutton her gown, to toss her gloves away. She had never behaved so badly in her life, but suddenly she wondered, why not?

She had obeyed her father and her husband after him. Obedience had never gotten her far. It had brought her to the road she traveled now, fleeing for her life into the forests of Derbyshire. Perhaps she might cast away more than just an ugly bonnet. This flight was more than just a desperate measure to save herself. She could change her life.

Something about Pembroke's presence had always inspired madness in her. As a girl, she had been ready to throw all of her life away and follow him to the Continent and beyond. They had planned to marry and live in Italy, where he would hire out his sword to the highest bidder, where she would bear their children and learn to speak Italian. This madness had seemed almost commonplace when he described it to her all those years ago. Now, sitting across from him in his traveling chaise, she began to feel the rising excitement in her soul once again.

She could not be with him again, that much was abundantly clear. But she could live her own life. She did not have to seclude herself in a quiet cottage for the rest of her days. She could actually enjoy being free.

Arabella felt a rising excitement, a rising joy fill her heart, stealing her breath. She fought it down, trying to be sensible, but to no avail. She kept her hands folded demurely in her lap, but it did not help. She was free, and she might do anything at all with that freedom.

It was enough to make her swoon if she had been the swooning type.

They arrived at Pembroke House just as the sun had begun to set. Though the moat had long since been filled in, the castle looked like a picturesque medieval fortress with modern windows dominating the walls like winking eyes as the slanting sun caught them in its light. The house sat on a bluff surrounded by a well-kept park of oaks and hawthorns. Ivy clung to the old walls, and wisteria rose against the gray stone to bloom white and purple in the fading light.

They both held their silence as Pembroke helped her down from the carriage. The warmth of his hand on hers made her shiver, but she kept her gaze scrupulously away from his. Her unbuttoned gown was hidden beneath her black pelisse now, but she could feel the open air on her skin, the softness of the silk against her throat. It made her feel wanton.

Arabella ignored her own strange reaction and craned her neck to gaze up at the high walls of the house, taking in the sweet scent of wisteria. It had just begun to bloom, and even as day slid into dusk, the heavy perfume of those flowers reached out to touch her where she stood.

She had never before been to his childhood home. She might have been mistress of that place if her father had not promised her elsewhere, if Pembroke's father had not been such a spiteful man. When they were young, she and Pembroke had met at a dance at the assembly hall in the village. He had come to her house to court her once or twice, but they had soon broken that off in the face of their fathers' disapproval. It seemed that the Earl of Pembroke would not receive the daughter of a slave trader, much less allow her to wed his heir. Though Raymond Pembroke would one day be an earl in his own right, her father had set his sights higher for her, and in the end, he used his ill-gotten gains to buy her a duchess's coronet. Pembroke's father told him that he need not waste his time courting a tradesman's daughter, a slave trader's daughter at that.

She wondered what her life would have been like if Pembroke had been allowed to court her openly. They might have married in the village church. They might have three or four children by now. She forced her thoughts into silence, that long-ago loss like a sword point driven into her lungs. She must have shown something of her pain in her face, for Pembroke was beside her in an instant, offering his hand.

He steadied her, and she took comfort from the warmth of his touch on her fingertips. There was no lust between them in that moment, only a shared sympathy, unremitting pain. She thought she saw a shadow of what she felt pass over his face, but then his butler Codington appeared at the doorway of the house, and the moment was broken.

Pembroke's man came down the steps and bowed before them. Arabella was shocked to see him, for he had been in London at Pembroke's townhouse only three days before. If Codington remembered her from the time before, she could discern no sign of it. He was as cool and polite to her as he would have been to any guest of Pembroke House.

For some reason, this indifference was painful, too. He had been her friend once, of a sort. She supposed that Codington was her friend no longer. And who indeed could blame him? She had made his master suffer for years. Had she been in his place, she would not have forgiven her either.

Pembroke must have seen the surprise on her face at the emergence of his butler, for he smiled, clearly grateful to have something easy to talk about. "Codington prides himself on his ability to move troops even faster than Bonaparte."

The older man seemed to notice nothing shocking in the fact that he had traveled over three hundred miles with lightning speed. His voice was as indifferent as if he were addressing an empty chair. "You are welcome to Pembroke House, Your Grace. Your room has been prepared, and I believe you will find everything in order."

"Thank you, Codington."

"I will see you at dinner, Arabella." Pembroke raised her hand, pressing his lips to her palm. She shivered, the heat of his breath warming her to her toes. She thought to chastise him for his familiarity, but she could not seem to find her voice.

Arabella struggled to maintain her façade of false calm as the housekeeper, Mrs. Marks, greeted her in the entrance hall. The older woman wore unrelieved black, but for a cap of Brussels lace that covered her hair. Her dark brown eyes were kind.

"Welcome to Pembroke House, Your Grace. Please come with me, and we will get you settled in."

"Thank you."

Arabella was surprised to find that though the exterior looked ancient save for the beautiful glass windows placed in its façade, Pembroke House was quite modern on the inside. The interior walls were all well-plastered and painted lovely shades of white and cream. Crown molding ran along the ceiling in every room, and though the house was filled with antiques, they were all from the last century and in pristine condition.

The sun was setting across the park, and Arabella stopped on the staircase to take in the view of the oaks with their new green leaves. The warmth of the day rose from the open window, and she took in a deep breath as she gazed down the bluff to where her father's house lay only two miles distant. She could see nothing of her childhood home, but she knew it was close. She would go there tomorrow and find the money she had come for. The sooner she was out of Pembroke's house, the better.

Mrs. Marks led her at once into a comfortable bedroom clearly meant for a lady, beautifully appointed with maple furniture and a soft cream rug. All was light and airy, the satin bedclothes embroidered in tones of ice blue and cream. Something about that shade of blue made Arabella feel at home, and she felt a strange illusion of safety close around her, as if she had been encircled by strong arms.

Arabella bathed in the tub of warm water Mrs. Marks sent up. Pembroke's household staff seemed determined to make her feel welcome. She wondered how many of Pembroke's mistresses this house had seen, how many country parties of debauchery, how many light skirts had come and gone like the tide. She smothered her jealousy and pressed these thoughts from her mind as she donned the one decent evening gown she had brought with her into exile. It was a completely inappropriate gown for a widow to wear, but her entire life was now far outside the pale of decency and propriety. Pembroke's words in the carriage still rang in her ears.

She really did look terrible in black.

The gown she wore now was a deep sea green, the only fashionable dress she had brought with her in her flight from her husband's house. Mrs. Marks had pressed it, and now Arabella stood before a full length of pier glass, smiling at her reflection. It was a vast improvement.

The scalloped edge of the bodice of her gown was demure, but it was low enough that she had been forced to remove the ring from the ribbon she wore and place it on a chain of gold. The gold chain had once been her mother's, and now it showed above the modest neckline. The scooped neck of the gown was cut wide so that her shoulders were displayed, and its cap sleeves left most of her arms bare.

She had not thought to bring gloves for the evening, but Mrs. Marks had taken that matter in hand as she had every other, so that now Arabella was clothed in elegance from her curls to the tips of her slippers. Mrs. Marks had even sent a woman to dress her hair, so that her usually plain locks, hidden always beneath a cap, were now displayed in simple curls that framed her face, with a larger mass of curls drawn to the crown of her head.

Arabella felt a moment of guilt at the thought of dead husband, lying in his crypt. But then she shook herself free of that remnant of her past. Why should she not wear a beautiful gown? She had spent her life hiding, first from her father and then from her husband. She was done with hiding. She looked well for the first time in her life, and she was determined to enjoy it.

She made her way down to the drawing room where she found Pembroke alone, staring into the back garden where his mother's roses had begun to bloom. The French doors were open, and Arabella breathed in the scent of roses mixed with wisteria on the evening wind. She came in as far as the door but then stopped and stared at him. He was so beautiful that he took her breath.

He too had changed for dinner and now wore a coat of midnight blue superfine with a black and silver waistcoat over skintight black trousers. Arabella noticed how hours on horseback had made the muscles of his thighs tighten into sculpted strength. She took in the sight of his broad shoulders, which almost filled the doorway he stood in.

When he turned to her, his dark blond hair fell into his eyes as it always did. Just as he had when he was a boy, he pushed that lock of hair away with one hand as he smiled at her. It was his smile that stopped her heart.

Pembroke opened his mouth to speak, but the sight of her seemed to silence him. He simply stood looking at her in the candlelight. Arabella stepped forward, and he came back into the room as if to meet her halfway. But before either could take another step or speak a word, Titania's voice filled the room, breaking the fragile spell that had fallen.

Ten

"GOOD EVENING, YOUR GRACE. WHAT A PRETTY picture you make as you flee London for your life. For the love of God, Pembroke, you might have brought faster horses. I've been in the village a full day already, waiting for your arrival."

The open warmth that had filled Pembroke's eyes the moment before vanished so quickly that Arabella wondered if she had imagined it. The sardonic smile he turned on Titania could have melted stone. "We had no broom at our disposal, madame."

Arabella colored at his calling Titania a witch, but the courtesan only laughed, the boom of sound filling the room, warming Arabella where she stood. That laugh seemed to say that no matter what went on, all was right with the world. Arabella did not believe the promise of that laugh, but she wished that she could.

"Well, you're in a sour mood and no mistake. Three days on the road will do that to a man, I suppose." Titania's eyes took him in with a gleam of speculation. As Arabella watched her, she wished that she had even half of her self-assurance.

"Well, let's go in to dinner, and I'll tell you why I'm here."

Pembroke led Arabella in to dinner, but he barely looked at her as he seated her at table. A place had been set for Titania as well, and for a moment Arabella wondered if Pembroke had decided to kill two birds with one stone and have an assignation with his mistress while he helped Arabella escape Hawthorne.

The thought was like an icy sluice of water on her skin, but as she ate the chilled cucumber and dill soup a footman placed in front of her, one glance at Pembroke's face disabused her of that notion. Arabella found that she had trouble listening to all that was said as relief swamped her. From his looks and his voice, Pembroke did not seem at all amorous, merely annoyed.

"Before you think I've become one of those jealous, clingy women who can't stand to let you out of my sight, let me put your mind at ease. I still keep a theater in Drury Lane."

"The Duke of Hawthorne pays your bills there, I understand," Pembroke said without sparing a glance at Arabella.

Titania continued her tale. "Well, Prinny's been keeping us in greasepaint and costumes lately, if you must know, but no matter. My theater is doing well."

"My felicitations," Pembroke said.

"Don't be so sour. My theater company has decided to go on tour in the country for the summer, see the sights, take in fresh air…"

"Debauch country lads and lasses," Pembroke said.

Titania dismissed that dig with a wave of her spoon.

"For Midsummer's Eve, we are scheduled to perform in Pembroke village."

"Here?" Pembroke set his spoon down on the table. The footman came and cleared the soup away, bringing in the roast beef.

"Right on your doorstep. Isn't that divine?"

"I wish you much success, Titania, but what has this to do with me?"

"You're going to perform *A Midsummer Night's Dream*," Arabella breathed, the longing in her voice palpable to her own ears.

The conversation stopped dead as both Pembroke and Titania turned to stare at her. Arabella felt a blush rise from beneath the bodice of her gown all the way to the roots of her hair, but even her embarrassment at being the focus of their attention could not take away her pleasure.

"I have never seen a play," she said.

Titania's look softened. She reached across the table and squeezed Arabella's hand. "We will make the performance especially good then. I will be the Fairy Queen, and I would like to persuade Pembroke to stand in as my Oberon."

"You've gone mad," he said.

"Indeed, I have not, my…" Arabella thought for a moment that Titania meant to use an endearment such as "my love" or "my dear," but in the end the actress swallowed whatever she had been about to say. "My lord. It would be for only one night and you would be the hit of the village. They would speak of it as far as London for years to come."

"That's what I'm afraid of."

"You will be divine as Oberon. And as I said, it is only for Midsummer's Eve. One night's playacting will cost you nothing but time."

"I'm surprised you don't expect me to pay for the privilege," Pembroke said.

"Well," Titania smiled, "if you're offering…"

"I am not. Titania, as generous as your offer is, I must decline."

Pembroke's jaw was tight with anger. Arabella wanted more than anything to see that play. She wondered if this might put her in danger. All the *ton* would come to see one of their own performing with a band of players, and Hawthorne might come with them. He was a patron of Titania's, after all.

She pressed her palm onto the tablecloth as the footmen served strawberry ices. Arabella, like her dining companions, left her ice untouched. Perhaps she might see a rehearsal or two, collect her father's money, and flee for parts unknown. She might go to the sea, for she had never seen the ocean. And then, when the *ton* had left Pembroke village far behind, she might return and live there in peace as she had planned.

Titania did not give up on her own plans but hounded her lover like a dog on the heels of a fox. "Pembroke, how long do you think it will take for your gambling and drinking cronies to wonder why you've gone into the country? Hawthorne will hear their speculations, and it might occur to him to come looking for your duchess here."

"Perhaps."

"Her Grace clearly wishes to avoid him. Why she wishes to do so is not my affair. But if you were to perform one night for the joy of it, your time in the country would be explained away. Hawthorne is a patron of the theater, but he hates all plays. He would never come to Derbyshire simply to watch you make a fool of yourself."

Arabella flinched at Titania's choice of words, but Pembroke's face lightened a little. The tension in Arabella's shoulders eased. "You begin to make sense, Titania."

"I always make sense, Pembroke. You just don't always attend to what I am saying."

"So your troupe will come here and perform one night of Shakespeare with an amateur. Will that not cost you good money?"

"It will," she said. "But between us, there need be no talk of price."

It was Pembroke's turn to look embarrassed. Her fear of Hawthorne and her speculation about the *ton* of London was burned away. There was a heavy tension in the air that seemed to press on Arabella's lungs. She felt like an intruder. She was tempted to rise and leave them to each other, but her jealousy held her in her chair.

Titania's voice was as soft as Arabella had ever heard it. This woman slept with Pembroke for money, but it was clear that she loved him, too. Somehow, that made it worse.

"Rehearse with us now and then, when your affairs allow. Let my company camouflage your real reason for being here."

Pembroke sat in silence, his eyes on Titania's. Arabella did not think she could bear one more moment of that silence. Pain had come to twine with jealousy, and she had to fight them both to breathe. She could not bear the silence another moment, so she broke it.

"I would dearly love to see the play," Arabella said.

Her voice was quiet, but it severed the connection between Pembroke and his mistress. He turned to her as if he had just remembered that she was in the room. He smiled, and she felt the new, unaccustomed heat of desire begin in her toes, rising to cover the rest of her body like a river of fire.

"Will you help me learn my lines?" he asked.

Arabella forced a smile. His eyes had taken on a gleam of mischief, and for once she would meet him in the same spirit. She ignored the pain lodged in her throat, the jealousy that made it difficult to swallow.

Arabella reached for her spoon and took up a bite of the melting ice. The sweetness of the strawberry burst on her tongue, and for a moment she thought the pleasure of it would overwhelm her. It served its purpose though, to take her eyes and mind away from him. When she spoke, her voice sounded almost light, almost carefree.

"Of course I will help you if you need it. You will make a wonderful Oberon."

Titania's voice boomed. "Excellent! Then we will have a play. Good thing, too, since my troupe arrives in the village first thing tomorrow."

◦━◦

Titania did not stay past dinner. Pembroke offered to walk her to the front door. He stood close to her in the entrance hall, and Arabella found herself listening from the drawing room to all they said.

"Will you not stay?" Pembroke asked.

Titania waved one hand, but she spoke quietly. "No, indeed. One woman in the house is enough."

He did not answer that, so she went on. "I am perfectly comfortable at the inn."

A silence fell, and Arabella stepped to the door and peered out. Pembroke was kissing Titania, his lips lingering over hers as if to drink her in. Arabella made a concerted effort to turn back, to look away, but she could not seem to take her eyes off Pembroke and his mistress. It was Titania who drew back and who sauntered calmly to the front door, leaving her lover behind.

"Good night, Pembroke. See to your guest."

The door closed behind her, and Codington bowed himself out of the entrance hall as if he had seen and heard nothing. Arabella wondered how good servants learned that cool air of detachment and if Codington might be so kind as to teach it to her.

Arabella turned away from Pembroke and his entrance hall and went back into the drawing room. A few candles were lit, but clearly the staff expected them to go to bed early. It had been a long day, and she was sick at heart, but she knew that if she retired after watching Pembroke kiss his mistress, she would not sleep.

Brandy and two glasses had been set out on the sideboard. Arabella crossed the room and poured herself three fingers, as she had seen Pembroke do.

The scent of the brandy was harsh in her nostrils as she sniffed at it. She had never cared for the smell and cared for the taste even less. Still, she tipped the glass back and downed it.

"Arabella!"

Pembroke crossed the room in three strides, taking the now empty glass away from her. The heat of the brandy burned like fire in her throat and created a roiling mass of heat in her stomach, lingering with the remains of her dinner.

Arabella took a deep breath, determined not to be sick. She moved the French doors, pushing them open so that she could feel the cool night air on her face. She had not choked on the brandy, though she had wanted to. As she drank, she had not been able to draw enough breath to choke. As she felt an alcoholic languor coming to claim her, she laughed, taking in the scent of roses from the garden beyond.

Now that she had her breath back, Arabella also found her voice. "Will you drink with me, my lord?"

"No, Arabella, I will not."

She turned to face him, the breeze from the garden at her back, moving the silk skirts of her gown against her legs.

"I do not recall giving you leave to use my given name."

"I am your only friend in the world. I will call you anything I wish."

"Not harlot," she said. "Not mistress."

There was a long silence that seemed to twine itself around them, stuffing itself down their throats. Arabella wished for another glass of brandy. The drink had freed her tongue and had made her limbs heavy, but it had not touched her heart. Her heart was still broken. Perhaps that was why Pembroke had stayed drunk for so many years. Drink did not alleviate pain but simply made it bearable.

"You saw me kiss her," Pembroke said.

"Yes. Not that it matters to me."

"Of course it matters. It was rude of me and callous. I apologize, Arabella."

"You owe me nothing."

She closed her eyes as if to blot out the words they had spoken as well as the sight of him. As she listened, he crossed the room until he was standing directly in front of her. The warmth of his body surrounded her. When she opened her eyes, he stood less than a foot away.

"I'll go to my father's and find his money," she said. "I'll be gone soon after, and you need never see me again."

"But what if I want to see you again?"

"That would not be a good idea," she said, her voice harsh in her own ears, like the voice of someone else.

"Do you hate me then?" he asked.

"I hate myself."

"We have that in common."

She laughed, and she heard her own pain in it. "You hate me, too?"

"No," he answered. "Self-loathing has been my only companion for years."

"And Anthony Carrington," she quipped.

He did not rise to the bait but nodded. "Yes. Except for Anthony. And now for you."

"You have your mistresses to keep you company."

"One woman is much the same as the next."

Arabella wanted to make some clever retort, but her wit failed her.

"All women are alike, but for you," Pembroke said.

"I'm the one you never had."

"The one I loved once."

The finality of the word *once* was what undid her. She began to slip down against the French door, as if her knees could no longer hold her up. She had the good sense to slide into a Queen Anne chair that stood to one side of the garden doors. The soft cushion seemed to buoy her up, even as the hard back of the chair dug into her spine, reminding her that she had a backbone and that it was her choice whether she would use it.

With the death of her husband, her world had changed. With the Duke of Hawthorne chasing her out of London, she had been swept into another world. She had grown up under the harsh reign of her father and had languished in silence for ten years beneath the boot of her husband. But neither man had ever threatened her life. The duke had threatened her very existence, and nothing would ever be the same.

As she sat in Pembroke's drawing room, Arabella began to wonder if the path she was on was not a disaster. Here in this place, beyond any future she had ever imagined, she saw for the first time how much she hated her life. That quiet life of desperation, taking whatever scraps were offered, was gone forever. If she chose, she could build a new one.

The brandy had given her another gift, the ability to face her life as her own responsibility. She could no longer look to her father, her husband, or even to Pembroke to give it shape. She would shape it herself.

After ten years of being entombed alive in marriage to an elderly man who could not love her, a vibrant new life beckoned to her. She did not know what that life would look like, but she knew that she wanted it.

Pembroke had not spoken again. He stood staring down at her where she sat, helpless in his Queen Anne chair. She saw him differently, too. He was a casualty of her father's cruelty, just as she was. She had always blamed him for not coming to her rescue so many years ago, for believing the worst of her, for not answering her letters, for turning away. But now, as she sat drunk in his country house, that old anger began to slip away.

"I am sorry," she said. "I am sorry that I hurt you."

He stiffened, his back straightening against the onslaught of her simple words. It was as if she had stabbed him, as if she had taken a knife out of her reticule and driven it into his heart. He still felt something for her then, if only anger, if only pain. She was responsible for that pain as much as her dead father was. She stood, unsteady on her feet, and went to him.

There were few candles lit, so the room was bathed in shadow, with pockets of warm light given off by a candelabrum by the door and another by the window.

The silk of her gown brushed against her skin like the touch of a butterfly's wing as she began to walk to him. Her stays hugged her ribs beneath her bodice, but instead of a confinement, they felt like a lover's embrace. She had never been embraced by a lover, save in her dreams of Pembroke.

Pembroke stood in silence, watching her.

Arabella felt the lawn of her shift brush against her thighs. The silk of her gown whispered as she moved, and she wondered why she had never noticed that sound before. The room was strangely silent, a quiet so deep that she did not know if they would ever find the end of it.

The ruby Pembroke had given her so many years ago seemed to burn like a brand against her skin beneath the bodice of her gown. She did not feel as if the ring would stop her, but that it urged her on.

Arabella raised herself on her toes, laying her hands on the solid firmness of his upper arms for balance as she took in his scent of cinnamon. Pembroke did not pull back or push her away but stood frozen in place as if he had been encased in a sheath of ice. He did not even seem to breathe as Arabella pressed her lips against his.

She did not know what else to do, so she kissed him, putting all her love, all her loss and sorrow, into the pressure of her lips on his. She knew that she was clumsy. She also knew that no one would ever love him as much as she did, that day or ever.

Pembroke gripped her arms, his strong hands making her feel even smaller than she was. She had begun to totter on her toes, for she had to stretch far to reach his lips. But instead of pushing her away as she had been so certain he would, Pembroke drew her close, bringing her into the circle of his arms, lowering his head, bending down to take her lips with his.

His kiss was gentle, as soft as hers had been, but the heated touch took her breath, and she gasped, opening her mouth beneath his. Pembroke pressed inside, stroking her tongue as if to soothe her, as if to savor her, as if she were the one taste he had hungered for all his life.

His hands pressed against the small of her back, drawing her flush against him as his lips devoured hers. As she followed his lead, she remembered the dream of Pembroke in her bed, and she kissed him as she had learned to kiss him in that dream. At first, he jolted a little with shock, but in the next moment he drew her even closer, his hands moving up her back into her hair, trapping her head so that she could not pull away from his questing lips even if she wanted to.

He tasted of the strawberry ices they had eaten. He tasted of mystery and danger, as if he held a whole world within the circle of his arms, a world she had never seen, not in her dream and not in the years she had spent in her husband's bed.

She soon forgot both her husband and the dream she had of Pembroke. There was only the man she loved, his arms around her, his chest pressed hard against her breasts, and his thighs bracketing her own so that she could feel the heat of him through the soft silk of her gown.

For one heady moment she thought he might draw her down into the shadows of the settee before the unlit fire, that he might cover her body as he had in her dreams. Instead, Pembroke moved back, but he did not let her go. He stared down at her, drinking in the sight of her face just as she drank in the sight of his. Arabella smiled at him, unable to hide her delight, not knowing why she should feel as she did. Nothing was solved between them, and nothing ever would be. But he had given her one of the greatest gifts of her life. She would remember their kiss until the day she died.

Her body was uncomfortable. Her gown and stays,

which before had felt so sensuous against her skin, now felt too tight and hot, as if she had worked in the garden during the heat of the day. Her mouth hungered for another taste of his. She could still feel the contours of his tongue as she ran her own over the smoothness of her teeth.

As she was thinking these things, Pembroke took a step back from her. He kept his hands on her arms in case she faltered. She saw the unhappiness in his eyes, and she pressed her fingertips to his lips. She spoke quickly, before he could give voice to his thoughts and ruin the moment for her.

"It's all right," she said. "I won't throw myself at you again."

In the end, it was she who stepped away from him. She took up one of the candles by the door to light her way to her room. Arabella moved into the corridor beyond the drawing room and began the long, slow climb up the wide formal staircase. She did not look back because she did not want to see Pembroke's eyes. It pained her that the kiss that had brought her so much joy had brought him only regret.

Arabella pushed the thought out of her mind. She had had enough of pain. She renounced it. From now on, she would embrace joy. There was so much joy in the world, and she wanted more of it.

Eleven

PEMBROKE WATCHED ARABELLA WALK UP THE STAIRCASE of his father's house, the short train of her evening gown trailing behind her on the mahogany stairs. He stayed in the doorway of the drawing room for a long time, listening to the tick of the grandfather clock on the landing above. When it finally hit the stroke of midnight, he forced himself to walk up the stairs to his bedroom, alone.

Arabella slept in the room he had set aside for her, the room he had decorated to match the color of her eyes. Her room was down the hall from his own bedroom suite, something he had not considered until the moment she kissed him.

He could still taste her lips if he closed his eyes. He could smell her light perfume. Or perhaps she wore no perfume at all. Perhaps if he divested her of her silk and lawn, her skin would give off that perfume simply of itself. The thought made Pembroke catch his breath, and he cursed himself.

Reynolds seemed to catch something of his mood, for his valet helped him undress in silence. Wearing only his trousers and lawn shirt, he dismissed his man, who bowed once before leaving for the night. Pembroke prowled the edges of his bedroom, crossing into the sitting room where he kept a bottle of brandy.

He poured himself a liberal amount, half a glass, before setting the decanter down. Pembroke warmed the brandy between his hands, lifted it to his lips, but he did not drink. The scent of the heavy liquor turned his stomach. All he could think of was the way that same brandy had smelled on Arabella's sweet breath when she had leaned up on tiptoe to kiss him.

She could still turn him inside out. Years later, after she betrayed him and left him for another, she need do nothing but crook her little finger and he came running, a dog come to heel.

He set the glass down and forced himself to lie on his bed. He stared up at the gold-and-white canopy above his head, alone in the vast expanse where he slept and where he indulged in love play. Never before had he faced a sleepless night in that bed, for always when he came to the country, he brought a great deal of distraction with him to drown the silence.

He thought of throwing on a coat and going to Titania in the village. He might sate his longing for one woman in the body of another. He might even stay out long enough in the morning for Arabella to know that he had been gone.

He wanted to hurt her. He wanted to smash her calm, to decimate the serenity of her smiles. He could not bear to see that calm, that serenity, when he was left with nothing but pain.

Why had she kissed him? Why, after days of protest and slurs against his whores, had she pressed her lips to his? Did she hope to muddle his mind? To wreak havoc on what was left of his life? If so, she had done it, in spades.

Pembroke lay against the bolster holding his breath, listening to the silence of the house as if he might hear Arabella's soft tread on the carpet outside his door. He had left his door unlocked, as if in a mad, vain hope that she might come to him. Had she been any other woman who had offered herself to him, he would have gone to her.

But she was no ordinary woman. She was Arabella, the only woman on earth who mattered.

Pembroke turned over on his side and covered his head with a pillow. Perhaps if he lay perfectly still, his body would grow bored of its hunger for her and go to sleep. He lay beneath the covers for an hour before sleep slowly stole over him, bringing him almost at once into a dream.

He knew it was a dream because, in it, he was not angry. Though there was no moon, the windows of his bedroom gave a milky light. It was the dark of the moon, so the moonlight that covered his bed like an enchantment was simply a figment of his mind, a part of his dream.

Pembroke knew he was dreaming because in the shadows Arabella stood before him in a nightgown only the most daring courtesan would ever have worn. At first glance, the lawn night rail seemed demure, save for a neckline that dove between her breasts, tied with a light blue ribbon beneath them. But when she moved, the gown caught the light, and he saw that it was almost completely translucent.

Pembroke stared at Arabella's body beneath the soft lawn as she stepped toward his bed. Her small breasts rose high above that blue ribbon, and Pembroke wanted to reach for her and unwrap her. He hungered to draw the gown open and to feast his eyes and his lips on the curve of her breasts.

As if Arabella could hear his thoughts, she raised her hand to that ribbon, slowly untying the bow. The gown opened beneath her hands as she drew it back and down her shoulders. The lawn pooled at her feet, and she stepped toward him, raising herself onto his bed without hesitation.

"Arabella."

She drew close to him on the bed, as naked as he was.

There was no hesitation in her eyes, no pretense of modesty, no embarrassment. He feared for a moment that his dream would change, that Arabella would suddenly transform into someone else, one of the knowledgeable courtesans who so often frequented his bed. But Arabella did not leave him. She kept her shape and her soft blue eyes.

For years he had remembered those eyes as being as blue as ice, like the winter that had descended over his heart. Since she had come back into his life, Pembroke had begun to think of those eyes as the color of light blue flame, a fire that might consume him.

Arabella kissed him then, and it was not a courtesan's kiss but the clumsy kiss of an innocent. Pembroke drew her against him, reveling in the feel of her curves.

She was slight; her breasts rose in peaks to press against his chest. Her belly was soft, and her thighs beckoned him. He pressed himself against her but did not draw her beneath him as he wished. He did not want to frighten her.

He bent his head to teach her how to kiss, and she followed his lead, catching on quickly, just as she had in the drawing room. The cavern of her mouth was sweet against his tongue, and she pressed her lips to his eagerly, opening her mouth under his to give him access to all her secrets.

Arabella moved close to him, wrapping her arm around his neck and drawing him down on top of her. Pembroke tried to pull back, tried to keep his weight off her slender frame, but Arabella only smiled, coaxing him with her hands and lips to lie on top of her again.

"I love to feel your body on mine," she said. "I feel safe from all the world when you lie with me."

Pembroke shuddered, his control beginning to slip. He ached to possess her completely. A part of his mind urged him onward, telling him that one more conquest would count for little in the long endless trek of his life. But Arabella was no conquest. Pembroke knew, even in the dream, that it was she who conquered him.

He groaned and pressed his face into the soft satin of her hair. Her long hair lay against his pillow, spread out like a fall of honey against the white of his linen sheets. She shifted beneath him so that his erection fit between the contours of her thighs.

"I do not mind if you hurt me," she said. "I know that the marriage bed is pain. But you are worth it."

Pembroke kissed her then, his lips pressed hard against hers as if to eat up her words, as if to take away her years in her husband's bed, all the years they had been apart.

He woke abruptly to the light of dawn covering his bed. He turned from the rays of the sun toward his dream, but it was gone. He could not get it back. His body was still hard, aching with need for her soft sweetness. His heart ached more.

He lay on his back as the hunger of his body slowly subsided. He thought of the empty years of Arabella's marriage, and what those years must have cost her. Perhaps she was well paid for the pain she had caused him. Perhaps a duchess's coronet was not the prize she had thought it would be.

Pembroke told himself not to be a fool. Arabella had made her bargain years ago, and now they both had to keep it.

But he found that he could not be angry with her anymore. Though his heart still bled, and no doubt always would, he did not have to cherish his anger.

After all the years he had tried and failed to die on the Continent, every mad raid he had led, every cavalry charge that had left his men dead on the field while he still lived, now, finally, he could let his bitterness go.

Perhaps the core of his fury had slowly burned away in the heat of countless battlefields, in the heat of brandy and women and gaming. Perhaps he had sinned enough to drive it out of his system, the way brandy dried out after a few days of sobriety.

Pembroke had defined his life by his bitterness, by

the woman he had lost. But now that Arabella had returned to his life, he wondered if he had more to live for than anger and regret.

⌑

He found Arabella already seated at the breakfast table dressed once more in her demure gown of dark blue muslin. Her soft, honey-colored curls were caught in combs at the nape of her neck, and a ribbon of dark satin was woven through her hair. Her light blue eyes met his, and he felt the power of her gaze run through his body like lightning.

"Good morning," she said, smiling as if she had just awakened from a night of blissful sleep. For the first time since they had begun their trek into the country, she looked rested and almost happy. He could think only of how her hair had looked in his dream, spread out like a fall of honey against his pillows. His body hardened in response, and he cursed himself once more for a fool.

"Tea?" she asked, completely unaware of the battle he waged silently as he stood in the doorway, unable to move either forward or back.

"No," he said, his voice sounding strangled to his own ears. "Coffee."

She did not wait for the footman to bring it but rose herself and poured his coffee from the silver urn that stood on the sideboard. She brought brioche and butter and placed both alongside the china already set down for him.

She seemed calm, unconcerned, as if nothing at all had passed between them. And yet he stood in the same room, his lust riding him. He could not draw her into the vortex of dark desire and hedonistic pleasure that he lived in. Left unchecked, the darkness in his soul would eat her alive, just as it was devouring him.

"Arabella," he said. "I must apologize for last night."

She lowered her toast and jam, looking at him inquisitively, for all the world as if she did not remember to what he referred. She did not speak but set her toast down on the plate in front of her.

"I took a liberty," he continued. "I know you have no wish to be my mistress. In the future, I will respect that. I give you my word of honor that I will not touch you again."

A shadow crossed the light blue of her eyes, but it was gone before he could be certain of it. She smiled, calm serenity radiating from her.

"I accept your apology," she said. "But it is unnecessary. If you recall, it was I who kissed you."

Arabella sipped her tea, and the warmth in her eyes drew him in. "Sit and eat, Pembroke. I am heading out to my father's house within the hour. Once I have his money in hand, I will be out of your hair and out of your life."

"I'm going with you."

She met his eyes, and it was as if their cornflower blue pierced his skin. Then she smiled, and he felt as warm as if he stood in the summer sun. No doubt he was losing what was left of his drink-addled mind.

"All right," she said.

As he watched her delicately nibble on a slice of toast, he realized that he had no idea how he would keep his promise not to touch her.

Twelve

THOUGH ARABELLA HAD NOT BEEN ON HORSEBACK IN years, she could not stand to be confined to a carriage on that beautiful day. So she rode a gentle mare to her father's house, as Pembroke rode his warhorse, Triton. The spring seemed to rise up out of the ground to greet her, the air so much gentler than the staid, closed air of London. She had been trapped in the city too long. She was happy to be free of it.

Before breakfast, she had walked in the rose garden. The warmth of the day had come upon her like a blessing as she took in deep breaths of the fresh air rising on the breeze from the river. Pembroke's mother was many years dead, but her roses still bloomed red, white, and gold, all different shapes and types, another form of immortality. Pembroke was another of that good lady's contributions to the world. To leave the world a garden and a child was no small thing.

Arabella found herself longing for her own mother as she stood among those blooms, thinking of the one time she had gone with her to meet Lady Pembroke. Arabella had been a child of five and her mother had brought her along on an afternoon call. The lady had been gracious, as her own mother was, and she had been kind. Arabella wondered if she might take a cutting of those roses for her own garden someday. She would ask Pembroke, once she knew where her cottage would be.

Her mount, a white mare named Blossom, moved slow and sedate over the long, worn paths between her father's house and Pembroke's. During the summer they had spent together, they had walked those paths a hundred times. They had eaten picnics by the river and strolled beneath the spreading oaks.

Pembroke and Arabella spoke little on their journey for he seemed lost in his thoughts. She hoped he was not still embarrassed about that morning or about the kiss they had shared the night before.

Never in her life had she thrown herself at a man. She never thought to do so again, though the experience had been intoxicating. Pembroke had responded to her kiss and had even kissed her back, just as he had in her dreams. But he was used to women with far more wiles and experience than she would ever possess.

She drew her mind away from such thoughts and looked at the verdant beauty all around her, the shades of green of the summer trees. If she never saw another city again, it would be too soon. Those ten years trapped in her husband's townhouse had been all of any city she would need for a lifetime. She was contemplating the beauty of the country all around her when they crossed the gate onto her father's land.

Of course, it was not his land anymore. Her father

was five years dead, and his estate had passed into her dower portion, which was a part of the larger Hawthorne duchy. Under normal circumstances, as far as she was concerned, Hawthorne might have kept her father's estates and welcome. But he had forced her hand with his threats to marry her, by bringing a knife into her bed.

Arabella had had her fill of those who would take from her, giving nothing back but grief. She would build a new life. Finding her father's cache of gold was only her first step into a larger world, the world of her freedom.

"Are you sure this gold even exists?" Pembroke asked.

Arabella looked at him, raising one brow. He had spoken her thoughts aloud, as if they were in conversation already. He had done that many times when they were younger, but she did not like it that he could still do it now.

"I am sure," she said, keeping her eyes turned front. Her father was many things, one of which was cagey. He had never trusted another man in all his life. He had never trusted her. He had sold her to the duke, hoping for entry into the world of the *ton*, which would have no part of him, but as soon as the duke's debts were paid with Swanson slave trade money, her husband had cut her father off completely, as if he had never existed, as if she had come from her mother alone.

Her father had been bitter about that, no doubt, for he had always been a bitter man. After her wedding, she had never seen him again. But she had known him well, as any victim knows her master. She knew his ways and the workings of his mind. What once had been a matter of survival now would serve her well. She had watched him in secret and knew the combination of his hidden safe. Her father would never have told another living soul about it. If the house was still standing, that money was there.

When they approached her father's house, she stopped Blossom in her tracks and took a moment to catch her breath. Swanson House gleamed in the morning sun, its red brick warm and inviting. That facade was a deception, as it always had been throughout her childhood. Before her mother passed away, there had been love and laughter between those walls. Her mother had died the year Arabella turned six, and the sun had not entered those walls again.

As she looked at the house that had been her prison until her seventeenth year, her scars throbbed against the soft linen of her chemise. She shifted her shoulders, but the pressure still lay on her back like the lash of her father's riding crop.

So be it. She was here. She could accept that her freedom must come at a price. The visitation of old demons was a small price to pay, though she was sure that it would not be the last.

Pembroke had drawn his horse close to hers, placing himself between her and the house. He watched her face, and Triton stood still beneath him.

The stallion's stillness was not one of idleness but a deadly readiness that came before battle. He had picked up on his master's mood and now stood ready to charge into the thick of an enemy's lines. Arabella wondered what Pembroke had seen on the Continent, what he and Triton had lived through in their shared quest to set Europe free from the marauding armies of Bonaparte.

"Are you well?" he asked, the smiling lines around his mouth suddenly grim. His blue eyes surveyed her as if looking for weakness, as if delving for answers to other questions he could not ask.

"I am well," she said. "It has been a long time."

"You did not come back after you married?"

"Never."

That one word held more truth than she had ever meant to speak. She turned her gaze from the seeking blue of Pembroke's eyes to the house behind him. The grouping of maples and hawthorns was simply a park, the graveled drive that led through the gate to the mansion simply a road. She squared her shoulders and kept her gaze on the redbrick house before her. She waited in silence until her demons fell silent.

"I am ready," she said.

Pembroke nodded once then urged Triton forward. The stallion did not leap ahead but kept a slow pace in front of Blossom as if he meant to keep himself and his master between Arabella and danger.

Perhaps she had grown too fanciful in the last week as she fled Hawthorne's threats on her virtue and on her life. Whatever was true, she felt infinitely better that Pembroke was with her. No matter what else lay between them, he would protect her as much as he could. There was something solid and vibrant about him that drove away the darkness of this place. She was grateful for his strength as she stepped into her past.

They rode to the stables and found them empty. No horses filled the many stalls, and no groom waited to greet them. Pembroke frowned, displeased, but Arabella was not surprised. Her husband had ignored this estate since it had come into his hands. The Duke of Hawthorne had no use for a smallish country house in the wilds of Derbyshire.

"Follow me," Arabella said. "If there is anyone still here, they will be in the kitchen building."

Pembroke seemed to disagree but said nothing as she took the lead. Triton did not like following Blossom but calmed at once when Pembroke murmured to him. Arabella ignored both the males in her company and rode on.

She came to the kitchen behind the house. The small building with its garden was hidden from the mansion by a row of high hedges. The scent of boxwood filled her nostrils, taking her back to the carefree days of her early childhood, when her young mother had chased her among those shrubs on the way to find some bread and honey in the kitchen. It seemed that she might find her mother waiting for her around the next turn of the path. It occurred to her that the mother she remembered had been years younger than Arabella was now.

She stopped outside the garden's picket fence. The fence had once been white, but now the paint had peeled away, leaving the gray, weathered wood beneath. The garden still bloomed with thyme, rosemary, and marjoram. Arabella could hear the hum of bees from the hive just beyond the next rise. She waited as Pembroke got off his horse, tying Triton to a fence post. He looped the leading rein casually, as if he truly did not expect his horse to leave him behind. No doubt Triton never would.

Pembroke reached for her and drew her down from the sidesaddle. Blossom stood as still as a post until Arabella was safely on the ground, then she lowered her head to munch the sweet green grass at her feet. Pembroke looped her reins over the fence as well, though she would not wander off as long as Triton was there.

Arabella opened the kitchen gate and walked through the garden, careful to keep to the paths between the neatly laid squares of vegetables and flowering herbs. The scent of that garden gave her pause, covering her with the breath of the past.

Mrs. Fielding came out of the kitchen then, still neat as a pin in spite of the pure white of her hair. The last ten years had aged her considerably, but the cook of Swanson House walked without a stoop, her slight, spry frame still wrapped in an apron that was too large for her. She bent down to pick a bit of rosemary, but one horse whinnied at the other, and Mrs. Fielding looked up, shielding her eyes from the morning sun.

"Miss Arabella? Is that you?"

Arabella did not speak but crossed the distance to the woman who had been her only haven in the years after her mother died. She meant to offer her hand, to press the elderly lady's free palm between her own. Instead she wrapped her arms around Mrs. Fielding as tears coursed down her cheeks.

Mrs. Fielding dropped the herbs she had picked

onto the ground. She held Arabella close, pressing her hands against her back, stroking and soothing her as if she were a child still and had run to her after a beating. Mrs. Fielding said not a word but offered her strength as she always had to a girl who had nothing in the world, and no one.

Arabella was the first to pull away. "I am very happy to see you."

Mrs. Fielding smiled, wiping her own eyes with the edge of her too-large apron. "We thought you dead or worse," she said, "gone off to London with that old devil."

"Better than the devil I knew," Arabella quipped.

At first, Mrs. Fielding looked frightened, as if old Mr. Swanson might hear the girl's words and beat her for them. But when she remembered that the old man was dead and buried, she laughed a little. "The old duke wasn't bad to you, was he?"

"No, Mrs. Fielding, he was kind. As kind as his nature would allow."

Mrs. Fielding harrumphed at that. She had seen enough of what passed for the occasional, halfhearted kindness of the cruel in her time. She wrapped one arm around Arabella's slender waist and drew her toward the kitchen. "And who is this fine young man you bring us?" Her brown eyes gleamed with mischief and with pleasure. "Might this be the young lord from over the way? The young man I had picked out for you to marry?"

Arabella blushed and Pembroke stepped forward, smiling. Charming old women was one of his many talents. Arabella's heart ached to see it, a deep pain that was harder to bear than any other, a pain so broad that she thought she would collapse beneath it.

"I would have married her, too, if the duke hadn't carried her off," Pembroke said, the lilt of his tone so like his voice when he was a boy.

Mrs. Fielding smiled up at him as if she were a girl of fifteen. "And you still might," she said.

Pembroke's laughter boomed as they entered into the whitewashed walls of the kitchen. Arabella's blush grew deeper, her embarrassment overwhelming her pain. Seeing her blush, Mrs. Fielding finally let that fruitless subject go.

"Sit here and drink some tea. What brings you here, Miss Arabella? Or ought I to call you Your Worship now, or some such?"

Arabella laughed. "Just Arabella, please, Mrs. Fielding. My days as a duchess are behind me."

"And good riddance," Mrs. Fielding said. "Now you can come home and live among decent people, God be praised."

Arabella did not contradict her but drank her tea. That was indeed what she hoped for, if she could elude Hawthorne and his schemes for her future.

Pembroke sat at the old oak table in the kitchen as well. The sunlight streamed through the open doorway and lit his hair with gold. His blue eyes smiled at her over the mug he drank from. Earl or not, he seemed not to care that he drank from earthenware.

Ten years had fallen from his shoulders at the sight of her old cook. He looked light and at ease, though that might just have been his joy in the spring day and happiness at the thought of finally being rid of her.

Mrs. Fielding sliced off hunks of her fresh white bread, covering it with newly churned butter before handing a slice each to Pembroke and to Arabella.

"You still need fattening up, Miss Arabella. Have they no decent food in London either?"

Pembroke laughed again, but this time he silenced himself by taking a great bite of the bread. Arabella savored her own, the butter melting on her tongue, covering the soft white crust with inexplicable sweetness. She blinked back tears. She could not be overcome by her love for her old savior or by memories. She had come back to Swanson House for only one reason, and she must see it through. Now that she was there she had only one fear, that by some strange mischance, her husband had found the cache of gold first.

"Mrs. Fielding, after my father died, did you ever see the old duke come to Swanson House?"

Mrs. Fielding's eyes ceased to sparkle, and she sat down heavily on the other side of the table across from Pembroke. "Aye, we saw him indeed. Just twice. Once after the old master died, and once again three months ago."

Arabella almost could not hear herself think over the sound of the pounding of her heart. She took a fortifying sip of tea and another bite of bread under the watchful eyes of her old cook. She thought to ask another question, but Mrs. Fielding spoke on, as if a dam had broken. Her words flowed out in a torrent, and Arabella found that she could only listen.

"The old duke had little use for this place. He said it was part of your dower portion and no good to him. He sold off the horses and the cattle, the best furniture, even your mother's spinet, God rest her soul. He drank us dry of every bottle of port and Madeira your father ever put by, and what he didn't drink, he carried off with him to London."

Mrs. Fielding spat out the word *London* as if she were spitting on the devil. Arabella was shocked at her vehemence, but the old woman was not done yet with her tirade.

"His High and Mighty Grace turned out all the staff but myself and the old steward, Grayson. He said that we two might stay and keep the house in order, like he was granting us a boon. Most of the others found places elsewhere, but some had to go to Manchester to work in the factories."

Mrs. Fielding shuddered, and Arabella could not blame her. She knew little of the industry that had become a blight on the landscape, but she had heard nothing good. Pembroke sat listening to this litany of horrors with no expression on his face at all. For a moment, Arabella wished she had not brought him. She was ashamed of her husband and of his dismissive cruelty to the people who had lived on her family's land for generations.

"The tenants are all well. They keep planting the corn, wheat, and barley and bringing it in. I've had to shut the house up. With no one to keep it, it has become a moldering tomb."

Mrs. Fielding broke off to sip her own tea. Arabella finally spoke. "Perhaps that is fitting."

The old woman looked into her eyes. Arabella felt as if her soul was bared to the woman who had seen her through so much pain. It had been Mrs. Fielding who had dressed the wounds from her beatings. There had only been two bad enough to leave scars, but the old cook knew of the years of cruelty and offhand slaps that Mr. Swanson had delivered to his daughter from the age of six onward.

"Perhaps it is," Mrs. Fielding said. "But this land is yours, as is this house and all in it. It was wrong of the old duke to sell it off and to turn out the staff like stray dogs."

Arabella felt tears rise in her eyes. "It was wrong of him. I am heartily sorry for it."

Pembroke caught her hand in his, and there was no hint of lust in his touch, only compassion. Her palm and fingers disappeared into his great paw, and the warmth of his touch gave her immeasurable comfort. She felt her tears recede.

"Well, none of the evil was your doing, Miss Arabella. You're the one to suffer with your dower portion gone. Though the furniture and wine cellar have long been sold, the land is still here. That's something, after all."

"Indeed," Arabella said. "Mrs. Fielding, you said that my husband came here twice. When he visited the second time…"

"In the dead of this winter he came… well, in early March of this year. You know how cold the wind blows even then, and the snow just melting on the roads. He came alone on horseback. I'd have thought a ride like that would kill a man as old as the duke. When he arrived, he was coughing up blood. I was sure he had the consumption, and I thought it the judgment of God."

Arabella flinched and Pembroke pressed her hand.

"I am sorry for speaking so plain, miss. But he was a bad man, and not worthy to kiss the hem of your gown, no matter how many coronets he wore." Mrs. Fielding was defiant.

"How long did he stay?" Pembroke asked.

"A good two days, though I think he'd have left sooner if he had not been so ill. He spent all his time in your father's library. It was the one room he left alone in the whole house."

Arabella felt sick. If her father's money was still in the house, it was in the hidden safe in the library. If her husband had found it, that cache of gold would have become one more part of his duchy. She shuddered but pushed her fear aside. One step at a time. She would deal with disaster when she was certain it had come.

"May I see the house, Mrs. Fielding? I might find something left of my mother in there."

From the look on Mrs. Fielding's face, Arabella knew the futility of that. The only things she had of her mother's was the locket she had tucked at the bottom of her traveling bag and the gold chain wound around her throat, holding the ring Pembroke had given her. Mrs. Fielding stood and rummaged in a tin can above the stove. She pulled out an old iron key and handed it to Pembroke along with a can of oil.

"The house is yours, or should be, if the world was not an evil place. Go and look if you like, Miss Arabella. May it bring you comfort. Then come back here and have a slice of pie. I have a few apples left over from last fall's harvest, tucked away in the root cellar. I've cinnamon and cloves. I know apple pies are your favorite."

Arabella blushed, for Pembroke smelled of cinnamon. The scent had been her favorite since she was a little girl. "Thank you, Mrs. Fielding. That will be most welcome."

The old lady drew her near and pressed Arabella close to her heart. "I am glad you are here. But don't linger overlong in that house. It's ever been a dark place, and the last few years haven't made it any brighter."

Arabella remembered the long, trailing staircase that led into the shadows of the upper floors. Her father had not allowed many candles or lamps to be lit, even in winter, so the bedrooms and the corridor that led to them had always been shrouded in darkness. She felt the cold fingers of her father's hand on the softness of her upper arm. She shuddered as the illusion passed, but she still felt cold, even standing in bright sunlight.

"I won't linger, Mrs. Fielding. I promise you that."

Thirteen

ARABELLA AND PEMBROKE LEFT THE WHITEWASHED neatness of Mrs. Fielding's kitchen and traced their steps back to the path that led into the formal garden. Though the hedges had been clipped recently, most of the flowers beds were overgrown with weeds. Arabella could see evidence that one man had tried to keep them up alone, and failing, had left them to flourish as they would. One path was clear of weeds and encroaching plants: the shell-lined walk led to her father's back door.

She drew back at first, her breath leaving her lungs in one sudden exhale. She stood looking at that door, the same door she had snuck out of so many times to visit Pembroke. Her father had caught her the last time she tried to sneak away, the night she tried to leave this place and her father behind. He had not struck her on the face that night, for her wedding was arranged for the morning.

Even as the old duke slept upstairs in the guest suite, oblivious, her father found her with her hand on the latch, her single bag packed and on her arm. Her father had twisted her arm behind her back in the downstairs hallway, dragging her to his library, where he took a cane to the bottoms of her feet so the blows would not show, punishing her for her attempt to run away.

Mr. Swanson had not laid the cane on too hard, but the blows had hurt. What had hurt more was the knowledge that Pembroke waited for her, and that she would never be able to go to him.

She had tried to send word to him, but just before her wedding ceremony her father had brought that letter to her room. He had intercepted it in the hands of the upstairs maid, turning the girl out of the house on the spot. He had showed Arabella the letter, then burned it before leading her down to the parlor so that she might marry the Duke of Hawthorne.

Arabella stood frozen before her father's back door, the memory of that horrible day coming back to stab her like knives, one in her back, another in her heart.

Pembroke, the man who had been hurt almost as much as she was by that terrible day, now stood beside her and offered her his arm. "Are you all right?" he asked. "Will you sit on this bench while I go in and look?"

His expression held no mockery. She could see no hint of his old resentment, his old bitterness. He was more like the boy she had known in that moment than in any year since. It was almost worse to see him as he once had been and to know that he did not love her anymore, as that boy once had. If he still loved her, he would have come to her all those years ago. At the very least, he would have answered her letter. Though his anger may have fled, he had not forgiven her.

Arabella fought her way back against the tide of memories, the wave of pain that swamped her. She could not mend the past, only build her future. She forced herself to focus on the here and now, where she was, and why. "No," she said. "I am going with you."

Pembroke oiled the lock and slid the great key into it. He turned it, and the bolt slid free as he pushed open the large wooden door. The only light in the house beyond came from the doorway they stood in. All of the curtains in the house were drawn. Arabella was sorry that she had not thought to bring a lamp.

Pembroke reached into his jacket pocket and drew out two thick candles and a flint. He lit them, handing the first one to her before lighting his own. Arabella found herself smiling.

"How is it you thought to bring these?" she asked.

"The house has been unoccupied for years," he answered. "And I learned on the Continent that it is always best to be prepared for anything."

"And is there a pistol tucked away in another pocket of your coat?" Arabella asked.

It was Pembroke's turn to smile. "Do you think I should have brought one?"

"Let us hope not."

She turned to the doorway then, and after only a moment of hesitation, she stepped into the darkness of her childhood.

❧

No spirits haunted the old house. No madmen lurked along its corridors. Arabella smiled at the memory of all the gothic novels she had read. Clearly Mrs.

Radcliffe and her ilk were as fanciful as her father's tenants who all believed in fairies.

The sound of her footsteps was loud on the wooden floor of the entrance hall. All the carpets had been taken up and sold. The old duke had sacked the house, plundering it of all that might bring him a profit. Arabella thought of her mother's china from the Orient, of her silver from India, but after a pang of nostalgia, she pushed those thoughts aside. She was here not to unearth the past but to claim her future.

She passed through the hall, turning her head to look at the wide staircase that led up into the darkness. She shivered, thinking of all the years she had avoided that staircase, taking the servants' corridors as much as she could, trying to avoid her father and failing. Arabella turned her back on the staircase and its shadows and continued into the right wing of the house where her father's study lay. The paintings that had once lined the hall were long gone, leaving dark stains on the walls.

The door to her father's study stood open as if waiting for her. The candle in her hand cast a feeble light, and she stopped in the doorway. Pembroke came to stand beside her, raising his candle above her head.

She could see into the room then, the old leather sofa still sitting by the empty fireplace. The rug had been taken up and dust covered the mahogany floor. She pressed back the memory of being called before her father for infractions, both major and minor. Her back stung with the memory of the riding crop her father had struck her with. Her shoulders ached, and she shrugged the memory away.

She stepped into the room that held so many of her old demons and set her candle in an empty holder on her father's desk. The books had all been taken down from the shelves and sold, but the great walnut desk remained. A lamp sat on its surface and she used her candle to light the wick. To her surprise, the flame caught and burned bright, for there was still a bit of oil in the base of the lamp.

She turned to the windows behind the desk and pushed back the heavy velvet drapes. Sunlight shone in through the dirty windows and dust rose from the velvet, choking her as it covered her hands, her face, her hair. She stepped back and brushed it off ineffectively, until Pembroke offered her his handkerchief. She wiped her face and fingers, smiling up at him without thought. "Thank you."

He stood staring down at her, dust caught in his golden hair. He reached for her and she jumped, but instead of taking a liberty, he simply wiped a smudge off her cheek. The simple gesture touched her heart as if it had been punctured. She breathed deep, trying to control her emotions, but only swallowed a mouthful of dust.

She turned without a word to the desk, the only table left in the room. Pembroke paced the edges of the study, raising the lamp as he examined the bookcases, looking for hidden compartments. Arabella knew he would find nothing. If there were compartments, her father would never have hidden money in them.

She sat in the cracked leather chair behind her father's desk, shivering as if his specter had touched her hand. She opened the top drawer, surprised to find it unlocked. Pembroke gave up his silent perusal of the empty bookcases and came to her side.

A voice from the corridor made Arabella jump, her hand pressed against her beating heart. Pembroke looked completely calm, but she could feel tension along his arm as he stood beside her, careful to keep his body between her and the door. Arabella caught her breath as her father's steward, Mr. Grayson, stepped into the room.

"Your Grace, I offer my condolences on the death of your husband," Mr. Grayson said. He bowed to her, ignoring Pembroke completely.

"Thank you, Mr. Grayson. Pembroke, may I present Thomas Grayson, my father's steward. Mr. Grayson, the Earl of Pembroke."

Mr. Grayson turned his gaze to Pembroke and bowed slightly, though he did not seem to feel much respect. "Your lord father has been dead these five years. I am sorry to hear it."

"You would be the only one."

Grayson's eyes were the color of rainwater, cold and distant. But when Pembroke spoke so irreverently of his father, a small smile touched the harsh corners of Grayson's mouth. "Indeed."

The steward turned to Arabella then, straightening his back. He still wore immaculate black breeches and tailcoat, along with a waistcoat of black. Though his clothes were well brushed and cared for, Arabella could see that they were twice mended. His linen had yellowed, giving his face a sallow cast even as he stepped into the sunlight that fell over the desk from the window behind it.

Arabella remembered this man from her childhood

as always silent, always dour. She had assumed that he
followed her father blindly, that he had thought her
father righteous in his cruelty, both to her and to the
rest of the staff.

She saw now that Mr. Grayson simply held to an
exacting standard of service to his master and did not
look beyond it. She felt a little of the tension leave
her shoulders as one more demon from her childhood
faded in the light of day. Memory was powerful but
not always accurate.

"Your Grace, when the old duke came, he took
everything. But he did not find your father's safe. I
saw to that."

A light entered her heart at those words, and she
felt a smile coming over her face. "He did not find it."

"No. I kept a watch on him and checked after him.
Your father's safe is untouched and hidden still."

Arabella wanted to leap to her feet and dance. If
she had known how, she would have jigged like an
Irishman, leaped like a lord. As it was, she clutched
one hand in the other to stop them from shaking.

"Thank you, Grayson. I will never be able to thank
you enough."

Grayson bowed and moved to leave them, but at
the doorway, he turned back. "I make it my business
never to reach above my place. But we had word from
the new duke today. He is looking for you."

Arabella felt panic close her throat. She swallowed
hard so that she might speak. "Yes," she said. "I know
that he seeks me."

Grayson looked into her face. "You do not want
to be found."

"No, I do not."

He nodded once. "You are safe among us. We will not tell him of your visit. Not myself, nor anyone here. I give you my solemn word."

The pressure in her chest seemed to ease, and she took a deep breath of the dusty air. "Thank you, Mr. Grayson."

He nodded, embarrassed by the warmth in her voice. "You may rely on our discretion in this house, Your Grace, out of respect to you and your father. But the new Duke of Hawthorne made it very clear that he is set on finding you. I think he may make inquiries in the village. I cannot speak for what they will tell him."

"I understand, Mr. Grayson. Thank you."

The older man left then, his iron gray hair combed in place, tied at the nape of his neck with a black ribbon. He looked like a specter from another time. Arabella did not take her eyes off him until he disappeared into the darkness of the corridor. Pembroke did not leave his place beside her.

"What a ghoul," he said.

Arabella realized that the old man had been completely disrespectful to Pembroke, not giving him his due as earl but treating him as the ne'er-do-well upstart that her father had called him when they were young.

She opened her mouth to apologize only to find Pembroke's gaze on her face, searching her eyes. His hand reached for her and brushed a honey-colored curl out of her eyes. "Are you all right, Arabella?"

His touch was electric, as if lightning had come

down to the earth and focused on the skin of her cheek. She could not catch her breath. Heat rose in her face and burned beneath her belly. She felt that fire rise within her as it had in her dreams. She could think of nothing but how it had felt to have Pembroke lie on top of her, pressing her into the mattress of her feather bed.

Arabella knew that they had only been dreams, but now she felt as if she were living in one. All her contempt for mistresses everywhere had fled. She could only feel his touch on her cheek and the warmth of his body as he stood close to her.

She tried to find her voice but failed. She could think of nothing glib to say, nothing to ease the sudden tension that had risen between them.

She thought of the kiss the night before and remembered the taste of his tongue on hers. She stared up at him as if she had taken complete leave of her senses, which she supposed she had.

They stood together in silence for a long moment before he spoke again. "I will write to Anthony. He will keep Hawthorne off you."

Arabella started, alarmed. "The Earl of Ravensbrook? Angelique's Anthony?"

"The very same. Though I believe neither of them considers him to be 'Angelique's Anthony' any longer."

Arabella colored. "No. I suppose not."

"Anthony is close with the Prince Regent. Prinny may be able to help, or at least advise us on what course to take. We will not abandon you to Hawthorne. You are not friendless."

"We cannot reveal this matter to the Prince of Wales," Arabella said. "He and Hawthorne are connected. He will encourage me to marry the duke, keep my title, and keep the money in the family." She clutched her fingers in their leather riding gloves. She gripped her own hand so tightly that the circulation was cut off. Pembroke drew her fingers into his warm palm.

"We will go to Anthony first," Pembroke said. "He will stand with me on this, as in everything. He and I will consider what is to be done."

"This is my burden. I cannot ask you to do more than you have done. I have asked too much of you already."

Pembroke kissed her then, his lips firm on hers, and fierce. This kiss was nothing like the one from the night before. It was not intoxicating, not seductive, but strong. She felt his frustration through the touch of his lips, through the touch of his hand on hers. He did not draw her close but pulled back almost at once, and for a moment Arabella wondered if he had kissed her simply to gain her silence.

"I do as I wish to do, Arabella. You are in my keeping, and I will protect you. Gold or no gold, we will find a way to set you free from Hawthorne. I swear it."

Arabella shivered. In spite of the sunlight from the window behind her, the shadows of the house rose along the edges of the walls of that room as if to choke her. She was overwhelmed by both her present and her past. She wanted only to be alone, to sit by a quiet fire, a bit of lace coming together between her hands.

The madness she had witnessed in the last week had begun to overwhelm her.

Pembroke seemed to see something of this hopelessness in her face, for he kissed her again, swiftly, but this time his lips were gentle, offering comfort, drawing her thoughts from her fear.

When he pulled away, Arabella found that her mind was clear. She could not stay, but she did not want to argue with him either. Hawthorne was coming for her, and she must be gone. Her voice was level and calm when she spoke. "Pembroke, take me out of here. I never want to step inside this house again."

He smiled and raised her hand to his lips. "I will lead you out of here. As soon as we have your dowry in hand."

She knelt beneath the old walnut desk, and Pembroke held the lamp for her so that she could see. She ran her fingers along the floorboards until she found one loose. She pulled it up easily, revealing the safe. Her hands shook as she worked the dial, but the combination had not changed.

The hidden safe beneath her father's walnut desk opened easily. She drew out a steel box filled to the brim with golden guineas, a box so heavy that she almost could not lift it. Pembroke knelt at her side and raised it to the desk. She opened the strongbox and stared at the gold within. Arabella had never seen so much money in one place in all her life.

"Well, now I can pay you for our room at the inn," she said.

Pembroke laughed, closing the box. "I think I can afford to keep you, my lady duchess. Now let us leave this place. I am beginning to get hives from all this dust."

Arabella laughed with him as she extinguished the lamp. That she could laugh in that place told her truly that her father was dead. She held her candle high and followed Pembroke out of the house and back into the sunshine of the formal garden. They blew their candles out and she left them on a table inside by the door, closing the house up behind them.

Arabella felt as if a part of her past was sealed in that house along with the dust. No matter what became of her in the days to come, she would never enter that house of darkness again.

Fourteen

PEMBROKE LOADED THE GOLD GUINEAS INTO HIS saddlebags, leaving the strongbox with Mrs. Fielding. After eating a piece of hot apple pie covered in soft white cheese, they rode back to Pembroke House. Mrs. Fielding came out to wave them off, and Arabella waved back. Pembroke would have liked to sit in that kitchen a little longer and eat more of her apple pie. Blueberries would be in season in a few months, and no doubt Mrs. Fielding would be making blueberry tarts.

Both horses were well rested after their afternoon of munching grass. Mrs. Fielding had brought sugar cubes and apples, so their mounts had had a more pleasant time than either Pembroke or Arabella. When Arabella approached, Blossom pressed herself against her, offering her forehead to be petted.

"Sweet girl," Arabella murmured.

Pembroke watched her openly, but she did not turn to look at him, lavishing all her attention on her horse. Something had fallen away from her in her father's house. She had left some burden behind in those shadows when she had locked the back door on all that dust. She had not wanted to look any further than her father's library, than the safe under the desk. She had the money to start a new life now. She did not need him anymore.

Or at least, she seemed to think that she did not. The distance between her and Hawthorne seemed to have soothed her into forgetfulness. From his dealings with the Hellfire Club, Pembroke knew the man better than most. Hawthorne would not give her up if he was determined to have her.

Pembroke needed to send a messenger to Anthony. The Earl of Ravensbrook would come to the wilds of Derbyshire if Pembroke asked him. He wanted all his forces arrayed against Hawthorne in case he came to find her there. It would not be long before someone in Titania's troupe mentioned that a duchess was living with him in country seclusion. Almost a love nest.

Pembroke swallowed a rueful smile. She might be living under his roof at the moment, but Arabella had made it very clear that she wanted nothing to do with him.

They rode slowly over the road between his house and her father's. The forest was quiet save for the wind in the trees and the rustle of branches above their heads. A few birds sang, but even their songs were quiet, as if they sang in a cathedral and did not want to disturb the holy place. As Pembroke looked around at the light summer green of the oaks and hawthorns that surrounded them, he remembered how sacred he had once found it, when he was young and happy.

As much to clear his own thoughts as to engage

Arabella in conversation, he said, "The actors will be settling into the inn in the village. Would you care to join them for dinner on the green? Titania sent an invitation this morning before we rode out."

He had expected her to balk at the thought of eating with his mistress two nights in a row, but Titania was not what caught her attention. Arabella slanted her blue eyes his way, a smile playing across the beautiful curve of her mouth. If she had not been so far away on her own mount, he would have kissed her.

"I suppose the actors want a look at you, to see what amateur they'll be getting."

Pembroke found his own heart lifting. When they were young, she had never had the confidence to tease him. He found that he liked it. "Madame, I will thank you to know that I performed not one night but two while I was at Cambridge, and to great applause."

"Two entire nights! That is renown indeed."

Arabella could not seem to stop herself from laughing, the joyous sound filling the air as they came to his stables. She shook with laughter even as Pembroke helped her down from her horse.

She reached to pat Blossom in farewell, but as she stood in the circle of Pembroke's arms, he found that he did not want to let her go. He left his hands on her waist, the warmth of her body heating his palms through the leather of his gloves. Her laughter died, and she stared up at him, her eyes riveted to the curve of his lips.

He knew he should not touch her. He and Anthony would defend her from Hawthorne, but once that matter was settled, she would move on with her life, and he with his. He knew now as he stared down into the cornflower blue of her eyes that he could never have taken her as his mistress, yet one more woman in a long unbroken line, a woman like any other. Arabella would always be the one woman, the only woman, for him. The fact that he could not have her did not change that.

She had abandoned him and married another. She had broken his heart. But now that he had opened his fist and let his bitterness slip away, he found that he did not hate her for that anymore. Whatever pain she had caused him, a seventeen-year-old girl had done. He could barely remember his eighteen-year-old self, much less hold him accountable for all that had happened in his life since.

Time was an ever-moving river. Time had left his love for Arabella behind long ago. The fact that he carried it still, tucked in his heart, was relevant to no one but him.

It was Pembroke who broke the moment, stepping back from her and drawing his hands from her waist. "We leave for the village in two hours' time. Will that be long enough for you to dress?"

Arabella laughed, but her laughter was breathless this time, a feeble attempt to hide a deeper emotion. He wondered in that moment if she could possibly want him as much as he wanted her. He knew she did not love him, but lust was a different thing.

Before he could follow that thought down a long and winding road into fantasy, Arabella said, "I have little to be vain about, Pembroke. I am not one of your London ladies who take hours with their coiffures. I will be ready and waiting on you in the entry hall, I suspect."

Pembroke smiled, his eyes lingering on her face, caressing her hair. Her honey-brown hair was curled again that day, tucked under a bonnet she had borrowed from Mrs. Marks. Even the servant's brown bonnet trimmed in a simple blue ribbon could not dim the soft loveliness of her face, the clear blue of her eyes, like the sky of a country he had never seen. He longed for her suddenly, not the girl she had been but the woman she was. His longing was like a vise on his heart, closing off his lungs. For a moment, he feared he could not speak, but as always, he managed to cover his emotions. His pain was no one's business but his.

"I will see you then," he said.

Arabella went into the house at his side and walked quietly to her borrowed room. He watched from the entrance hall below as she climbed the staircase. He absorbed the unconscious sway of her hips beneath the dark blue of her demure gown. She was a woman of combined beauty and quiet strength. No wonder he had fallen in love with her so many years ago. No wonder he was in love with her now.

And she would never know it.

The irony of that was not lost on him. He wanted a taste of brandy so badly that his hand shook. But he did not take it. Instead, he stood alone in the summer sunlight of his entrance hall and rode the wave of drink lust until it passed. That desire for brandy would never leave him, he knew. He would simply have to face it as a man, one day, one moment at a time.

❧

Pembroke had given her a rosewood box in which to keep her father's money. Mrs. Marks left it for her after Arabella had finished her bath, saying that the lord had wanted her to have it, for it had been his mother's.

Arabella, still wrapped in linen towels, stepped across the room and caressed the smooth surface of the well-polished box. She opened it to find her treasure neatly stacked within, her future laid out in gold guineas, the money that would buy her freedom for the rest of her life.

It was not a lot of money by the standards of her father or her husband, but she had never held so much money of her own in her life, nor had she ever thought to. But now that her husband was dead, she walked her own path. Elation rose in her heart like a bird taking flight. The sight of her gold made her dance, her bare feet slipping along the cream and blue carpet. Her borrowed lady's maid gave her a sideways glance, but the smile Arabella gave her seemed to warm her, for she left off looking frightened and smiled back. She stopped dancing when she remembered Hawthorne. He was coming for her, and sooner or later he would find her in Derbyshire. She must be gone before he did. But she did not want to leave yet.

She wanted to ask Pembroke why he had never written back, why he had ignored her letters. He had left for the Continent and the war without another word passing between them. She had left him and married another, but he had never acknowledged the truth that her fate had not been her own choice.

Arabella leaned out the open window that looked

out over the expanse of the estate behind the house, the scent of Pembroke's mother's rose garden rising on the warm evening air. It took hours for the sun to set this time of year, and the slanting sun bathed the world in buttery light. The green of the Forest of Arden beckoned to her from across the expanse of Pembroke's lawns and flower gardens. She wanted to walk there again now that she was free.

Maybe that night she would. Maybe there, beneath the old king oak, she would ask him why he had never written her back.

With the help of Clara, the housemaid who had been temporarily promoted to assist with her hair and her clothes, Arabella was indeed ready half an hour early, but when she stepped into the entry hall, she found Pembroke waiting for her. He was dressed in a coat of midnight blue superfine that seemed to intensify the blue of his eyes. His man had tried valiantly to conquer the lock of hair over his forehead but had failed. Pembroke peered out from under it as he reached up to toss the errant lock of hair aside.

"You are a vision," he said. His voice was serious, and when she checked his expression for some form of mockery, she found none. A long silence stretched between them, a silence in which time stopped.

Arabella rallied, forcing a smile. "I have only the one gown."

She was wearing the green silk from the night before, a gown she had loved too much to leave behind when she fled her husband's house.

"You would be beautiful in anything, but that shade of green is lovely on you."

"Thank you."

Arabella knew a practiced compliment when she heard one. In Pembroke's eyes she saw no hint of desire, but neither did she find the warmth that had sprung up between them that afternoon.

Perhaps that warmth had been Pembroke feeling protective or nostalgic for the days when they had been friends. Arabella straightened and brought another false smile to her face. No matter how much she wanted to know the answer to that question, she would not ask. She needed to face the past once and for all, and then let him go. But she would have dinner first. She took the arm he offered and let him lead her to the open carriage.

They rode in silence to the village green. Pembroke seemed lost in his thoughts as he looked out over his land as they drove. Though the evening was cooler than the day had been, a delightful warmth still lingered. The scent of wisteria seemed to follow them down the lane from the great house, but as she looked up, she noticed that wisteria still grew wild in the trees above their heads. It had flowed out from the estate, untended and unencumbered, to fill the world with white blossoms and a delicate, sun-warmed scent. Arabella leaned back against the cushions of the carriage and breathed deeply. This country was home, as no other place would ever be.

She did her best to put Pembroke from her mind. She kept her face turned to the open window, wishing the top was down so that she might feel more of the wind on her face.

She heard the actors before she saw them. Great

bellowing laughter echoed across the village green where long tables had been set up, covered in white cloths. Bouquets of wildflowers filled earthenware jars positioned at intervals on the tabletops. Actors and stage hands mingled with the villagers who had come to meet them and to see what all the fuss was about.

There was a feeling of excitement in the air that Arabella never remembered in the village before, not even on Midsummer festivals when she was a child. Of course, never before had a troupe of actors come all the way from London to perform a play on Pembroke commons.

Titania stood like a queen, directing the staff from the pub as they set out meat pies and pastries and distributed vast jugs of mead and cider. The great men of the village had been invited to this impromptu dinner along with their wives. The mayor wore his ribbon of office stretched across his large paunch. Actresses sat with the most handsome of the village's young men, chatting with them as they shared mugs of cider.

Arabella wanted to be among them suddenly, to feel part of a group as she never had in her life. When she was a child, her father had not let her interact with the villagers, no matter what the festival. Tonight, she would change that.

Pembroke took her hand and drew her out into the evening's fading light. He did not seem to notice when she tried to pull away, but kept her by his side as he spoke.

"Good people, welcome to our feast."

Arabella thought that he sounded like a character

from Shakespeare. Though Titania was queen of all she surveyed, Pembroke was king. He had arranged the entire evening and no doubt had paid for it all.

She turned to smile at him, but he did not look down at her. Pembroke kept her hand firmly on his arm, pressed down by his own, as he greeted first the mayor, then the town aldermen, and all their wives. He introduced her as Arabella Hawthorne, and no one said a word about her husband or his duchy. They treated her with deference, but not because she wore a coronet. They bowed and whispered about her because she stood beside Pembroke. If they remembered her father, the slave trader, they were polite enough not to mention it.

She noticed then that she had caught the eye of some of the players. The men were smiling at her a little too fondly, and the women stared at her, drinking in every detail of her gown and gloves, even of the dyed slippers on her feet. A few of the women narrowed their eyes in open disdain before turning avaricious eyes on Pembroke.

Arabella was taken aback as she saw them practically lick their lips at the sight of him. He was handsome, rich, and an earl. What more could a Cyprian of the stage ask for in a protector?

For his part, Pembroke seemed not to notice any of them. Only Titania was acknowledged as she approached them, offering Pembroke her hand to kiss. He obliged like the gentleman he was, smiling at the queen of the evening from beneath his errant lock of hair. But even as he greeted his mistress, Pembroke did not let go of Arabella's hand.

"You have outdone yourself," Pembroke said to Titania.

"It has a lovely bucolic flavor, does it not? Perhaps we should have chosen *As You Like It*."

"Then I would not have the chance to play Oberon," he said.

"And that would be a great loss to the theater."

Arabella wondered if Titania was being sarcastic, but then Pembroke laughed, the warm sound filling the clearing where they stood. People from the village turned to listen to their lord's laughter and they laughed as well, not knowing the joke but happy to have him home.

Arabella looked around at the villagers. In spite of the economic trials that had come to England since the war, the people of Pembroke Village seemed well dressed and well fed. She wondered for the first time if he had helped their businesses and farms flourish. His father would never have bothered. But as Pembroke had told her more than once, he was not his father.

When they sat down, Pembroke kept her hand pressed to the table beneath his own, as if sure she would escape if he let her go. She was beginning to feel stifled by his odd behavior. He would not look at her, but he would not release her either. Surreptitiously, she tried to pull her hand away and failed.

Most of the diners were sitting on benches, but chairs had been brought out of the inn for Pembroke, Titania, and herself. Titania's actors sat ranged around them like a royal court. Pembroke seemed perfectly at ease with so many theater folk, but Arabella found her natural shyness rising to silence her. She was not used to dealing with people she did not know, much less people as flamboyant as these.

"We are happy to have you here among us, Your Grace," one man said, his dark hair gleaming against the cream linen of his coat. "It is not every day that actors dine with a duchess."

Titania tossed back her dark red hair and laughed. "Speak for yourself, Bart."

The rest of the company laughed with her. Arabella smiled, taking a sip of her cider.

"Madame Titania, I am happy to be here. I have never met a group of actors before. It makes me eager to see the play."

"Since it will be your first play, we will make it a good one."

"Your first play?" A different actor, this one young and blond with a gleam of mischief in his eye, raised his glass to her. "A virgin then. I would not have thought it possible."

Other actors laughed aloud, and a few of the actresses exchanged looks of derision before slanting their eyes at her.

Pembroke tensed, his hand crushing hers against the tablecloth. Arabella felt the color in her face rise. She was not used to being addressed so casually by men she did not know.

Before Pembroke could speak, Titania reprimanded the man. "Cliff, that's enough out of you. One more word and I'll banish you to the painting brigade."

"I apologize, Your Worship. Meant no harm." He hiccupped.

Arabella forced herself to smile. "No harm done."

She took a deep breath and found that she was not offended, merely surprised. Perhaps she could make her own way in the world after all. Perhaps she need not hide away in a cottage of her own for the rest of her life. Clearly there were many more types of people in the world than she had ever met. The world seemed to lie before her like a vast expanse behind an open door. She might do anything, be anyone. She might do as she pleased, now that she was free.

It was a heady thought.

Titania spent the rest of the meal doing her best to put her at ease, and Arabella was grateful for the kindness. She never forgot that Titania was Pembroke's lover. No doubt he would visit her that very night. But even as she fought down her jealousy, Arabella could not look at the confident, beautiful Titania with her vibrant red hair and theatrical gestures without wishing she was more like her. Molly, the name she had been born with, simply did not suit her. Titania seemed much more appropriate.

As the evening wore on, Titania's indulgence seemed to buy Arabella a measure of acceptance among the actors. Arabella knew she was not beautiful enough to attract their interest, with her pale face and her thin frame, but a few of the men among them nodded and smiled to her as if she were indeed a beauty, though each man kept an eye on Pembroke, careful not to offend him. Arabella almost laughed when she noticed that, for though he was treating her like something he owned, Pembroke had no interest in her.

Though he irritated her by treating her like a piece

of his property, she could not help but admire him as
Pembroke spoke with ease with all who sat at the table
with them. He was as confident and full of life on the
village green as he was at his own dining table. This
could have been accounted for by the simple fact that
he was the Earl of Pembroke, but the respect these
people showed seemed to go deeper than that.

Just as the men seemed to respect him, all the
women seemed desperate to catch his eye. They did
not seem to care about his open relationship with
Titania, or for the fact that he had not left Arabella's
side all evening. One particularly insistent woman
came up in the middle of the meal, her low-cut gown
more like that of a serving wench in a brothel than an
actress from London.

"My lord," the woman said, shouldering Arabella
aside as if she were not there. "You have not been to
the theater in an age."

"I was there just last week, Cassie. Perhaps you
didn't notice me."

"I would notice if you'd been there. I've been
pining for you."

Pembroke's skin colored beneath his tan. Arabella
released her annoyance with her next breath, choosing
instead to lean back in her chair to watch the show,
enjoying his discomfort. She had heard rumors of
his great prowess with the ladies, both with countesses and ladies of ill repute, but she had not seen
evidence of this charm. She caught Titania's eye over
Pembroke's shoulder, and the red-haired Cypriot
winked in commiseration.

Arabella turned her gaze back to the actress who

had captured Pembroke's attention. Cassie's gown was a bright yellow, which matched the brassy yellow of her hair. As the flame of a nearby lamp flared, Arabella blinked. Such a color surely did not exist in nature. Perhaps it should not exist anywhere.

Arabella felt her irritation rise as she watched the woman lean in closer to Pembroke, pressing her ample bosom against his arm. "I'm playing a fairy in this production, my lord. Since you are to be my king, perhaps I might help you learn your lines?" Her hand slipped beneath the table, only to be caught in one of Pembroke's own and brought back into view.

Arabella felt her temper rise like a flash fire, and she swallowed it down. She had never known herself to have a temper in her life, but it seemed that Pembroke brought it out in her.

Fortunately Titania spoke up before Arabella embarrassed herself. "Cassie, you won't be playing anything in this production if you don't stop making a cake of yourself. Sit down and mind your place and give his lordship some peace, for the love of God."

Cassie glared at her producer before simpering once more in Pembroke's face. "If you have need of me, you have only to call," she breathed, pressing her bosom against him.

"Thank you, Cassie. I will keep that in mind."

The woman flounced away, leaving a cloud of cheap perfume behind her. Titania reached for a jug of mead, and Arabella did not protest when she poured a bit of it into her tumbler. "Cassie is a force of nature," Titania said.

"A gale force wind," Pembroke agreed.

"Good riddance," Arabella said.

Titania laughed, and Pembroke looked shocked at her outburst as Arabella hid her face behind her tankard. She drank her mead and felt the sweet heat of it warm her stomach and all her limbs. Though it went down as easily as cider, it seemed to be a bit stronger. Titania watched with a smile as Arabella drank then leaned over to fill her tumbler again.

"Titania," Pembroke said, a warning note in his voice.

Arabella did not heed that warning but drank deep, enjoying the taste of the sweet mead on her tongue.

"A drop of the elixir of the gods never did anyone any harm," Titania said mildly.

Arabella kept drinking, a happy tingling coming into her hands and feet. Warmth suffused her, and as she looked over the company, she smiled over them all, her shyness beginning to slip away.

"That's nothing to do with the gods, that's honey liquor," Pembroke said.

Titania only smiled, and Arabella smiled back at her. "Try a bit, Pembroke. It might sweeten your mood," Arabella said.

Titania laughed when she heard that, passing the jug to Arabella, who filled his empty tankard. "Now we shall all have the elixir of the gods."

Pembroke did not drink but watched her, a dark light coming into his eyes. Maybe it was simply a trick of the shadows cast by the hanging lamps, but the look made her shiver. Arabella knew that she must speak with him seriously about the past, confront him, and clear the air before she left Derbyshire for good, but she could not seem to keep her mind on that worthy goal. Instead, all she could do was wonder if it would be a sin to ask him to kiss her, their past be damned. If so, she thought it was a sin that she could live with.

She would not be his mistress, of course. She had sworn that, and she meant it. But one more kiss could do little harm.

It might even do her good.

Titania raised her voice so that she might be heard across the green. "This has been a charming evening. Thank you for welcoming us so splendidly to Pembroke Village, my lord. We will do you proud and give you a Midsummer's Eve that you and yours will never forget."

A cheer rose from the villagers and the actors raised their voices along with their tankards. Titania nodded, graciously accepting their accolades. Arabella could easily imagine her at the foot of a stage in a great theater, taking bows before her audience, drinking in their applause.

Titania caught her eye and smiled. The woman seemed to feel no rivalry toward her, only open affection. Arabella did not know whether to be touched or insulted. But a rosy glow had come over her since she had finished her two tankards of mead. She smiled on Titania as if she were a long lost sister.

Titania stepped toward her and helped her stand, steadying Arabella as she rose to her feet. The ground suddenly seemed very far away, but she caught her balance quickly with Titania's hand on her arm.

"My lord, I believe your lady fair will need an escort to see her safe home."

Arabella looked up at her. "I am not fair."

Titania touched her cheek. "I think his lordship disagrees."

"Titania," Pembroke said, his voice low with warning. His mistress only smiled, letting Arabella go. Pembroke offered his arm and Arabella took it.

"Good night, Madame Titania. I will see to it that he learns his lines."

"I am glad to hear it. I leave our Oberon in your capable hands."

Titania bowed, her eyes on Pembroke's. Some silent communication passed between them that made him frown like thunder as Titania laughed. For once, Arabella did not feel jealous. Wherever he went later that night, whatever he did with Titania in the nights to come, he was with her now. Arabella clung to that thought as tightly as she clung to his arm as he led her toward the carriage.

She thought of the Forest of Arden, and of the king oak where he had once proposed to her. "Might we walk, my lord? It is only two miles and it is such a lovely night."

"Arabella, you are not quite steady on your feet."

"I am fine, Pembroke, I assure you." Arabella drew herself up straight in an effort to convince him, even as the earth seemed to sway beneath her in gentle waves.

Pembroke still hesitated, clearly reluctant to walk into the night with her. Arabella raised her eyes to his. She did not press herself against him as the actress Cassie had, but as she looked at him, he seemed to waver in some contest against himself. She did not know which side of him won.

"All right, Arabella. If you would like to walk, we'll walk."

"Thank you, Pembroke."

Titania overheard their exchange and turned away, smiling. Though Arabella was surrounded by a warm haze of mead-induced relaxation, she took perverse pleasure in the fact that the actress Cassie was glaring at her.

Their Forest of Arden lay between the village and his home, an enchanted place. She had been afraid to walk there in the light of day, to embrace the memories that would come to haunt her and the burden of all her regrets. But all that pain seemed very distant that evening. The warm night air beckoned, and the arching branches of the oaks seemed to wave to her in welcome. Perhaps the combination of the forest and the mead would keep away the pain. Perhaps she could walk into the past and revel in it, if only for an hour. It seemed so little to ask.

She steadied herself on Pembroke's arm and strolled with him into the shadows of the tree-lined path that led back to Pembroke House, stepping into the forest of her dreams.

Fifteen

PEMBROKE AND ARABELLA KNEW THE PATHS ALONG THE forest well, for they had traveled them often together the summer they were courting. The summer air was warm, so Arabella allowed her shawl to fall to the crooks of her elbows, leaving her shoulders bare. She would have stripped off her kidskin gloves, but she had not brought a reticule to put them in, so she left them on.

The full moon was rising over the treetops, casting a milky light along their path. Arabella took in deep drafts of the night air, enjoying the freedom of walking in the country unencumbered. The path was lined in columbine and fennel, the scent of those flowers rising to greet her like old friends. She would never have had such freedom in her husband's house, and after ten years of marriage, she found that she savored it.

It was so surprisingly easy to be in Pembroke's company, almost like the peace of being alone, but infinitely better. There seemed to be no anger, no recriminations, no bitterness between them now. She knew that she must bring up that pain again and ask him about the letters she had sent. But instead, as they walked in the moonlight, Arabella pretended that they were ten years in the past, that all the years of pain and separation had never happened. She imagined that they had married and now walked this path alone as man and wife.

She knew she was a fool, but the moonlight and the mead beckoned to her, allowing both her worries and her scruples to slide away. Once they arrived again at Pembroke House, she promised herself that she would set such fantasies aside. But for now, she would live as she wished. Though reality waited for her on the other side of this forest, this was a blissful moment, an hour apart, and Arabella meant to relish it, to drink it in without spilling a drop.

She reached out and took Pembroke's hand. His glove and hers separated them, but she could still feel the steady warmth of his touch.

Pembroke did not look down at her or speak but walked with her in silence. With the clean night air and the motion of her walking, the mead she had drunk began to burn away. She was left with a feeling of warmth and joy, but her senses had returned to her. She was grateful because she did not want to miss one moment of this night.

The spring green of the oaks and hawthorns around them was dimmed in the moonlight, turned to milky blacks and grays. Sunlight brought out the verdant greens of the land around them, but the night, with its scent of jasmine and the occasional swoop of an owl, had beauties of its own.

Arabella stopped beneath a king oak tree, the same

great tree where they once had pledged themselves to each other.

She felt the ruby ring beneath the bodice of her gown warm against her flesh. She laid her hand over it, taken back as if by magic to the time in her life when the world lay at her feet, when the man she loved held her hand in his and all the joys of the world seemed possible.

Arabella looked up at Pembroke and saw a shadow of the boy he once had been. It was as if their younger selves had never left that place but had haunted it, suspended in time, caught in the moment before everything between them was shattered into dust.

Pembroke, standing beside her with his hand in hers, seemed to feel it, too.

Arabella looked up into his face, where the boy and the man both lay reflected in his eyes. She had not forgotten that boy. She would never forget. Once she left to build her own quiet life, she would never know another man like him.

She stood beneath the great king oak and wondered if she was bold enough to kiss him twice.

❧

Pembroke stared down at Arabella, watching as the wind moved the shadows over her face. Her skin was as milky white as the moonlight that shone on her. He knew that she was flushed from drinking mead and from the walk, though he could not see the pink of her cheeks in that dim light.

He had knelt to her there once, long ago. He almost could not remember that boy, his younger self, who had been so full of plans for the future, so full of hope. It seemed as if that boy had not died, as Pembroke had always thought, killed by disappointment and betrayal and by all the sin that Pembroke had indulged in from that day to this. That boy had lived, waiting for him to return to the foot of the great oak with this woman beside him.

Arabella was the love of his life. Pembroke had always known it, even in the midst of his bitterness. He had always mourned her.

His friends changed mistresses and paramours as often as they changed hats. For years, he had done the same, hoping to set himself free from his obsession with her. But nothing he had ever done had been enough. There was no woman on earth who would ever be able to free him. Arabella was the love he had lost, and he knew, standing with her once more beneath that king oak, that he would never love another.

For the first time in his life, this realization did not bring pain with it. Now that his bitterness was gone, he no longer blamed her for the ruin of his life. But he knew just as well that he could not keep her with him, not in any form. He needed to be free of her. He needed to live without pain. He did not think it possible, but he had to try. And he could not do that standing here in the dark with her, the curve of her lips inviting his kiss.

He knew this, but he did not bundle her out of there. He did not walk away.

Her green gown was transformed into a milky gray, the sheen of her throat bathed in the moonlight. He had sworn that he would not touch her again, but beneath the magic of that tree, all oaths seemed superfluous. He knew he was a fool. Almost desperately, he searched his soul for the bitterness of his regret, for his anger at the loss of all the years of his youth. But he could not find them. All that mattered in that moment was the love he felt for her.

Pembroke fought himself even as he drew her close, his hands on her upper arms. Her flesh was soft, warm beneath his palms in spite of the cooling breeze that rose around them. He moved slowly, giving her ample chance to resist him if she wished, hoping that she would, but Arabella did not pull away.

Her lips were warm under his, as soft as a moth's wing. She tasted of sweet mead and of the beef pastries they had eaten on the village green. He meant to kiss her only once then let her go. He meant to kiss her in memoriam for the past they shared, in an attempt to say good-bye.

But she did not let him.

⁓

Arabella felt a powerful warmth rising in her, a reckless desperation that seemed to take over her senses. From somewhere she took in the scent of night-blooming jasmine, its heady perfume filling her mind like a drug, like an enchantment meant to banish fear.

She knew all the reasons she should step back and away from him, all the reasons she should never have touched him to begin with. But she took in the scent of his skin with each breath, the cinnamon she had not eaten in years, because it had always made her think of him.

The past seemed to fall away from her as she kissed

him, as if she had really sealed it away when she closed the door of her father's house for the last time. There, beneath that tree, she felt as if she were under an enchantment, as if in the magic of that moment, she could have anything she wanted. And the only thing she wanted, the only thing she had ever truly wanted, was him.

She pressed herself against him, not as a wanton woman would but as a woman who had waited a long time to be kissed. She opened her arms to him, raising them to clasp his neck. Her fingers wove into his hair, the warmth of her touch making him shiver.

Suddenly as bold as another woman, as bold as the woman she longed to be, Arabella opened her mouth beneath his and ran her tongue along his lips. She felt him try to hold back, and she feared for one horrible moment that he would pull away from her. But then his mouth opened over hers, and she heard him groan as he surrendered.

Pembroke's tongue plundered the soft, warm recesses of her mouth, driving into her even as he drew her hips close against his so that she could feel the strength of him burn through her clothes and his. She shuddered with sudden need as one of his hands reached up to cup her breast. She felt her need rise through the pores of her skin as he clutched her close, his hands everywhere at once. She felt as if she had been caught in a flash tide, as if the dam of her loneliness had burst, letting in a flood of warmth and light.

She moaned beneath the onslaught of his mouth, pressing closer, shifting against him, her body hungry for something she did not understand. Pembroke knew what she wanted though, and at first he moved as if to draw her down onto the leaves and the moss that grew against the base of the tree. But then he changed direction, moving with her as in a dance until her back was against the king oak, seeming too distracted to bring her body beneath him on the ground.

Instead, he pressed her against the tree, and her shawl fell away. She felt the rough bark dig into her back, snagging the silk of her one good gown. Pembroke's hands moved over her, and her body cradled him easily, until she could feel the heat of his arousal nestle against the cleft of her thighs. He reached down, drawing her gown up as his hand slid along her leg until it reached her garter. She trembled with desire, and for one heady moment it was as if she stood on the edge of a cliff, ready to leap.

Then he pulled away.

Her body was hot where he had touched her. She could still feel his strength all along her flesh, a heat that she had longed for all her life.

"Make love to me," she said.

She had nothing left to lose, and she knew it.

Pembroke stared at her, his eyes devouring her body beneath her gown. The cool moonlight filtered in through the branches overhead, no longer casting enchantment but counseling reason. She felt the cool bath of that light on her skin as she watched him fight for control.

"No," he said. "You are not my mistress. You are not my whore."

"What I am, what I will be, is my own business. Don't leave me here with nothing."

He turned and walked away. For one stunned, horrible moment, she thought that he would leave her where she stood, alone in the dark, with only moonlight and her own humiliation for company. He stopped at the edge of the clearing. No matter what else might be said of him, Pembroke would never leave a woman to walk alone.

"Come with me, Arabella." He did not look at her but kept his eyes on the path that led back to Pembroke House. "I'm leaving this place, and you are leaving with me. This is madness, and we will leave it here behind us."

"You're doing this to punish me," she said, not moving. "And maybe I deserve it. But haven't the last ten years been punishment enough?"

He did not answer her. She felt the beginning of tears at the back of her throat, but she would not give in to them. She was cold now in spite of the warm breeze rising from the river, and the king oak dug into her back, giving her courage. She was sick of tears.

"Why did you never write to me?" she asked.

"I do not make it a habit of writing to married women," he answered.

"I am not just any woman, or so you said. Was that a lie too?"

He turned back to her then, his eyes blazing across the distance between them. He took one step toward her but stopped himself. He stood in a pool of moonlight, and for a moment he really did look like Oberon. He had cast an enchantment on her all those years ago, and she was still trapped in it.

"You never answered my letters," she said. "The

day I was taken to London, I wrote to you. I wrote to your London house, to your father's house in Derbyshire, even to your club. I never got an answer."

She could not read his face, for a shuttered look came over him, as if he enclosed a great deal of pain, pain he would not let her see.

"I received no letter from you. Most likely because you never wrote one."

"And now I am a liar, too?"

"You have always been a liar. You were a liar when you said you loved me. You were a liar when you said you would marry me."

Arabella felt her tears rising, but she pressed them down. He had not received her letters. Perhaps they had been lost. Perhaps his father had burned them.

She bent down and picked up her shawl. It was light, summer-weight linen embroidered with bluebells and green leaves. She had made the shawl herself one lonely night in winter, sitting by a fire in her husband's house. She wrapped that shawl around her now, wishing it was heavier, wishing it was armor that might keep out her pain. Though the summer air was warm all around them, she shook as with an ague.

Pembroke did not speak but walked to the path. She forced herself to move and to follow him. He did not touch her again but strode back to his father's house in silence. She said nothing as she tried to keep up with him, for her mind was one great bruise.

If he would not listen to her, there was nothing left to say.

Sixteen

PEMBROKE WATCHED AS CODINGTON OPENED THE FRONT door for Arabella, then he turned away. He walked to the stables, his strides devouring the ground beneath his feet. He wanted to run, to put as much distance between himself and the woman he loved as he could. But he knew from long years of running that he could not move fast enough or far enough to escape her.

He saddled Triton himself, dismissing the sleepy groom with a silent wave of his hand. His mount tensed under him as if ready for battle, until he smoothed a hand over his neck and murmured to him the old command to stand down. He had no battles to fight tonight. No battle he could win.

He rode into the village, the sound of Triton's hooves on the rutted road like thunder in his ears, drowning out the hideous loop of thought that would not leave him. He tossed Triton's reins to a boy waiting outside the inn, then strode up the stairs two at a time. Titania was in her sitting room, drinking a brandy, a second glass at her elbow as if she had been waiting for him.

"I already poured your favorite," was all she said.

"I don't take brandy any longer," he answered.

"Leave it then. I'll drink it later."

He did not look at her but paced the small room like a caged lion, circling and coming back but never even looking at the chair she had waiting for him or at her new night rail of transparent linen and lace.

"You know you're a damn fool," she said, drinking her liquor.

Pembroke faced her then, taking in the soft fall of bronze hair around her shoulders, the deep shadow of her generous cleavage, the outline of her voluptuous body beneath her gown. There was a time when he would have had it off her in a trice, her body under his in the next moment. But now he stood and looked at her as at a sweet he no longer craved.

"I am a fool for not bedding you, you mean?"

"You are a fool to have love show up on your doorstep twice, only to turn it away."

He did not lie to Titania. For some reason, he had never been able to lie to her.

"She does not love me."

"I beg to differ, my lord."

"Hearing you beg is always amusing, Titania, but I am not in the mood tonight."

"That much is clear."

He started pacing again, and she watched him. "She loves you, Pembroke. Only you're too blind to see it."

He stopped pacing and sat down beside her. For a moment, he considered drinking the brandy laid out for him, but though his hand shook with desire for it, with the thirst for that clean burn on his tongue, he fought it down. He did not touch the glass.

"She says that she wrote to me after her marriage."

"No doubt she did."

"I would have received those letters, Titania, at least one of them. She is lying for her own amusement. Or to make me suffer. Or both."

"Hmmm…" Titania took a sip of her own brandy. "The duchess does not seem the vindictive type."

That word on his mistress's lips seemed to snap something within him, some tether to the past, the last vestige of his fury. He watched it spin away, a splinter carried on an outgoing tide. He felt drained and listless, as if he had fought a long battle and lost.

He sighed and leaned his head against the tall back of the wooden chair he sat in. Titania was blessedly silent, and the only sound in the room was of coal falling in the grate. "She left me without a word and married another."

"You still believe she married an elderly man of her own accord?"

"To become a duchess instead of the wife of a disinherited youth? Yes."

But even as Pembroke spoke, his words sounded false in his own ears. He no longer believed that. As he sat, staring into the fire with his mistress beside him, he wondered how he ever had.

"I think you need to speak with her again," Titania said. "And this time, do not run away."

Pembroke did not say a word but stood at once, pushing his chair back from the table. He leaned over her, pressing a kiss into the softness of her hair. His lips just brushed her temple, and he felt no desire to kiss her mouth or to do anything else with her. The scent of cornflowers filled his nose, as if Arabella were standing beside him.

He left Titania sitting where he had found her. As he closed the door behind him, he heard her say, "Whatever happens tonight, don't be late for rehearsal in the morning."

❧

Arabella did not sleep. She tried to lie down, but she knew it was a futile effort.

Pembroke had left her at the front door to go to his doxy in the village. As much as she liked Titania, the thought of him touching her, or any woman, made her throat fill with bile.

At least she preferred bile to tears.

So after lying for two sleepless hours in her borrowed room, she drew on a dressing gown and went down to the front hall. Codington had not gone to sleep either. She knew that he would not sleep until his master was home. She did not see him, but she sensed his presence as if he stood in the room with her. She ignored the thought of the older man who had once been her ally and kept to her seat at the edge of the entrance hall, as if she were a tradesman who would not be shown inside.

She sat in the hallway for only half an hour before Codington emerged as if by magic and opened the door for his master.

"My lord, the duchess has waited up for you."

Pembroke turned to her, his blue eyes cold. "So I see."

Codington melted into shadow, leaving them alone.

"What do you want, Arabella?"

She felt her tears rising then, knowing that she would leave his house on the morrow, knowing that she would never see him again. She could not leave him without telling him what had happened, some short version of events, whether he ever believed her or not.

"My father forced me to marry the duke. I did not know about his plans until the night before the wedding, when I was supposed to come to you. I tried to escape my father's house, I tried to send word, but I failed. I am sorry."

The last three words were torn from her throat, leaving her bleeding. But some small light came over her heart for a moment as the words were spoken. She saw from his shuttered look that he had not truly forgiven her, that he did not believe her. But she had told him the truth. Now she could go.

Save for one thing more.

She stepped forward, drawing the gold chain from around her neck. His mother's ring was still warm from the touch of her breasts. She held it in the palm of one hand, clutching it reflexively, knowing it was the last piece of him that she would ever have.

She looked up into the shuttered blue of his eyes, the one errant lock of hair falling across his forehead as it always did. She did not reach up to brush it aside, for she had lost that right long ago. Instead, she opened her hand.

"This is yours," she said. "I hope that whoever you give it to will make you happy."

❦

Pembroke stared down at the ruby ring in her hand.

The light in the hallway was gentle, cast by a pair of candelabra beside the door. He could not tell himself that his eyes were playing tricks for he could see that they were not. His mother's ring gleamed in the light of those candles, as bright and untarnished as the day he had first given it to Arabella.

He could not speak, so he did not. He simply took the ring from her palm and held it up to the light. The ruby flashed, and he remembered his mother laughing. He felt as if she were beside him in that moment, caressing his hair. But then she was gone, and all memory of her presence went with her. He was left alone with the woman he loved. She had lied to him for the second time that day. No doubt to spare his feelings, to assuage her guilt before she left him. The fact that he loved her had not stopped him from losing her twice.

Arabella waited, but when he did not speak, she turned and walked up the stairs alone in the dark. The shadows swallowed her, and Pembroke sat heavily in one of the Queen Anne chairs beside the door, one of the chairs his mother had chosen when she decorated that house before he was born.

The ring was heavy in his hand. It seemed too heavy for a slight woman like Arabella ever to have worn it.

Codington was beside him. "Will you step into the sitting room, my lord?"

"No," Pembroke said.

"Into the library?"

"No, Codington. I am going to sit in the front hall until my legs work again."

There was a long silence, and Codington did no leave. He stood like a sentinel beside him. Pembroke was not sure how much time had passed before he noticed the silver tray the butler offered him.

"What's this?" he asked.

Codington did not reply at once but lowered the tray for his inspection. Three yellowed letters lay on it still sealed, their wax beginning to flake away.

"These letters came long ago, my lord. Just before you left for the Continent. One came to your club another to the London house, another here. I gathered them all and kept them from you."

Pembroke reached out with one finger. The bits of yellowed paper did not vanish but lay still on the silver tray, like bodies of the long dead.

"I interfered in your life, my lord. I stood between you and that woman. I do not know what these letter say, nor do I care to know. She left you, and these were the only word she sent after she married His Grace, the Duke of Hawthorne."

Pembroke could not remember a time when Codington had spoken so much, not even when he was a child. He waited for his anger to rise, for outrage to overtake him at the high-handedness of the man who had been like a father to him all his life.

But he felt only a sense of wonder as he touched the letters again, this time reaching down to pick them up. They were brittle in his palm, against the calloused pads of his fingers, as if they might flake away into nothingness the way their wax seals had begun to do.

"You were trying to protect me," Pembroke said.

"I feared for your life, my lord. I feared what migh

come of more interaction with that woman. So I kept the letters from you."

"But you did not burn them, or return them, or throw them away."

"No, my lord. They are yours, after all."

Codington withdrew the tray and stood ready as if for a firing squad. "I have no defense for my actions, my lord. I will tender my resignation, effective immediately if you wish. Or, if you prefer, I will stay until a suitable replacement can be found."

Pembroke looked at the man who had loved him all his life, the man who had placed himself between the boy Pembroke had been and his father during the worst of the old earl's drunken rages. He knew without a shadow of doubt that he would not have survived his childhood without Codington's interference in his life.

For some reason now, after all this time, he did not feel betrayed that Codington had kept such knowledge from him. Whatever those letters held, they would have hurt him then, all those years ago, as they were hurting him now. He knew that his old butler had hoped to keep him from yet more pain.

Life is pain, and to run from it is only to prolong the worst of it. Pembroke could feel the worst of it rising from the letters in his hand. Still, he knew that he would read them.

"I do not accept your resignation, Codington." Pembroke rose so that he and his butler stood eye to eye. Codington's blue eyes met his own, and Pembroke was not surprised to see that there were tears in them. "Thank you for protecting me. I have to pay the reckoning for loving her, but I may not have had the strength to do it then. I have the strength to do it now. Thank you for bringing these to me."

Codington swallowed hard, his tears running down his expressionless face in two rivers of salt.

"Will that be all, my lord?"

"For tonight. Go to bed, Codington. I will see you in the morning."

"And the letters?"

"I will read them now."

Seventeen

Pembroke was gone when she came downstairs in the morning. She had her bag packed and on her arm, intent on leaving for the inn in the village, where she might catch the mail coach heading away from there. But when she stepped into the hallway with her satchel in one hand and a bag containing her golden guineas in the other, she found the letter he had left for her on a silver tray outside her borrowed bedroom door. It said almost nothing.

It said only, "Please stay."

She set her heavy case down on the cream carpet and read the note again. She turned it over as if it were a cipher, searching for something more, some clue as to what it meant, as to what he wanted from her now.

She found none.

But she placed her still-packed bag on its stand in her room and went downstairs. She did not turn to the breakfast room, and Codington did not emerge to confront her. She opened the front door herself and stepped out into the warm air of summer.

The morning light was like a caress on her skin. She

took in a deep breath of the rising breeze, the scent of wisteria tickling her as she walked down the long drive away from the house, toward the village. She had almost no clothing. Before she moved on, perhaps she might find something in the village. Something that was not black.

She pushed away the pain that rode her and waved to the people working in the fields. Some of them called to her by name and raised their caps to her. She remembered few of these people from her childhood, for she had never mixed in with the folk who worked the land. They had kept away from her, a slave trader's daughter, as from a plague that was catching, and her father had kept a sharp eye on her, save for the one summer when he had arranged her marriage to the duke.

Arabella pushed away all memory of her father, not wanting to poison the summer day with such filth. Instead, she thought of Pembroke.

As she walked beside the hedgerow, her sturdy boots covered in mud, she wondered what her life to come would be like once she was gone from this place and from all who knew her, once she never saw Pembroke again. The thought of living without him was like a knife wound in her chest, one that made her fight for breath. She wondered what Pembroke had to say to her. Perhaps, finally, at the end, he was ready to listen.

Mrs. Bonner, the village seamstress, greeted Arabella warmly as if she had never known who her father was. Arabella found a few well-made, pretty gowns of soft muslin for her day dresses and one sturdy gown of light blue worsted—simple gowns that a duchess never could have worn. She never wanted to wear black again.

Out of nowhere, she felt a moment of searing guilt that she was flouting convention completely, leaving mourning for her husband behind only a month after his death.

She took a deep breath to steady herself. She had lived too long under the shadow of others. Hawthorne had seen to it that she was ruined already. No one in decent society would receive her again. She might as well get on with her life and live and dress to please herself. When she had escaped to Bristol, when she was living under another name, no one would know her or care.

There was one gown, though, that she should never have tried on. It was too beautiful for her life now or for the life to come. But she tried it on anyway.

Arabella faced the mirror in a formal gown of blue watered silk, taking in the sight of her small, high breasts nestled beneath the scalloped, low-cut bodice. The high waist flattered her slender figure, accentuating what few assets she had. The blue silk matched almost exactly the color of her eyes, and the pink silk trim brought out the color in her cheeks.

Arabella smiled at her reflection as Mrs. Bonner made adjustments to the gown. She knew that she would take this dress, along with the others. She would think of the future later, but she would wear this gown tonight.

With pins between her teeth, Mrs. Bonner said, "You are a vision, Your Grace."

"Thank you, Mrs. Bonner."

"And shall I send the bill to Pembroke House?"

Arabella colored at the implication that Pembroke would pay for her clothes. "No. I will pay for the dress myself."

The seamstress colored with pleasure when Arabella paid her at once and in gold. She gave Mrs. Bonner a little extra money to arrange delivery of a few of the gowns to Pembroke House that very afternoon.

Arabella could not wait even a few hours to be rid of her borrowed bonnet. She bought a new one made of white straw trimmed with silk cornflowers and light blue ribbon. She donned at last a gown of sprigged muslin decorated with cornflowers that Mrs. Bonner had been able to adjust to her figure while she waited.

Arabella had to make do with the leather boots she had brought with her into exile, but at Mrs. Bonner's request, the cobbler came by to measure Arabella's feet. So she had the pleasure of ordering new boots made, as well as new slippers. Arabella savored having ready money on hand, being able to pay her own bills without having to appeal to her husband for her meager quarterly allowance. She signed the bill of sale for her new wardrobe herself, savoring the taste of freedom her own money brought. The golden guineas in the bag at Pembroke House would pay for a modest life for the rest of her days. She was not sure yet if she would invest them in the City or simply bury them along with herself in an unknown town. She did not have to decide today. But her father's gold, bought by the misery of others, would also buy her freedom.

She stepped out in her new muslin gown and pelisse, the sun warming her as she turned her face to the light. It was already noon, and she had begun to get hungry, for she had avoided Pembroke's table. He would be in rehearsal until the evening and not free to speak with her until then. She decided to savor the last few hours alone in her home village with a stroll to the pub. It was a different place with her father dead and her freedom close at hand.

The day was warm and bright, with no evidence of the frequent rains she remembered from her childhood in Derbyshire. Perhaps even the weather had come under an enchantment, bringing sunlight and warmth, deep greens and fragrant flowers to the village commons without the price of rain. Arabella knew that all things must be paid for, but not that day.

She walked down the high street of the village, greeting shopkeepers as she passed. The baker pressed a roll into her basket, wrapping it in brown paper to keep it fresh. It was warm from the oven, and Arabella could feel the heat of it through her kid gloves.

Along one side street, she noticed a little stone cottage set back from the lane. She turned down the street to look at it, but the high wall in front of the house blocked any view of the garden. The wall was not forbidding the way the garden wall seemed at Swanson House, but instead seemed to offer shelter, a sanctuary behind its stone. Arabella had never had sanctuary in her life, save for the last few days with Pembroke.

The bright, cheerful blue of the wooden gate stood out from the gray stone of the wall. She pressed her hand against the latch, and it opened without a squeak of protest.

Beyond the gate lay a tiny cottage set back in its own garden. The flowers had not been tended in quite a while, but Arabella saw columbine and thyme, rosemary and goldenrod. A profusion of blooms welcomed the kiss of the sun as flowers mixed with herbs along the neat path that led to the cottage's front door. The roof was of gray slate, and when she peered inside a front window, she saw that the interior walls were whitewashed. It seemed like a house from another time, an enchanted place where one might live in quiet, where one might be happy.

The scent of roses reached her and she breathed in their languorous perfume. Red roses climbed the western wall, entwined with yellow pease blossoms. Both flowers would get the best of the afternoon sun. Arabella stood for a long time, drinking in the sights and smells of that cottage. She knew that she could not stay. Hawthorne was on her heels or soon would be. And she needed to be away from Pembroke before he crushed what was left of her heart. But she wanted a home like this. She longed for it, for a place to belong, with almost a physical pain. Perhaps in Bristol she would find one, a little house that looked out over the sea.

Arabella turned her back on the white cottage with the sharp click of the gate closing behind her and made her way back to the high street and to the public house that faced out onto Pembroke village green. She saw the actors eating under the trees at the same tables where they had all taken dinner the night before. Pembroke and Titania were among them.

She froze, like a coney in a snare, her only thought

to turn back. But Titania rose from her place among her players and waved to her with one lazy sweep of her arm. "Your Grace," Titania called to her. "You must come and sit between us, if you have no objection to taking your luncheon with actors and riffraff."

As she spoke the last word, Titania looked not to her company but at Pembroke. The lead actress was once again in full possession of her power. She sat enthroned like a queen surrounded by her court. Caught in the gaze of Pembroke's mistress, Arabella lost her voice.

"You must join us, Your Grace," Pembroke said.

His blue gaze held hers, running first over the new muslin dress she wore, as if he were thirsty on a hot day and the sight of her was cool water. He drank her down in one long draft. Arabella was caught in the fire in his eyes as Pembroke crossed the green to her and took her arm. He escorted her carefully across the close cropped grass and drew out a chair for her beside Titania. She sat before her knees gave way.

She felt the warmth of his arm on the table beside her as he reached for a flagon of ale. He poured her a cup of cider and served her a meat pasty off the tray in the center of the board. All the while, Pembroke kept his eyes away from her and his ears on the conversation at the other end of the table. Though he did not look at her again, she knew that he was aware of her as she was of him. A thread of heat ran between them, and Arabella felt a frisson of hope. Perhaps they might finally talk when they were alone again. Perhaps they might both put the past behind them and begin to heal.

Two actors were talking about the rustic scene toward the end of *A Midsummer Night's Dream*, when they acted a play within a play. Arabella had read this masterpiece of Shakespeare's over and over again, though she'd never seen one of his plays performed. She tried to take her mind off Pembroke and listened avidly as the actors spoke, wondering how it would be to see one of her favorite scenes acted out before her.

Titania smiled wryly, catching Arabella's eye. She looked at Pembroke, who still did not spare a glance for Arabella but who kept her plate and cup full. Titania raised one elegantly curved eyebrow, and Arabella found herself wondering if the actress minded seeing her lover sit so close to another. She felt a spike of jealousy in her own spleen and swallowed a sip of ale to cool it.

As luncheon finished and the stage manager called for rehearsal to begin, Pembroke turned to her for the first time since the meal began.

"I wish you would stay and watch." His lips quirked in a smile. "I need you to tell me if I'm making a fool of myself up there."

Arabella found herself smiling. "We wouldn't want that."

"No, we would not." His eyes were bright with mischief, but beneath that she saw a need that matched her own. He leaned down and kissed her hand before turning away.

Pembroke crossed with the other players toward the makeshift stage just built on the green. He moved with authority even there, though he listened to the professionals and took the advice they offered him about how to position himself on stage, how to enter, and how to exit. Arabella was listening to all this with half an ear, watching Pembroke all the while. She did not notice Cassie until the actress sat down beside her.

"Well, Your High and Mighty Worship, what's a fancy duchess from London doing among the likes of us?"

The woman's eyes were sharp on Arabella's face, all trace of the warmth that she had worn before Pembroke gone.

"There's some from London who might like to know where their duchess is. You'd best leave out of here quick-like, or that someone might come looking for you."

Arabella felt all the color drain from her face. Her mouth was as dry as chalk, so dry that she could not speak. She swallowed hard, blinking in the face of this woman's malice, but she could not bring herself even to rise and walk away. She could not even blink as she stared into Cassie's hate-filled eyes.

"While you're at it, you might stay away from a girl's mark. Pembroke's mine next, and everyone here knows it."

The iron voice of Titania filled the space between them, forcing Cassie to her feet. "Pembroke belongs to himself, my girl. Her Grace does not arrange his love life, and neither do you. Now take yourself to the stage or I'll dock you this afternoon's pay."

Cassie swallowed whatever she had been ready to say next. She walked away from them, but not before casting one last evil look at Arabella.

"Thank you," Arabella said. "I did not know what to say."

"There's little to say to the likes of her, Your Grace. Put her out of your mind. You've got bigger fish to fry."

Arabella watched as Cassie took her place on stage with the other fairy women. She drew her gaze from the girl reluctantly, almost afraid that something terrible might happen if she did not keep her eye on her.

She knew that she needed to be gone. In the morning, after she had spoken to Pembroke and had gotten a decent night's rest, she would disappear. No doubt the vulgar woman was right. If Hawthorne had not heard where she was already, he soon would.

"You are kind, Madame Titania. You need not trouble yourself on my account."

Titania tossed her head, the sunlight catching the bronze buried in her red hair. "It is no trouble at all to keep a troublesome actress in her place. Believe me when I tell you, if you give an inch, they'll take a mile. If I left her to her own devices, next I saw her she'd be wearing my own gowns and swanning about like the Princess of Wales."

Arabella laughed at that. She caught Pembroke's eye across the green and she felt her face flush with pleasure. Just the touch of his gaze took her breath away.

Titania noticed the exchange and the pink that had risen in Arabella's cheeks. Her smile took on a new light, and she lowered her voice, which was filled with the kindness of an elder sister.

"Your Grace," Titania said. "It seems Lord Pembroke

can't keep his eyes off you, especially when you are not looking."

Arabella felt the blush in her cheeks flood her neck and chest, heating her skin all the way into the bodice of her new gown. "You must be mistaken."

"I am not. And it seems you feel the same way about him."

Arabella did not answer but kept her eyes downcast, her hand on her mug of cider.

"It is not my place to interfere, and you certainly need no advice from the likes of me. But there are times when men don't know their own minds. Sometimes they need to be told what to think. That's why they have us."

"But he is yours," Arabella said.

The actress smiled, and for a moment Arabella thought she saw some fragment of pain there, but it was gone in a moment, so she doubted herself.

"As I told Cassie, Pembroke belongs to himself."

Arabella felt a moment of sudden longing, that she might go back in time and make Pembroke truly hers. But that was impossible. The best she could hope for was to reclaim some small part of their friendship, to tell him the whole truth so that they could both get on with their lives.

Titania did not say anything more on the subject but rose to her feet. "Since his lordship has asked you to sit among us for the rehearsal, I wonder if you might assist me. I need a prompter, and my usual girl is sick in bed."

Arabella felt a new kind of pleasure rise at the thought that she might be of use. She had never been of use to anyone in her life, save to her father when he married her off. "What is a prompter?" she asked.

"When an actor can't remember his line, you read it to him. Other than that, you read along as we work and watch the play."

Arabella felt nerves rise along the nape of her neck. She had never drawn attention to herself in her life and did not know how she would feel with the actors' eyes on her.

But the thought of helping to put her favorite play onstage, even in this small way, made her smile. It would feel good to be useful.

She followed Titania to the front of the stage, where a chair had been placed for her with a cushion. A girl from the inn came by with more cider, and Arabella felt almost at home. She was sure that she would be self-conscious as the rehearsal began, but everyone seemed to know their place and hers and moved about accordingly. Even Pembroke blended well with the troupe despite his rank.

The first time an actor asked for his line, she gave it to him without hesitation, her voice loud enough to be heard, but not so loud as to draw focus away from the stage. Titania, standing on the makeshift platform in the guise of her namesake, nodded her approval, and Arabella felt a surge of pride.

For the first time in her life, Arabella felt as if she were part of something larger than herself. Though she kept her eyes on the printed pages in her hands, her attention was drawn again and again into the scene as the actors played it out over and over. Each time they brought out different nuances in the words, some treasure buried in Shakespeare's poetry. Arabella was enthralled.

The afternoon flew by on a sparrow's wing. She had taken off her gloves and slipped them into her basket to protect them from the ink of the pages. When she gave the script back to Titania, her fingertips were coated in black. Titania clicked her tongue when she saw it, but Arabella only smiled.

"A small price to pay to be able to sit through such a wonderful rehearsal."

The afternoon had made her wish that she might stay and see the final production, and dance with the villagers on Midsummer night. But Arabella knew that she could not.

Pembroke waved to the actors as they turned from the stage and headed to their rooms before taking their dinner on the green. They had been invited to dine with the troupe again, but she heard Pembroke decline.

Cassie flirted shamelessly with Pembroke, batting her long lashes that had been blackened with kohl. Arabella felt a touch of fear as she watched Pembroke with the woman who had threatened to reveal her whereabouts only a few hours before.

Her throat was suddenly dry again, and she felt a prickling on her neck that made her want to look behind her. She refrained out of force of will. She would not be bullied by a two-bit actress, nor would she give in to fanciful fear. She was going to leave on the morrow, and no one would know where to find her. She would be safe from Hawthorne if she ran. She was sure of it.

Pembroke smiled absently at Cassie, but his eyes

shifted away almost at once to meet Arabella's gaze. He nodded to Cassie politely before he left the stage, coming down from his perch to stand at Arabella's side.

The actress shot another venomous glare at Arabella and flounced away. It was safe to assume that if Pembroke did have an assignation later that night, it was not with the frazzled blond.

Pembroke stood close beside her without speaking. He took up her hands and made an effort to rub the ink of the script away. His attempt was fruitless, but he did keep her hands in his.

"I will leave you two to your evening's revels," Titania said. "Until tomorrow."

She bowed to both of them and turned to the public house, the prompting script in her hand. Arabella found Pembroke staring down at her, her fingers cradled gently in one large hand.

"We need to talk," he said.

"Are you finally willing to listen?"

"Yes."

He stared at her, his blue eyes heating like dark flame. He leaned closer and her heart leaped in her throat. For one moment she thought that he might actually kiss her there in front of all those people, but he did not. He only took in a deep breath of the scent of her skin, as if she were a flower that had just opened.

He did not speak again but took up her basket and led her to his waiting carriage, which stood open to the evening air, its top down. The sun had begun its slow descent beyond the forest, and the moon was already rising. The coachman lowered the steps, taking her basket from Pembroke. But it was Pembroke who lifted her into the carriage before he took his place beside her.

Pembroke sat close to her, his thigh pressed against her own. Arabella felt his body heat radiating from him as if he were his own sun. But she was not repulsed by his closeness, as she had once been repulsed by her husband. On the contrary, Pembroke's heat made her want to draw closer, as to a fire in winter. Pembroke took her hand in his. He did not speak of the past, as she thought he might.

"I am sorry that the ink stained your skin."

Arabella smiled. "It will wash, my lord."

"My lord, is it? I thought we established that with you, I am Pembroke."

Arabella kept her eyes down, savoring the touch of his hand over hers. She relaxed a little, realizing that he did not want to air their old differences with his coachman listening. They sat in silence for a moment, the dusk rising from the grasses and the wildflowers along the roadside. Pembroke did not let go of her hand.

"How did you like the play?"

"I loved it."

Pembroke cocked an eyebrow, looking up at her from under the errant lock of hair that had once again fallen over his eye. "Love is a strong word, Arabella."

"It was wonderful," she said. "There is something truly beautiful about a play. The beauty of such a performance lies in the fact that it will last for only one night. It is insubstantial, a phantom that with our next breath is gone, just as one day we will be."

Pembroke stared at her as if he had found another

reason to admire her. But this time she did not feel the need to blush or look away. She had always told him her thoughts when they were younger, no matter how outlandish, no matter how odd. And he had always listened. He had never mocked her but had considered her words and answered them. She felt as if she had gone back in time as he answered her now.

"Shakespeare said something of that in *The Tempest*," Pembroke said.

"'We are such stuff as dreams are made on, and our little life is rounded with a sleep,'" Arabella said.

"I never knew you loved Shakespeare."

"Yes, you did," she said.

Their Forest of Arden rose between them, and all the walks they had taken together in it. They had read *A Midsummer Night's Dream* to each other over the course of a week, each reading different parts, skipping over the bits with the young lovers, the bits that made her blush. Arabella found that she was not blushing now.

He did not answer her, but she saw on his face that he remembered, too.

In a futile attempt to keep the past at bay, she kept talking about Shakespeare. "I've been alone a long time," she said. "There was little left to me in the last few years but to read."

She had never spoken of the dark vistas of her married life to anyone, not even Angelique. But she needed to tell him how it had begun. She needed to tell him why she had abandoned him.

"I would like to speak with you alone," she said.

"I know," he said. "There are things I must tell you, too."

She straightened her shoulders. "At dinner then?"

He took her hand in his as he helped her down from the carriage. "At dinner. I'll see you in an hour."

Her voice seemed to have deserted her, so she turned away and moved into the house. As she climbed the mahogany staircase, the soft carpet silencing each step, she felt almost as if she were running from him. It seemed that she could feel his gaze on her body even after she had closed the door to her bedroom behind her.

Eighteen

Mrs. Marks sent up a hip bath and warm water, and Arabella bathed by the fire. She took down her long hair, and washed away the grime of the last few days. She rubbed herself dry and sat at the vanity table while Rose, the upstairs maid, carefully dried her hair. She tied it at the nape of her neck in a simple blue ribbon, letting the honey-colored mass fall down her back, a few wisps soft against her cheeks and temples, framing her face.

She was ready early to greet Pembroke, but she did not go downstairs right away. She stood in front of the full-length glass in her borrowed room, considering the fact that she no longer looked as mousy as she had throughout her married life. The sun was still setting, and the windows were open, the warm summer breeze bringing in the scent of the roses below.

Arabella looked at herself in her new light blue gown. The cobbler had even managed to finish the matching slippers, so she was dressed from head to toe in new clothes, for her new beginning. She did not know where she might wear that dress in the future, but she was glad that she had it for this one night.

There was a knock on her door, and for some reason she did not call out to tell Mary to enter but went to open it herself. Pembroke was standing on the other side.

He held out the letters to her.

They were yellowed with age, their wax seals broken and all but flaked away. She saw those letters and took a step back, as if they were a disease that might be catching.

"You had them," she said. "You had them all this time, and you called me a liar."

She hit him then, her small fist a ball of pain. He did not dodge her blows but took them, pushing her back and into the room, closing the door behind him. She ripped the letters from his hands and tore them into bits, tossing them on the cream carpet at her feet, trampling them with her new slippers.

Pembroke drew her close then, and when she tried to strike him again, he caught her hands in both of his.

"I did not have them. Codington did. He gave them to me last night."

Arabella shook as with a fever, one that would not burn away until it killed her. She sank down where she stood, her knees giving way. Pembroke picked her up and carried her to an armchair by the fire. The wingback surrounded them both, shutting out the rest of the world.

She did not lean against him, but she did not try to pull away. Her strength had gone. She let him hold her hands.

"I am sorry, Arabella. I am sorry I did not come for you."

She was weeping then, deep, overwhelming sobs that rose from her gut and her spleen, carrying her fury and her pain with them. She did not hit him again, but let him draw her close. She leaned against his fine coat, her tears staining the dark green felt. His hand was in her hair, stroking and soothing her as nothing else could.

"Forgive me, Arabella. I should never have believed your father and his lies. I should never have believed my father. I should have come for you, no matter what seemed to be. I should have stolen you away from your husband's house. I should not have left you alone."

Arabella clung to him. She pulled her hands out of his grasp, but she did not hit him. Instead, she wrapped her arms around his neck as she had always longed to do, pulling him close, her tears watering the soft linen of his cravat. And still she sobbed. She was not certain that she would ever stop.

It was a long time before her pain began to fade. She saw the irony of this moment; the man she had hurt, the man whose life she had destroyed, was holding and comforting her. He had not known of her father's betrayal. He still did not. She would tell him, finally, a burden that she could at last lay down.

"Raymond, I must tell you of my wedding day."

He swallowed hard. She felt the movement of his Adam's apple against her cheek as she clutched him close. His voice was rough with unshed tears. She knew that he did not want to hear it, just as she did not want to tell it. They had both had enough of pain.

But he must know, so that he could choose finally to let her go.

❦

Ten years before, the last day of her freedom, the last day of her youth, Arabella had spent with Raymond. On that fine day in midsummer, he kissed her beneath the king oak and gave her his mother's ring. She wore that ruby on her left hand for the first and the last time.

On that day so long ago, she kept her hand closed in a fist, certain that if she was not careful, it would fall to the grass and she would lose it completely. In the light of the setting sun, the dark red stone gleamed like heart's blood. She pressed her fist to her breast, as Raymond kissed her again.

"Meet me under the oak. I'll have horses waiting."

"I will."

He did not walk her home, for he was not allowed on her father's land. She went alone, planning to pack her things, one small bag, just a few bits of her mother's lace, a few gowns, a pair of slippers. All she needed to take into her new life with him, the life they would build together.

When she snuck in through the back door, her father was waiting.

"It's about time you came home," was all he said.

Arabella stared at him, his wide shoulders ramrod straight, his graying hair the color of polished pewter. His light blue eyes held her still, like a bug under a pin, impaled and dying. For a moment, Arabella was sure that she could not move, could not breathe. Only when he looked away could she take a breath.

She did not try to run then, when she might have gotten away. Instead, she followed her father into the house to the front parlor that had not been used since her mother died. An old man sat by the fire there though it was midsummer and warm.

The house as always was dark and cold, the fire meager, only three candles lit by the hearth. The old man did not seem to mind but stood as her father did, his cool gray eyes assessing her as she had once seen a horse assessed at the fair in the village.

"This is His Grace, the Duke of Hawthorne. Come and greet him, daughter."

Arabella flinched. He only called her daughter when he thought to beat her. She felt the sting of old wounds on her shoulders as she stepped forward to take the old duke's hand.

Hawthorne bowed as if they met in a ballroom, surrounded by bright lights and soft laughter, dancing and merriment. He kissed her fingertips, his lips leaving a trace of spittle on the back of her hand.

She felt her dread rising. Her father had never brought anyone home before. She curtsied, her eyes cast down to hide her fear. She knew her father could smell it on her, but she might escape a beating if he did not see it in her eyes.

"The duke has graciously condescended to marry you on the morrow. You may hold your tongue. I can only imagine how pleased you must be to become a peer of the realm, the wife of such a man. I have no doubt that you are grateful that we have arranged such a stellar match for the likes of you."

Arabella stepped away from the two old men, her

mind whirling. She had never seen this man before in her life. She would not marry him, tomorrow or ever.

She knew then that she would have no time to pack a bag. The fragments of her mother's memory and of her old life would have to be left behind. If she could get to Pembroke, if she could reach him, she would be safe, no matter what her father said, no matter what bargains he had made.

She still wore her cloak of dark blue wool. She murmured something polite and curtsied again, drawing her cloak close about her. She stepped into the hall as if to go to her room, but her father must have seen some hint of defiance in her face. When she turned not toward the staircase, but to the back door of the house, her father caught her arm. He dragged her up the stairs himself, while the old butler stood looking on, silent and dour.

As always, the house was ill lit. Her father carried a lamp in one hand, gripping her thin arm in the other. She had never fought him in her life, but she fought him then, desperately trying to tear herself away, as she would have torn away from a bear trap if caught in the woods. She could not think of failure, only of escape.

"I know you've been sneaking around with the earl's son," her father said. "That's all well and good for childish pleasures, but you will be a woman on the morrow and you will obey me every moment until then. You will marry the Duke of Hawthorne as I bid you. You will put a smile on your face tomorrow morning, and you will swear to obey him for the rest of your life."

Arabella saw the key in his hand and knew that he

meant to lock her in. Despite the years she had lived
with him, in spite of the beatings she had received at
his hands since her mother's death, for the first time
she stopped struggling and asked for mercy.

"Father, I love him."

He did not hesitate. She wondered for a moment if
he had even heard her speak. He pushed her into her
bedroom, the cold hearth filled with ash.

Her father struck her once, raising a welt on her
cheek. "Love is just a pretty word. You will marry
where I bid you."

He slammed the door to her room, locking it
behind him. Arabella could not take those words as
her epitaph. She hammered her hands bloody against
that door, hoping some servant would hear, take pity,
and set her free. But the entire household was as afraid
of her father as she was, and no one came.

He heard her though, and he came back with a
supple willow wand, a wand she had not seen since
she was a girl, since he had taken to beating her with
his riding crop.

"Take off your shoes," he said.

"I will not."

So he called in his valet to hold her down and he
took her shoes off himself and beat the soles of her
feet as his man kept her pressed into the threadbare
carpet. It was not a bad beating as some of them went.
He stopped after ten strokes. She knew then that he
was serious about making her marry on the morrow.
There would be no time to escape.

Arabella sat up all night, alone in the dark. Just
before dawn an upstairs maid came to dress her hair

and to help her into her wedding gown, a blue silk gown of her mother's that now fit.

She slipped a letter to Raymond into the basket that had held the remains of her breakfast bread, asking the girl to hand the letter to the cook. Mrs. Fielding would see that Pembroke received it.

In an hour, Arabella's father came to take her downstairs to be wed. He drew out the letter she had written, telling Pembroke why she had not come to him.

"You cannot defy me, Arabella. I am your father, and I hold your life, such as it is, in my hands. You will obey me as God has ordained. You will come downstairs now and take an oath to obey your husband for the rest of your life. Forget this boy. He is dead to you, or I will make him so."

Arabella could not be certain he truly meant that he would kill him, but in that moment, she believed him. She watched as he burned her letter to Pembroke. He drew a flint from his pocket and struck a spark that ignited the small blaze. When it was gone, with all her hope, he took up the fire tongs and scattered the ashes before he led her down to the drawing room to marry the Duke of Hawthorne.

⤜⤛

Pembroke pressed his hand to hers. He felt his mind wheeling in circles like a great bird, looking down on that long-ago day. He saw her father as he had once seen him, a huge, imposing man whose ambition burned like a brand, raising blisters on all it touched. He saw her face as he had seen it on her wedding day, thin, pale, and drawn, her eyes downcast except when she had looked at him.

That day he had been so filled with pain, so overcome by anger and despair that he had not truly seen her, not really. He had seen only a woman who had betrayed him, an avaricious woman who had played him for a fool, lying to him one night only to marry another man the next day. He had been a boy of eighteen, unable to see past his own wounded pride and his own pain. But now Pembroke looked back down the corridor of years and saw Arabella as she truly had been. A seventeen-year-old girl, lost and alone, with no man to defend her, not even him.

Pembroke wept, pressing his hands to his face. He knelt beside her chair and laid his head in her lap, his tears staining the linen of her napkin. Arabella pressed her fingers into the softness of his hair. He felt her soothing touch like a balm on his soul. He raised his head and wiped away the last of his tears.

"I have always loved you," he said. "I never stopped, not for one moment, from that day to this."

The silence stretched between them as he looked into her light blue eyes that matched the room around them, the room he had designed just for her, when he had been certain that she would never see it.

Arabella pressed her lips to his forehead. Pembroke felt the last of the open wound on his heart heal.

"I love you, Raymond. I always loved you, even when it was no longer my right."

She stood as if to run from him, and he rose to his feet with her, still not letting go of her hand. Pembroke pulled her to him, holding her within the prison of his arms. He did not tighten his grip, he did not try to distract her with desire, with the press of his lips on hers. He wrapped his arms around her but gave her room to move, room to breathe. He would not smother her, but he also knew that he would never let her go.

Arabella stopped fighting him and leaned against his chest. She rested her head just above his heart. He could feel her breath and her heartbeat, like the wings of a tiny bird, frantic to be free. Finally, her heart slowed and her breathing became even. He wondered for a moment if she had fallen asleep, she was so quiet as she leaned against him.

"Marry me, Arabella."

She shook in his arms, and when he looked down at her face, he saw that she was not weeping but laughing, the light of joy on her face.

"I cannot marry you," she said. "I will never belong to a man again. And Hawthorne is coming. I cannot be here when he arrives. But thank you for asking me."

"I will protect you from Hawthorne."

"And who will protect you? From a duke of the realm? From a friend of the Prince Regent?"

"I'll call him out. I'll kill him for touching you."

"He would kill you."

"No, he won't."

Arabella knew Hawthorne too well to believe that. No matter how mad he might be, he was a crack shot. Hawthorne had killed at least one man in cold blood on the dueling field, and she knew it would not trouble him to shoot one more. It might even give him pleasure.

"No," she said. "I will not marry again. I must be gone."

"If you think I am letting you go now that I've found you again, you are lying to yourself."

She laughed louder then, her old, free laugh from her belly. He held her close and felt the vibration of her laughter through his own body, coaxing out his own.

"I love you, Arabella." He needed to say those words again and to have her hear them.

"I love you, Raymond. And I am still leaving."

He pressed her lips closed with his own, knowing that he did not have the strength to argue with her anymore.

He had waited for her ten years already. He would keep waiting for as long as it took. Now that he had her back, he felt as if his heart had grown large enough to encompass the whole world. She would marry him, no matter what she said. He would see to it.

He kissed her until she was leaning full against him, soft and pliant. When he drew back from her far enough to look down into her eyes, she sighed and smiled at him.

"Be my mistress then," he teased. "Live with me in sin. Let us have twenty bastard children together and be the talk of the *ton*."

Arabella laughed, raising her head. He saw the light in her soft blue eyes. "Twenty children?"

"Too few?" He smiled down at her, smoothing her caramel hair back from her face where it had come loose from its ribbon. "We can compromise on the number of children," he said. "I want only to be with you."

She did not speak at once but lay her head back down on his chest. Her breathing was even and calm, her body warm and soft against his. Pembroke took the moment in, giving thanks for it even as it passed.

This moment was what he had waited for all his life. This moment was why he had not died in Spain, or Italy, or Belgium. He had lived so that he might one day stand with her like this.

Arabella pulled back a little so that she might look up at him again. This time her eyes were clear. They bore no tears and held no fear. Only her love shone on him, reflected in the ghost of a smile that touched her lips.

Nineteen

PEMBROKE KISSED HER AGAIN, HIS TOUCH AS SOFT AS A butterfly's wing. Arabella sighed and opened her lips beneath his, so that his tongue might enter.

The kiss began soft but did not stay that way. In the next breath, Pembroke's hand moved up her back and into her hair, drawing the ribbon out, her hair soft between his fingers.

Arabella moaned at the feel of his hands in her hair, pressing close to his hard body that she might take in all of him at once. She knew that no matter how long she was given to be with him, she would never be able to get close enough.

Her fingers rose between them, running over the muscles of his chest. His waistcoat and linen shirt blocked her touch, but she could still feel the heat of him rising through the layers of his clothes. When she reached up to touch his cheek, his cravat got in her way. She drew back a little so that she could see to begin to unravel it.

Pembroke laughed, his breath gone. He took her hands gently in one of his and drew them away from the linen at his throat.

"Arabella, I was joking when I said I would take you as my mistress. You will be my wife."

"And I told you that I will never marry again. Why don't we save this argument for another time, and let this night be what it will?"

She smiled up at him, knowing that he fought with himself over his rediscovered honor. She saw his desire for her in the heat of his eyes. She felt it along the palm of his hand where he held her by the waist, as if wanting to draw her close and push her back all at once.

Arabella pressed herself against Pembroke without warning, wrapping her arms around his neck, her fingers in the soft blond of his hair. The nape of his neck was bare, his blond mane close cropped for war, but she found a few curls buried in the military style that he had not given up in all his years of debauchery.

Pembroke moved to pull away from her, and she clung to him as a burr might to his clothes. Her hands were tenacious as she wrapped her arms around him tighter. She had spent all her life alone. She wanted this night.

He stopped trying to pull away.

She saw a look of hunger cross his face, but she knew that it was not food he wanted. She pressed herself against him, suddenly remembering how her husband had mounted her in their marriage bed. She shuddered inwardly and pushed all thoughts of the old duke away.

"I love you, Raymond," was all she said. Then she raised her lips to his and opened her mouth over his.

The sound of his name on her lips worked like the

incantation of a spell, for he responded, sliding his tongue over her lips until she opened her mouth and let him devour her. His palms ran down her back and over the curve of her hips, pressing her thighs into the hardness of his body.

She felt his manhood high and hard against her belly, and instead of making her retreat, the feel of him against her made her want to get closer. With her husband, she had wanted to flee, but with Pembroke, even knowing the pain that was to come, she wanted to be nowhere but in his arms.

She drew back to take a breath and Pembroke met her eyes, his blue gaze dark with desire. Even then he tried to rein himself in, to retreat, to withdraw from her. She saw his honor war with his desire. She fought on the side of his desire, for it matched her own.

She felt heat in her belly and in her chest, expanding like a tide coming in to shore. She moved against him, not knowing what she wanted, knowing only that if any man could give it to her, that man was Pembroke.

"Do not leave me tonight," Arabella said. Her voice sounded like another's, some other wanton woman, a woman Pembroke might have taken into his bed on any night before this. But she was not any other woman. She was the woman he loved. She was the woman who loved him.

She pressed herself to him, letting her body move as it wanted to, as if she had never known another man, as if she was free to love him alone.

"Stay," she said.

Pembroke stopped fighting himself and his own desire, turning the force of that desire on her. His hands moved over her again, smoothing down the soft silk of her new gown. He pressed against her slender form, drawing her close to the fire.

The sun had long since set, and the fire and candles were all they had to light their way. Pembroke could not seem to get enough of touching her. He raised her in his arms, carrying her to the bed. The fire still burned in the hearth behind them, but it gave no light where the bed lay in its alcove of blue silk. Pembroke laid her body down on the soft feather bed, and pressed a kiss first to her forehead, then to her lips. "Stay here," he said.

He rose and looked down at her, his hair wild from where she had mussed it, his eyes consumed with wanting. His hand shook as he brought a candle close to the bedside. The long taper burned bright, casting a deep yellow light across the counterpane, across her body, across the blue of her silk gown. Shadows stretched as she did, and she saw her shadow as another creature, something outside herself that reflected her desire.

She stretched again, languidly, and watched as Pembroke's eyes caught fire. Arabella felt her own power then, for the first time in her life. With Pembroke, she was safe to feel it, to savor it, the joy of her own need for him, and joy of the need she inspired in him. She spread herself out along the soft contours of the feather bed then raised one hand, beckoning him to lie down beside her.

Pembroke did not move to join her at once, but stood staring. She saw in his eyes that he hesitated not because he doubted her desire but because he was drinking in the sight of it. Arabella raised herself on one elbow, patting the bed beside her. "Come here, Raymond. I have need of you."

He laughed then, and she shivered at the sound. It was not mocking laughter, but a surrender. He laughed not at her, but at himself.

He took off his coat and tossed it behind him on a chair. He left his waistcoat and linen shirt on, as well as his breeches. He took his boots off carefully, one tight sheath of leather at a time. Arabella sat up so that she could see him better, taking in the play of his muscles beneath the sheer linen of his shirt.

"I did not know what desire was until I saw you," she said to him.

Another woman seemed to have taken over her body, and yet she had never felt more completely herself. And it was not wine this time, or mead, for she had not taken a drop. This night she was drunk on her love for him and on the fact that, for this night, he was hers.

He sat on the bed with her then, his weight making a deep depression in the soft mattress. Arabella rolled toward him and caught herself against his thigh. She ran her hand idly over the muscles beneath the taut breeches, touching him as she had always longed to do. Before this, she had always been afraid. This night, she felt as if she would never be afraid again.

She did not know what to do, but she was not embarrassed by her ignorance. Her innocence was a gift she could give him along with her body, an offering in the face of all they had lost, of all that had been taken from them in the last ten years. They had lost time and youth, but they were together now, and that was an unlooked-for blessing.

Arabella kissed him gently then drew back to unlace her gown. She took off her bodice, kicked away the silk of her skirt.

Pembroke helped her draw each piece of clothing off, laying them carefully on the chair beside the bed. Arabella undressed until she wore nothing but her thin chemise and her stockings. She untied each garter and slowly rolled the stockings down her legs, tossing them aside.

She smiled at him, drew out the pins from her hair, and it fell around her face and shoulders like a veil. She pushed the caramel locks back so that she could see him clearly, so that he could see her.

He seemed to drink in the contours of her face, the curves of her cheeks, which she knew were pink with joy. She felt herself blush beneath his hand, but she did not turn away. She savored the heat as it rose beneath her skin, knowing that when he touched her, her skin would heat still more.

Pembroke stood to draw his own trousers off, as well as his waistcoat, so that he faced her in just his shirt. The edges came down over the tops of his thighs. The golden trail of hair on his chest disappeared beneath the linen, only to reappear as a golden fleece along his thighs.

Arabella did not back away from him even then. Her old fear did not rise to overwhelm her, and it was yet another victory. She longed to draw that shirt off him, so that she could see the hair on his chest. When he sat beside her again, she pressed her hand to his heart, moving his linen shirt out of her way so that she might lay her lips on his skin as she had always longed to do.

Arabella moved her lips across the heated warmth of him. The dark golden hair on his chest pillowed her cheek, and she ran her hands across his body. He stripped away the shirt so that she was left with just him and his beauty before her. He lay back and let her look.

Pembroke's blue eyes were filled with desire for her, but he did not move to touch her. He lay back and let her feast on him, first with her lips and then with her hands.

Arabella's eyes fell on his manhood nestled in its thatch of golden hair. She had never seen one before. The old duke, when he came to her, had always worn a long gown. In her marriage bed, she had closed her eyes and braced herself, praying for it all to be over quickly. But tonight, with the man she loved, she would keep her eyes open.

He gasped when she touched him. She flinched back, thinking that she had hurt him, but he laughed low, almost like a purr deep in his chest. She saw the heated light in his eyes darkening to a deeper blue. She kept her eyes on his and touched his manhood again.

The pleasure on his face looked almost like pain, and he groaned beneath her fingertips. He wrapped one hand around her wrist as if to stop her, and she bent down and pressed her lips to his fingers. The manacle on her wrist relaxed then as he ran his hand over her cheek. She turned her head and pressed her lips into his palm before she leaned down and brushed her lips lightly against his manhood.

Pembroke leaped then as if she had scalded him. He moved so quickly that she had no time to take her next breath before he had pulled her beneath him. He rose over her, his breath labored as if he had run a fast mile, the laughter in his eyes mixed with desire, and she found herself laughing too.

"Am I wrong to touch you?" she asked him.

He laughed low, the sound sending a shiver along her skin. "No," he answered, "you are not wrong. But if you do it again, I will not be able to control myself."

She smiled, running her hand along the line of his jaw. She pressed her lips to his throat. "Why should you control yourself?"

"I don't want to hurt you," he said.

"I do not mind if you hurt me."

"No," he said. "Pain does not belong in bed. Only pleasure."

He pressed her down against the soft feather bed. The shadows cast by the single candle lengthened over them as he moved above her, running his hands over her body, smoothing the skin of her arms, his palms coming down to cup her breasts. Arabella had never been touched that way in her life, and she gasped beneath his mouth as his lips ravished her, as his nimble fingers spread over the rosy softness of her breasts.

She had always thought her breasts too small to be of interest to a man, but Pembroke worshiped them, pushing her chemise aside to run first his hands and then his lips over them. She lost her breath completely when he took one of the taut peaks into his mouth, laving his tongue over it. Arabella thought she might never breathe again, but she did not care. His touch on her skin was more pleasure than she had ever known. If she were to die, let it be like this, with his body over hers and his hands on her skin.

Pembroke raised her chemise altogether then, and she helped him, gathering up her hair and drawing it aside so that he could bring the last piece of her clothing over her head. He tossed the linen away and feasted his eyes on her naked flesh. Arabella froze, thinking to cover herself, for no one had ever seen her naked before.

She forced herself to look into Pembroke's eyes, and when she saw his love for her mixed with the heat of his desire, she relaxed against the bedclothes, letting her limbs fall limp so that he might look his fill. She covered nothing but let him look, her own eyes following the planes of his body, the hard muscles beneath the skin of his chest and thighs, the power he held in check always, the power and desire that now loomed over her.

She did not feel small or frightened by him as she had always been frightened of her old husband. She felt in some way as if Pembroke's powerful body was an homage to her, for his strength was humbled by his desire.

Pembroke raised her up then and ran his hand along her back, drawing her close against his body. With his hand on her shoulder he froze, the desire in his eyes freezing with his next breath.

"Arabella. What is that?"

She froze with him, the beauty draining out of the moment, sliding down and away from her like warm water down a drain. She clutched at the warmth, at the joy she had experienced, but she could not hold it. Like all good things, it was not meant to last.

❧

Pembroke stared down at the knots and raised flesh along the smooth planes of Arabella's back. He sat up and drew the candle closer so that he might see them better. A network of scars ran across her shoulders, raised welts that looked to be old and long healed. Pembroke felt his bile rise.

"Hawthorne?" he asked. He could barely force the word from his lips. He felt as if his tongue had seized up, as if the interior of his mouth had turned to dust. He swallowed hard, trying to find his voice. He failed.

Arabella turned her scarred back from him, raising her fingertips to touch his face. Her hand was soft and warm on his flesh. He felt a soothing coolness follow wherever she touched him, as if a drop of her clear sanity was being smoothed over his flushed skin.

"It was not my husband," she said. "It was my father."

Pembroke felt tears rise in his eyes, and he let them come. He could not stop them from flowing anymore than he could have held back the tide at Brighton.

He set the candle back down on the table beside the bed, careful not to catch the silk hangings with its flame. He drew Arabella close. He kissed her lips clumsily, as if he was a green boy of eighteen and not an experienced man of eight and twenty. Arabella pressed her lips to his in a vain attempt to offer him comfort, but he would not be comforted. Pembroke drew her down onto the soft feather bed and turned her over, that he might look at her back.

The scars were high between her shoulder blades, as if Swanson had taken a riding crop to her bare skin. Pembroke had seen a man flogged once while on campaign. The scars that were left behind the whip were nothing compared to these.

"He only struck me once in this way," she said as if to soothe him, as if being tortured only once made the offense forgivable.

"Tell me," Pembroke said. He cleared his throat, but his tears kept falling. The salt fell on her old wounds. He smoothed his tears into her scars, as if his sorrow might heal her. "What else?"

Arabella understood him. She did not want to speak of it, but his hand was on hers. He could not plead with her, so he squeezed her fingertips as if to beg her with his touch. He could not find the words to ask it of her. His tongue would not obey him.

She looked over one shoulder at him, tears standing in her eyes. Pembroke saw her compassion and her deep love for him reflected there. Her tears were not for herself but for him.

"He struck me across the face now and then," she said calmly, as if reporting on the weather the farmers might expect next spring. "But such blows leave marks. So when I was of marriageable age, he would take his cane to the bottoms of my feet. He had read about that punishment somewhere in his library. I believe the Persians use that method of chastisement to keep their women obedient. Or perhaps it was the Chinese. He told me once, but now I have forgotten."

Pembroke listened to her words and they burned him worse than the sight of the blows had. He ran his fingertips over her scars, once, twice, again and again, moving his hand across them until he laid both palms across her shoulder blades, as if to block the sight of them out.

He sat up, forgetting his own nakedness and hers as he raised her with him. He drew her slender, tiny feet into his lap, caressing them, bringing them into the feeble candlelight. He saw no scars there, no bruising, but still his hands ran over the soles of her feet again and again, searching for old pain, as if his fingers spoke a mantra of healing that only he could hear. Arabella pressed her hand to his shoulder, her tears making two long tracks down her cheeks.

"I am long since healed," she said. "He died a long time ago."

Pembroke drew her into his arms and held her close, her soft body slender in the circle of his embrace. She leaned on his chest, her heart beating steadily against his, as small as a bird, as defenseless as a newborn lamb. Pembroke knew that there was evil in the world—he had seen his fill of it. But only now, as he held the woman he loved in his arms, did he understand the true meaning of evil and the depths that it would go to in order to vanquish good.

But Arabella was not vanquished. It was she who held him as he caressed her hair. She wept not for herself but for him. She clung to him as if his arms were the one safe haven she had in the wide world. Pembroke cradled her against him, kissing her hair, pressing the wisps down with his hands and his lips.

They always slipped from his grasp, and he laughed with the taste of her hair on his lips.

"I love you, Arabella Swanson."

"And I love you, Raymond Olivier. I am glad that you finally know it."

All thoughts of lust had fled. Pembroke drew the counterpane up over them both until they were cocooned in the soft silk and feathered down of her bed. He had bought that bed just for her. He had decorated that room with her image in his mind, choosing the colors of wood and silk that he thought would best match her caramel hair, her eyes, her fair skin. She was here now. She was his. Pembroke swore an oath to himself silently as he held her in his arms that, no matter what she said, he would never let her go again.

As they lay down to sleep, Pembroke said, "If he was not already dead, I would kill him with my own hands."

Arabella did not answer but pressed her palm to his chest, over his heart. Pembroke caught her hand in his and held it there, drawing her close, wrapping his arms around her so that she could not escape even if she wanted to. He knew now why he had closed her bedroom door earlier that evening. Not to keep the world out, but to keep her in. She would not leave him again. If she tried, this time he would follow her to the ends of the earth.

Pembroke absorbed this knowledge of himself as Arabella fell asleep on his shoulder, her breathing even, her tears dry on her cheeks.

ACT III

"I love thee. By my life, I do."

A Midsummer Night's Dream
Act 3, Scene 2

Twenty

ARABELLA WOKE TO SUNLIGHT ON HER FACE. THE curtains had not been drawn over the windows the night before because the upstairs maid had been locked out of her bedroom.

She smiled, stretching, reaching out to feel the heat of Pembroke's skin under her fingertips. He was as warm as an oven, and she burrowed beneath the covers to escape the light and to get closer to him.

He laughed, his voice low in his throat. "Good morning, Arabella. You are like a mole in the garden, hiding beneath these covers."

She laughed, her own voice scratchy with sleep. "Good morning, Raymond."

She hid her eyes against his shoulder but drew back to look at him as he pressed his hand to her cheek. He smiled down at her, his fingertips caressing her hair. Arabella realized then that she must look frightful. She had never before woken to find a man beside her. She smiled as Pembroke pressed his lips to hers. She did not care what she looked like, for the man with her was the one she loved. At long last, he was here, and

she was with him. She would not concern herself with
trifles like vanity.

His tongue found hers, swirling in the soft contours
of her mouth, as if seeking hers in a game. She
followed suit, until the game changed and they began
to devour each other in earnest. She remembered
then that she was completely naked, as he was. She
had never been naked with a man before either, not
before last night.

Pembroke must have felt her hesitation, for he drew
back. Though his breath came short as hers did, she
knew that he would only touch her if she wanted him
to. She ran her tongue over her lips, savoring the taste
of him that had not yet dissipated. She did want him to
touch her, and more. It was fitting that she give herself
to him in the light of day.

He smiled down at her, the errant lock of hair
falling into his eyes as he raised himself above her on
one elbow. She pressed her body against his beneath
the feathered counterpane, and watched the blue of his
eyes darken to indigo with desire.

"Are you sure?" he asked, his voice hoarse.

"I am sure," she said.

He kissed her then, slowly this time, meditatively,
as if to seal the bargain they had made. Arabella pressed
closer to him, pushing away everything save for the
way his strong body felt against her slender curves. She
had been given a second chance with him. She was
going to enjoy it for as long as it lasted.

Pembroke raised himself over her, and she thought
that he meant to press his manhood between her
thighs. She remembered little of the marriage bed

other than the pain, but she knew that her old husband had raised himself up on his elbows before impaling her with his failing member. The few times he had forced himself inside her, it had never taken him long to finish. She found herself wishing that it might take longer than a few seconds with Pembroke. Though she did not like pain, the thought of having him inside her made her shiver. She would endure more pain to keep him with her a little longer.

But Pembroke did not impale her with his member. He fell instead to kissing her breasts, his hands cupped beneath them, raising the delicate curves to his lips, first one breast and then the other.

Arabella lost her breath as he did that, pleasure at his touch rising within her like a wave on an ocean shore. She gasped as he took one of her nipples between his teeth. She opened her eyes wide and watched as his tongue slid over her breast, his hand caressing the other. He worshiped her breasts until she thought she might melt into the bed beneath him, and then his lips began to move lower, trailing down her stomach to her thighs.

Her body felt warm and lush in their cocoon of silk and linen, as if she had been transported to another world. The life she knew was far away, behind the white and blue silk of her bedroom curtains. Her world reduced itself to the room she lay in, to the bed where Pembroke lay on top of her, and finally to the place on her body where his lips slid down the inner curve of her thigh.

His mouth touched her then, and she reared up beneath him as if to escape the questing warmth of his tongue. Pembroke caught her and held her down so that she could not escape. He did not heed her fevered pleas to let her go but dove in deeper, kissing her secret places with his tongue just as he had kissed her mouth.

Arabella fought him for a moment but soon found that she might as well have fought off a bear. She was too feeble to win, and his tongue delving inside her only made her weaker. But behind that weakness, that languid, liquid heat, she began to feel her own strength building, a secret strength that she had never known existed.

It seemed there was within her a wealth of knowledge, a treasure of beauty stored up that she had never known. Pembroke knew of it though, just as he always knew things about her without her having to tell him. This time, she did not reveal a secret of hers only to find that he knew it already. This time, he revealed a secret to her.

She lay dumbfounded by the beauty within her as her pleasure built until she rose up once, crying out, a great wave of pleasure swamping her, taking her mind and her thoughts and tossing them aside as if they were nothing. Arabella lay back against the soft pillows of her feather bed, her breath gone, her voice gone. Tears were on her cheeks, but this time, they were tears of joy. She had never known such pleasure existed, that such strength and beauty lay hidden away inside of her. Pembroke had given her that. If she had the rest of her life to spend with him, she would never be able to pay him back, gift for gift.

That was what love meant, in the end. A debt you could never repay.

Pembroke saw her tears and drew her close, kissing them away. "I am sorry," he said. "I did not mean to hurt you."

She wiped her tears on the hair of his chest, the warmth of his heart beating beneath her cheek. She found her breath and smiled up at him. "You did not hurt me. I weep for joy."

Tears were in his eyes then and he pressed his lips to hers, a soft, lingering kiss that told her he would not touch her again if she did not wish it. But in spite of the pleasure his lips and tongue had given her, Arabella found that it was not enough. In spite of the pleasure that had built and faded, the pleasure that still lingered in her body like the glow of a dying fire, she wanted more.

She pressed him back against the bolster behind them, the pillows rising around them like a fortress, blocking out a little of the morning sun. Arabella followed him down into the little valley the pillows made, their white linen embroidered with silver and blue flowers. For the first time, Arabella saw that the blue of this bedroom matched the blue of her eyes.

Arabella kissed him, her mouth lingering over his, her tongue seeking his as he had taught her, her long hair falling over both of them in a wave of caramel and gold.

Pembroke's hands were on her arms, drawing her closer, opening his mouth wide under hers, taking her in as he accepted all she had to give. She pressed herself against him, the length of her slender body touching the length of his. The hard planes of Pembroke's chest and thighs cradled and supported her as he feasted on her mouth, on her tongue and lips, trailing down to kiss her throat, turning her over until she lay beneath him.

His blue eyes were dark with desire. He stared into her face, the smile he had worn before gone now, burned away in the heat that rose between them. She knew that he was going to ask her permission once again, and she knew also that she could not bear to hear him ask it. So she raised herself under him until her hips caressed his swelling manhood. She did not know how to draw him down and into her, but she made her desire known without words.

Pembroke laughed, a low, harsh sound that sent a wave of lust spilling down the edges of her spine. She shivered beneath him, for she saw that he needed no further prompting from her.

He rose over her, and this time she knew he would not turn back. His long, thick fingers slid between her thighs, and she opened them wider, as if to offer herself to take him in. Arabella did not care what he did to her or how it hurt. She wanted only for him to be inside her.

Her thoughts skittered away like fallen leaves caught in a blast of wind. Her breath rose in gasps as his fingers lingered between her thighs. Though desire had transformed his face into hard planes and angles, though his blue eyes were indigo as they caressed her breasts and hair and face, he was still the man she loved. He was still Raymond Olivier.

Arabella gasped beneath him as he tested her once more, his long fingers lingering within her for a moment before they withdrew, taking the heat of her with them. Pembroke raised those fingers to his mouth and sucked on them as he had sucked on her breasts. Arabella shuddered with pleasure to see him do it. She shook with longing as he lowered himself between her thighs, raising her hips to meet his.

He was gentle even as he slid inside her. She saw the tension in his jaw, the shaking of the muscles of his arms as he strained to contain himself, as he strove hard not to hurt her. Arabella opened her mouth to tell him that she did not care, that pain from him was worth more than pleasure from anyone else. But instead of words, instead of coherent thought and comfort for him, she found she could not speak at all. As he entered her, the hard length of him making him one with her for the rest of their lives, she could only gasp and then moan as her ecstasy began to mount.

Pembroke heard her moan, and a look of triumph crossed his face. But he did not give in to his own desire even then, but raised her hips and moved carefully between them, working against her body as if she were a puzzle he meant to solve. She felt it then, the deep fountain hidden within her, a place of hidden bliss broader than what she had found before when he had kissed her secret places. Pembroke, still watching her face, shifted the angle of his entry, and she moaned.

Pleasure built in her as a volcanic mountain rising suddenly from the depths of the sea. She did not climb that mountain but rose with it as Pembroke moved over her, using the rhythm of his hips against hers to drive her farther and farther into it. She felt the mountain that carried her shake beneath her as the waves of her ecstasy rose and crested. She came apart, calling his name over and over until she lost her breath.

Pembroke gave himself up to his own desire then, letting her hips fall beneath his as he drove himself into her again and again. He shuddered with his own satisfaction as he lost all control, and Arabella wrapped her arms and legs around him, drawing him closer, her arms behind his shoulders, her legs around his hips. Pembroke lay still against her, his breath coming in gasps, his weight across her as if a boulder from her mountain of bliss had fallen down to bury her.

She laughed a little under her breath, wondering how she could be capable of such glorious pleasure. Perhaps it was some magic, some alchemy that lay in Pembroke's power alone. She knew that she would never find out. She would never make love with any man but him.

He raised himself off her so that his weight did not bear her down into the softness of the feather bed. Arabella felt the loss as he withdrew from her, rolling onto his back. He kept his arms wrapped around her and took her with him, so that she lay sprawled across his body like a living blanket, her legs entwined with his.

"Where was the pain?" she asked him.

Pembroke met her eyes, drawing himself back from the lingering effects of his own pleasure. Used to debauchery, he caught his breath much more quickly than she caught hers. He pushed the long strands of hair back from her face, leaving his large palm against her cheek so that she could not turn away.

"What pain?" he asked.

"Always with my husband, I felt unspeakable pain. It lasted the whole time he was with me. I felt no pain with you. Nothing but joy."

She watched his blue eyes darken again, this time with anger and not with desire. He drew her down to lie across his chest, wrapping his arms around her as if to protect her from the world and from all the people in it.

"I am sorry he hurt you," Pembroke said. "I would kill him, too, if he still lived."

Arabella smiled, wondering why his threats to kill the men in her past made her so happy. Perhaps it was the tone of protectiveness in his voice when he made these threats against men who were dead.

"You will never know pain again, Arabella. I swear it. I will stand between you and what would harm you every day for the rest of my life."

She did not tell him the obvious truth that he could no more keep her from pain than he could keep the sun from rising. Pain came with life as breath did, but joy came too.

Hawthorne threatened to rise up before her, a specter born to drive away her happiness. She closed her eyes against him and against the memory of his knife. He would not find her. She would be gone when he came. But here, alone with the man she loved, she would not think of him. He might take her future with Raymond, but he could not take this moment.

Arabella and Raymond did not make love again but lay in bed together for another hour, reveling in the silence, in the fact that the door to her room was locked, that no one could reach them. She did not think of the loss of the past or of the loss to come. She simply lay with her head on her lover's chest, sweet touches the only talk between them.

Twenty-one

PEMBROKE AND ARABELLA WENT DOWN TO THE village, so that he might rehearse with the Shakespearean troupe, as he had promised Titania he would do. Arabella took up her script once more and watched him perform the role of Oberon, telling herself that she could not leave the village until Mrs. Bonner had finished with her new, modest wardrobe. She pushed the shadow of Hawthorne and his coming out of her mind and instead raised her face to the warmth of the sun, taking in the beauty of that summer day.

She watched the play, rarely needing to refer to the text, for after the first rehearsals, no actor seemed to need to call for a line. They moved in Shakespeare's world with ease, as if the dream the playwright had created was the real world, and the world beyond the stage was the illusion.

Arabella was not sure how, but the whole group seemed to sense the change between them. Pembroke was discreet, but his eyes lingered on her even though his hands did not. Titania seemed to know that she had been temporarily replaced. If she was jealous or angry, Arabella could see no sign of it. The beautiful actress simply pressed her lips to Arabella's cheek. "I knew you'd have him. I knew it the first time I laid eyes on you together."

Arabella laughed. "I wish you'd have told me."

Titania smiled as if the love between Arabella and Pembroke were somehow her doing. "And spoil the fun? The gods must have their way with us. There is no use in rushing fate. The fates rule our lives. We are but their playthings."

Arabella did not agree, but she pressed Titania's hand. "I am grateful to them then. I have never been so blessed."

One of the other actors overheard her words and spat into the dirt at her feet. "Avant," he said. "Don't tempt the gods. They cannot bear too much happiness."

Arabella did not believe in the old gods either, but she smiled and nodded at the actor just the same, for Barnabas seemed intent that she believe his words of warning. After a life of grim survival and disaster, for that one day, she savored her joy. Even Cassie's glare from across the village green could not dampen her spirits. Love colored her vision and touched everything she saw and every person she spoke to. She felt as if she lay under an enchantment indeed, but one not from the gods or from the fairies. An enchantment Pembroke had cast on her.

Though rehearsal went on, Pembroke came down from the stage and took Arabella's arm. She smiled up at him, bemused, as he led her to his phaeton without even a by your leave. Titania waved to them as they left, and Arabella was surprised to find a picnic basket tucked away behind the seat of the carriage. Pembroke sang in a deep baritone, bringing the birds down from the trees as they passed, carrying her into the country-side away from the village where no actors or villagers would follow. The light carriage had no top, and the early summer sun warmed them.

He brought out a picnic that Mrs. Marks had packed and spread a blanket for them on the grass beneath the oak tree where they had first pledged themselves to one another.

He offered his hand to her. "We never were allowed to dance, Miss Swanson. May I have this waltz?"

Arabella laughed and stepped into his arms. There was no music but the sound of the wind in the trees over their heads, and the sweet music of the river running nearby. Arabella fell into step with him easily, for though she did not know how to waltz well, Raymond did. She followed his lead and let herself move without thinking, an unaccustomed luxury.

The warm sun caught in the green of the leaves overhead, setting dappled shadow to dance across her face as Pembroke held her in his arms. He waltzed with her over the uneven ground as if tree roots and broken leaves did not exist, as if they were alone in a world of their own making.

He stopped suddenly but did not let her go. He held her close so that she could feel the heat of his body against hers and the beat of his heart.

"I had better stop," he said. "There are no Almack's ladies to keep me on my best behavior here."

"I find I like your roguish ways, Raymond. Feel free to practice them on me anytime you wish."

He laughed then, helping her down onto the picnic blanket. He handed her a glass of crisp white wine, pressing his lips to hers. They sat beneath the spreading arms of the old oak, sunlight filtered through the verdant green of the leaves as the wind moved the branches overhead. Arabella felt as if all the world offered its blessing to them, the great oak, the wind, and the sky. She kissed him, her lips lingering on his. It was Pembroke who pulled away, raising his glass to her.

"To Lady Pembroke, the only woman I will ever love."

She raised her glass to him and drank. "I had no idea you still held your mother in such high esteem."

"I mean you, minx, and you know it."

"I will be the lady of your heart, but I will bear no other title."

"I have loved you all my life. I will always love you. You'll marry me. You'll see."

She laughed, breathless. "No, I will not."

He leaned over and kissed her again, his lips tasting of the tart wine. She sighed against his mouth. "You will find I am very persuasive," he said.

"I have no doubt of that."

He took the wineglass from her hand and pressed her down onto the blanket, heedless of the fact that they were outdoors, heedless of the fact that anyone might come upon them and be shocked, as she was.

His lips lingered on hers with feather lightness, but his body bore down on hers, making her breathless. Desire pooled between her thighs as if he had conjured it by magic. She felt the warmth suffuse her body, making her pliant beneath him.

He drew back, his eyes on hers. "I will persuade you."

"No, you will not. But if this is a sample, I hope you keep trying."

He laughed then and bent to kiss her even as he raised them both up to sit. As they sat and ate together, his hands stayed on her, his warm touch lingering on her body as they ate, a glancing touch on her thigh, on her breast, on the softness of her hair. She wanted him with a consuming hunger, but she did not throw herself at him. She merely sipped her sweet wine and ate another strawberry.

He laughed at her restraint before taking her wineglass from her. He drew her close, and she let him, pressing her down against the nest of soft blankets beneath the tree.

His hand rose up under her skirt, caressing first her calves, running up over her stockings to her ribbon garters. Her heart pounding, she thought that he might loosen them, but he did not, his hand moving across her thigh, brushing against the thatch of hair hidden beneath the linen of her drawers. He reached up and began to slide his fingers past the linen, into the warmth of her body.

She gasped and half rose as if to escape him and the pleasure he offered, but he bore down on her as he had in her bed, pressing his body against hers, holding her prisoner as his knowing fingers played within the sweet warmth of her body. She cried out, and his lips swallowed the sound. She murmured and moaned, writhing beneath him as if to get away, but everywhere she moved, he moved to meet her, so that she came closer and closer to the bliss he offered.

She screamed once and shuddered beneath him, and his lips drank in the sound like wine. He did not stop moving as her pleasure crested but played her body as he might a violin, until the last note of her ecstasy had sounded and she lay limp beneath him.

"I love you, Arabella. And I will not let you forget it."

She pressed her lips to his throat, the only place she could reach. "What can I give to you, Raymond?"

He laughed, his body vibrating over hers. "I have had pleasure enough. Today, let me give to you and be content."

She did not agree with him but was too tired and replete with her own bliss to argue with him. She knew that he loved her, but she also knew that he meant to tempt her to abandon her future, and to join her life to his.

But she had been married once already. A wife belonged body and soul to her husband. She did not exist under the law but could be put away or ignored at his will. She could be cut off without a penny, no matter what dowry she brought to the match. A wife was nothing, a nonentity, a ghost. As much as she loved Pembroke, as much as she always would, she was alive. She had fought hard for her life, and she would keep it.

Even if Hawthorne were vanquished tomorrow, Arabella would never live under the boot of a man again.

❧

As the month of June wore on, drawing ever closer to Midsummer Night, Arabella chastised herself for being a fool. She knew that Hawthorne would come looking for her, and that she needed to be gone long before he arrived. Once she disappeared, Pembroke would no longer be a target of Hawthorne's wrath. And if she hid herself well enough, Hawthorne would never find her.

She saw the logic of this and knew that her father's golden guineas were enough to live on for the rest of her life. She must take them and go. So she told herself every morning as she woke. And every morning, she woke by Pembroke's side, and every morning he kissed her, and she was left telling herself that she would leave... tomorrow.

Their time together was a stolen season.

Since their picnic in the Forest of Arden the week before, he had not mentioned marriage again. For some perverse reason, this pained her, though she reminded herself that she could not marry him, or anyone, so it was just as well that they did not keep discussing a fruitless subject.

As long as she lingered there, Arabella had wanted to enjoy the village of her childhood as she had never been able to while her father was alive. She had wanted to exercise her new freedom that Sunday and go to the village church, but Pembroke had kept her in bed. When he went out to the players on the green that afternoon, she went down to the kitchen to make a tart, using one of Mrs. Fielding's recipes. If she had not had the sense to leave by then, she would go to church next week.

As Arabella stood in Pembroke's kitchen, the sunlight slanted in through the great wide windows that looked out on the herb garden. Mrs. Marks clicked her tongue to have a duchess below stairs making pastry, but Arabella ignored her.

She hummed to herself at the little wooden table Cook had set aside for her use. Her pastry was ready to go into the oven. She was making strawberry tarts as Mrs. Fielding had taught her to do, long ago. She slipped her pastry into the corner of the oven Cook had set aside for her, then turned back to her table to clean up the flour and bits of crust she had left behind, when a flurry of noise caught her attention.

Angelique Beauchamp stood in the kitchen door.

Arabella laughed with joy to see her, taking her friend into her arms with no thought for the floured apron she wore, or for Angelique's fine blue traveling gown.

"I should have sent word," Angelique said. "But I did not want Hawthorne to get wind of my doings."

"You are here, and I am glad to see you. Nothing else matters."

Arabella looked around the kitchen then and noticed that the under maid, Anne, had come down for her lunch but had chosen to linger, listening to them. Cook also listened as she basted the great goose that they would eat for dinner that night. Every evening meal was a feast in Pembroke's house since he had come home.

"Mrs. Bellows, we will go upstairs to the sitting room," Arabella said. "Please let Mrs. Marks know, and ask her to send up some tea and some of your good biscuits."

Arabella unwrapped the great apron she wore, laying

it carefully across her wooden table. The kitchen staff bobbed curtsies as she passed, and Angelique spoke low in her ear.

"I don't know how you've gotten Codington wrapped around your finger. He not only allowed me to come down to the kitchen to find you but had a maid leave her duties to escort me."

"Codington owes me."

Angelique raised one elegant brow.

"I'll explain later. It is too fine a day for melodrama."

"Speaking of penny operas, you and Pembroke are the talk of London. Hawthorne is livid to find the rumors he spread about you are coming true. Everyone says that Pembroke has spirited you off and made you his mistress."

Arabella laughed. "Well, I seduced him. He put up more resistance than one would think."

Angelique laughed with her, the seductive tones of her deep voice reverberating in the upper corridors as they climbed the stairs to Arabella's sitting room. "He loves you. No doubt that made things difficult. And you plan to marry," Angelique said.

"No. I'll never marry again."

"But you've loved this man all your life."

"And I always will. But love isn't enough, as you well know."

Angelique's face darkened, and Arabella caught her hand. "I am my own woman now, or will be as soon as I get Hawthorne off my scent. I intend to stay that way."

As they came up the servants' staircase, Arabella opened a hidden door into the main hallway. She crossed to her favorite sitting room, the parlor that looked out over Pembroke's mother's rose garden. She opened the door only to find that the room was not empty.

A young woman dressed in a traveling gown of soft brown trimmed in gold, her long blonde hair caught up in a snood shot through with diamonds, sat holding a fat little boy who looked to be about a year old. The baby lay sprawled against his mother's breast, breathing deep as he dozed. He had soft blond hair as his mother did, left to curl against his forehead and above his ears. Arabella caught her breath at the beauty of the picture the two made, and she felt a sudden longing for a child of her own. She pushed away the idea as ludicrous. A woman alone could not have a child.

"Good afternoon," Arabella said. "I am so sorry. I did not know Pembroke had visitors."

The beautiful woman rose to her feet and smiled, the warmth of her brown eyes seeming to take in Arabella all in one moment, as if she were pleased with what she saw. Arabella was not a formal woman for she was out in company very rarely. Her father had kept her mostly at home, and her husband had done the same. But she was sensitive to the moods of her friend. Angelique had not entered behind her but stood in the doorway, transfixed by the sight of the beautiful blonde woman, as still as if she had seen a ghost rise up from the mahogany boards at her feet.

Arabella turned to Angelique, shocked by the loss of color in her friend's face. She had never seen Angelique so out of sorts. She watched as recognition dawned in the eyes of the beautiful woman with the baby. The two women stared at each other, as if their words had deserted them completely.

"Welcome to Pembroke House," Arabella said, drawing Angelique into the sitting room after her. The windows faced south, so sunlight came through the panes of glass even in the early afternoon. The expanse of Pembroke Park lay below them, Pembroke's mother's rose garden giving way to green meadows dotted with sheep. Angelique looked neither at the beauty of the room nor at the park beyond. She fell into a chair close by the door as if her legs would no longer hold her up.

Arabella spoke to the woman with the child, who stared past her at Angelique. "I am the Duchess of Hawthorne. And you are?"

"Forgive me." The young woman's voice was as melodious as Angelique's, though not quite as low. She curtsied to her hostess, the baby still caught up in her slender arms. She looked too frail to hold on to such a healthy infant, but the weight of the boy seemed not to bother her at all. Her brown traveling gown caught the light as she moved, and Arabella saw that the heavy wool was shot through with strands of gold that matched the flecks of gold in the woman's eyes.

"I am Lady Ravensbrook, but you must call me Caroline."

Arabella froze in midstride as she crossed the room to greet her guest. She stared into the eyes of the woman who had stolen the love of Angelique's life. This was the girl from Yorkshire who had married Anthony Carrington, who for years had been Angelique's lover.

Even Arabella, as cloistered as she had been in her husband's house, had heard the gossip that had surrounded the Earl and Countess of Ravensbrook almost two years before. Anthony Carrington had left London for what was supposed to be a weeklong journey, only to disappear from town for months. When he returned for the Christmas season, he had brought into the city a very young, very beautiful wife. He had openly spurned Angelique at the Prince Regent's Twelfth Night Ball. Angelique had taken another lover at once, but all the *ton* knew that she pined for Carrington still.

"Oh my," Arabella said. "This is a difficult moment for you both."

Angelique snorted with laughter from her perch by the door. A tentative smile crossed Caroline Carrington's face. "Difficult is perhaps an understatement," she said.

Angelique laughed out loud then, rising from her delicate chair to cross the room to Caroline. She extended her gloved hand as a man might, to show she carried no weapons. Caroline shifted the baby in her arms and took the offered hand of her old enemy.

"We have met before. You'll remember that I am Angelique Beauchamp."

"Of course, Countess Devonshire. I could never forget a lady as beautiful as you are."

Angelique laughed again. "You are silver tongued. Have you any Irish in your blood?"

"Only French, on my mother's side."

"That explains it then. All French women can please with their tongues when they are of a mind to do it."

Arabella blushed to the roots of her caramel hair, but Angelique and Caroline laughed together, their careful rancor giving way to genuine amusement. Anthony Carrington clearly had a taste for strong women.

Angelique leaned down to look at the baby, enveloping Arabella and Caroline in a cloud of orchid perfume. "What a beautiful child. You must be very proud of him."

Caroline's countenance lit as with a sunrise, her brown eyes turning to look upon her son's sleeping face. "He is a wonder of the world."

Angelique extended her hand, touching the baby's cheek very lightly with one gloved finger. "Children are a blessing. You are a lucky woman."

There was such naked longing in Angelique's face that Arabella felt a lump rise in her throat. She had always assumed that her friend had taken precautions against child bearing whenever she was with one of her lovers, for her husband was ten years dead and a child would be more than inconvenient. It would be social suicide.

But for the first time Arabella saw that Angelique longed for children as much or more than she did. It was as if a window had opened into Angelique's soul, and Arabella could see past her strength and her seductive beauty to a hidden pain beneath the layers of the woman she thought she knew. Arabella reached out and took her friend's hand. Angelique did not shrug off her touch but caught Arabella's hand fast in her own, as if to take strength from it.

Caroline Carrington, who had triumphed over her rival in every way possible, did not look triumphant.

Nor did she cast her face into a mask of indifference or condescension. She reached out and laid her hand on Angelique's arm.

"Lady Devonshire, will you hold Freddie for a moment? He is very heavy, a bit too heavy for me."

This blatant lie drew Angelique's gaze to Caroline's face. But there was no triumphant mockery there, so Angelique opened her arms and took the baby into them. Freddie woke, his blue eyes opening to take in the ladies who stood over him. He smiled at his mother, before his eyes fastened on Angelique's face.

There was a delicate moment when Arabella feared the baby might weep to find himself in the arms of a stranger, but then Freddie smiled, a beacon of light cast onto Angelique's sorrow. Her friend seemed to heal a little as the baby's eyes rested on her. She drew him close and pressed her lips to the top of his head.

"He is beautiful," she said.

"I am blessed," Caroline answered.

"We are all blessed so long as he is in a good mood," a deep masculine voice announced from the doorway.

Caroline turned to the door with a smile. At the sound of that voice, its tone like velvet over steel, Angelique stiffened, baby Freddie still in her arms. Pembroke had entered, followed closely by Lord Ravensbrook.

Twenty-two

ANGELIQUE EXTENDED HER ARMS AND HANDED THE baby back to his mother. Arabella had always known that her friend was formidable, but she had never before seen her put on full armor. Angelique seemed to grow taller before her eyes and somehow more beautiful. If Arabella had not known better, she would have thought her friend an enchantress indeed, for in that moment Angelique became not just a beautiful woman relinquishing a baby who did not belong to her but a siren who might lead any man to his doom. But Angelique wanted to doom only one man: Anthony Carrington.

Caroline raised baby Freddie to her shoulder as she crossed the room to stand beside her husband. Though she and Angelique had laid their own weapons down, Anthony was another matter altogether. Arabella wondered, her throat tight with anxiety, if the peace the two women had managed to build in so short a time would be just as quickly decimated.

Pembroke did not intervene between them but stayed behind Anthony as if to watch his back. He had mentioned Ravensbrook to Arabella over the last few weeks as the one man in the world that he trusted. Now that she saw them together, Arabella knew that it went beyond that. In Ravensbrook, Pembroke had found a brother.

Ravensbrook was tall, even taller than Pembroke. He was dressed in a coat of deep brown that seemed to set off the hints of gold in Caroline's gown. His cravat was beautifully tied, his waistcoat and buckskins immaculate.

He took in the room he stood in and all who stood there with him, cataloguing them as if seeking for weakness, as if he were a bird of prey. His chestnut eyes softened slightly when they settled on his wife, but the moment passed in less than a breath as he turned instead to stare at Angelique.

Arabella was not a woman comfortable with confrontation. She had avoided it at all cost all her life. But she had begun a new life now, and she would begin as she meant to go on. If Ravensbrook was Pembroke's brother, Angelique was her sister. Arabella moved to her friend's side.

Angelique seemed to glitter with hardness, her limbs stiff beneath their seductive lines. The dark blue of her gown brought out the sapphire of her eyes, but Arabella could see over that sapphire blue lay a sheen of tears.

In the end, it was Freddie who broke the strained silence. He gurgled, one hand gripping the front of his mother's gown to steady himself as he turned back to Angelique. His eyes fastened on the woman who had held him only moments before, and his face broke into a smile that seemed to light the room. Angelique smiled back as she stepped forward to press her lips to the baby's cheek.

"Your son is beautiful, Anthony. I see that he takes after his mother."

Caroline laughed, and so did Pembroke. Arabella waited to see what Ravensbrook might do. His eyes did not smolder when he looked at the woman who had been his mistress for ten years. He did not seem to feel any lust for her, but neither did he seem indifferent. Angelique smiled as she looked up into her old lover's face, and then she turned back to his wife. "May I hold him a moment longer? Freddie is too beautiful to relinquish so quickly."

Caroline laughed, the dark honeyed tones of her voice filling the room with warmth. Arabella watched her anxiously but saw that she was sincere. "Of course. But don't feel that you must keep him long. He is a great brute and very heavy."

Angelique drew the baby close and kissed his forehead, walking with him to the settee by the empty fireplace. She sat with the baby on her lap for all the world as if she were a queen enthroned, surveying her domain. Ravensbrook smiled at her, and something seemed to pass between them, a private moment that Caroline did not notice. That moment seemed to mollify Angelique, to give her some measure of peace, for she turned back to the baby and jounced her knee beneath him, imitating a horse at a trot. She sang a little riding song to Freddie, who laughed and squealed with delight.

Caroline took her husband's hand and led him to

the settee opposite their child, drawing him down to sit beside her. The tea was brought in then, so Pembroke stepped farther into the room, though he still seemed flummoxed to find Ravensbrook, his wife, and Angelique in the same room and under his roof. Arabella saw that once more she must intervene.

She began to pour the tea, acting as hostess, since Pembroke seemed too out of sorts to do or say much of anything. She handed the tea around, beginning first with Angelique and then Caroline, serving the gentlemen next and herself last. There was nothing said in all that time, the only sound in the room Angelique's soft singing, the clink of china, and the baby's laughter.

"Well," Arabella said. "I'm a country girl and too sheltered to know the etiquette for a situation like this. So I suppose we shall simply have to go on as civilized people do everywhere and drink our tea."

Angelique laughed and the baby stood on her lap, reaching for her mouth with his fat fingers. She kissed his hands, one after the other, then handed him back to Caroline, who held out her arms for him.

"I am a country girl myself, and I agree that life is too short to worry with the past," Caroline said. "I propose that we deal with the matter at hand, namely, the new Duke of Hawthorne."

Pembroke shot a look at Ravensbrook, raising one fair eyebrow. The earl caught the look and spoke as if he and Pembroke were in mid-conversation already. "I try to keep things from her, but I've found that it's simply not possible."

"Now, if he would only stop trying, we might actually get one or two things accomplished."

Ravensbrook reached for her hand. "I think we have managed one or two things."

Baby Freddie opened his arms to his father, and Lord Ravensbrook took him up, pressing his lips to his son's cheek.

Arabella offered the biscuit tray to Angelique, though she knew her friend did not eat much sugar. Angelique looked down at the cookies as if trying to decide which to take. She finally selected one and laid it on her saucer, happy no doubt to find a reason to keep her eyes off Ravensbrook with his son. The painful moment spun out, as if it might never end, and then finally, the moment passed. Ravensbrook did not see the tortured look that crossed Angelique's face, which was all that mattered.

"The Duke of Hawthorne," Caroline said, taking up the reins of the conversation once more, "is a bother and a nuisance, but one the lawyers can't find their way around. Anthony, have you had any luck with the Prince?"

"No, love, I have not." He turned to Arabella and she froze, caught in the heat of his dark chestnut eyes. The force of his personality, the command in his gaze made Arabella feel like a rabbit caught in a snare. Just as she felt panic rise within her, Pembroke pressed her hand.

"The Prince Regent cannot help me," she said. "I believe he owes Hawthorne more than one favor." She forced her voice to be steady, breathing deeply so that she did not swallow her words.

Ravensbrook did not seem to think anything amiss with her voice or the way she answered, and Angelique caught her eye, smiling at her. No one else knew how difficult it was for Arabella to deal with strange men.

"I do not think that he cannot, I think that he will not," Anthony said. "At least not at the moment. You are right, Your Grace. The Prince Regent is pressed with problems of his own. The new duke is one of his most ardent supporters in the House of Lords and, more to the point, has bought a contingent of MPs in the Commons. Suffice it to say, His Highness is not at liberty to make an enemy of Hawthorne."

"So we are on our own," Pembroke said.

"Indeed," Ravensbrook answered. "So it would seem."

"I thank you both for the trouble you have taken. But there is no way to settle with Hawthorne," Arabella said. "I must disappear."

Pembroke stiffened beside her, his hand gripping hers as if he would never let her go.

Ravensbrook seemed to sense his friend's displeasure, for something softened in his face as he spoke. "Please do not fear, Your Grace. The Prince cannot help you, but we will. Having the Earl of Ravensbrook stand by you is no small thing."

"Once you are my wife, Hawthorne will not touch you. If he comes here, I will kill him myself." Pembroke's voice was as stiff as his back. He would not look at her but made this pronouncement to the room at large. Arabella tried to take her hand away from him but could not wrestle it from his grip.

"I beg to differ, my lord. I will marry no one."

She stared at Pembroke as if she could force him to look into her eyes with the strength of her will alone. After a few moments, she began to notice the awkward silence in the room and that Angelique and Caroline were exchanging wary smiles.

"Your personal affairs are your own concern, Your Grace," Ravensbrook said. "But the *ton* has heard of your foray into the world of the arts, Pembroke. It seems that most of our friends and acquaintances, even one or two of our enemies, are interested in seeing you play the King of Fairies on Midsummer's Eve. So interested, in fact, that they are all coming here."

Pembroke laughed, but his grip on her hand did not loosen. "Good God, you can't be serious. I've come all the way to Derbyshire to get away from those people. Surely they will not travel three days to see one performance."

"Indeed they will," Anthony said. "And the new Duke of Hawthorne will be among them."

Arabella took a sip of tea to tamp down her panic. When she set her empty cup on its saucer, she saw that her hand was shaking.

Angelique touched her arm before pouring fresh tea for everyone, beginning with Arabella. She pressed not one biscuit but two onto Arabella's plate before offering the tray to everyone else. Pembroke took two, eating them in quick succession as if to fuel himself for battle.

"Well, Hawthorne may come here if he wishes," Pembroke said. "If he wants to speak to you or even see your face, he will first have to come through me."

Angelique caught her eye. "He will have to come through me as well."

"There will be no need for such theatrics," Ravensbrook said. "My man will dispatch him if it comes to that."

"Or I will," Caroline Carrington said, dandling her infant son on her knee. Baby Freddie, who had been listening solemnly to all that was said as if he understood it, caught sight of his mother's beatific smile and gurgled with glee.

"I am sure that when His Grace is presented with our united front, he will simply retire from the field," Ravensbrook said.

The assurance in his voice, his utter confidence made her wonder if he was as powerful as he claimed or simply mad with overconfidence. Arabella caught Angelique's eye. As two women who had always been on their own, manipulating or dodging powerful men all their lives, they both knew that Hawthorne would not be so easy to dissuade.

Arabella drank her tea in two gulps. The warm liquid fortified her before Caroline leaned across the distance between them to place Baby Freddie in her arms. The weight of the child seemed to soothe her, and Arabella felt herself calm down as she looked into the baby's blue eyes. She felt anchored by the child in her lap and protected by the people around her. But she knew that protection was an illusion. In spite of their good intentions and all their resources, they did not know Hawthorne as she did. They had not seen the light of possession in his eyes as he tried to take her on her husband's bed with a knife in his hand. In spite of the warmth of the midsummer day, in spite of the baby in her arms, Arabella shivered. She needed to be gone. She had wasted too much time already.

Twenty-three

ANGELIQUE REFUSED TO STAY THE NIGHT AT PEMBROKE House. Anthony and Caroline had a guest suite set aside for their permanent use in Pembroke's home, and Angelique seemed to know that already. She kissed Arabella by the front door and took her own carriage back to Pembroke village, where she had leased a cottage for the week. Arabella wondered if it was the cottage she wanted so. She would visit her and find out.

Angelique left early, saying that she had business with Titania, for she was one of the first shareholders in Titania's Shakespearean company.

Arabella saw the lines of strain around her friend's eyes and knew better than to press her to stay. The sun was beginning to set when Angelique left just after supper. Arabella stood on the steps of the house, watching the shadows thrown by Angelique's carriage lamps fade as she drove away. Pembroke stood beside her, stepping out into the gloaming. Fireflies had begun to dance above the tops of the trees, lighting the night as fairies did in Titania's play.

Caroline and Anthony had retired directly after supper, and the baby had gone to sleep, whisked away by his nurse hours before, so Arabella and Pembroke stood alone on his front steps. Oaks and hawthorns cast deep shadows over them as evening fell.

"Shall we walk in the forest?" he asked her.

She took his hand in her small one. His fingers dwarfed her own, his great paw covering hers with a blanket of comfort and warmth. She did not know how she would leave this man, but she knew that she must.

She also knew that she would not leave until the morning. This night belonged to her. It belonged to them.

"No, Raymond. Stay inside with me. I want a finger of brandy."

He laughed. "Since when have you become a drinker, Arabella?"

"Since you gave it up."

She drew him back into the house, making him follow her step by step into the sitting room that looked out over his mother's rose garden. Codington stared at her as she passed and she nodded to him in an attempt at civility. They had not spoken since he had revealed the letters. She supposed it was just as well. Pembroke would need him when she was gone.

She closed the door to the sitting room in Codington's face, sealing them off from the world. Pembroke ignored the brandy on the sideboard and stood staring out at the garden. A dish of roses had been cut and stood on the table before the fire. Arabella went and arranged them again, pleased that the sugar water she had poured had kept them fresh.

Cut flowers were not meant to last, but these might last until morning.

She lifted one and crossed the room to him, careful to keep the thorns from stabbing her. He turned to her when he felt her warmth beside him, and she reached up and ran the soft petals of the rose across his lips.

"Red roses are for love, are they not?" she asked.

"So I have always heard." His voice was husky when he answered her, strangled with longing and with all that they could not speak of again. He seemed to realize that to coax her to stay, to bully or cajole her, would leave them both with a headache. Though his longing to keep her was palpable, it matched her longing for him.

She pushed aside all thoughts of tomorrow and lowered the rose to her own lips. "I love you, Raymond. Now and forever. I think that love is eternal for me."

"You never aged in my mind, Arabella. You have always been that slender young girl who lost her bonnet in the river."

She covered the rose with her hand and tore the petals free of their thorny stem. She cast the stem onto the Queen Anne chair beside them and took his hand in hers.

She brought him with her into the room, to the soft rug that lay before the fireplace. There was no fire in the grate, but she wanted one.

She tossed the petals onto the carpet, heedless of the expensive weave. She knew that he could afford to buy another one. She also knew that once she was gone, he would keep this rug where it lay.

Codington ran the household well. Though the fire was not lit, it was built properly in the grate, ready for a match. She took a taper from the box on the mantle and lit the kindling. It did not smoke but caught right away as she nursed it carefully, allowing the flames to grow.

Pembroke watched her light the fire in the grate. "Is there anything you cannot do? Bake pastry, light fires with the first match you strike, steal my heart."

She turned to him and took his hand in hers. She pressed it against her breast so that he could feel her heart beating. "You have my heart, Raymond, for as long as I draw breath."

"An even trade then," he said.

"I cannot say, though I am a tradesman's daughter."

He kissed her then, his lips lingering on hers as if he knew she would not stay, as if he knew he could not keep her. She opened her mouth beneath his and touched his tongue with her own, beginning the warm dance that she had come to love, the dance that she would never make with anyone but him.

She pulled back long enough to help him take his coat off, but he would not strip any further than that.

"Here?" he asked, cocking one eyebrow at her.

"Here," she answered. "I want to smell the roses and the smoke of the fire together."

He kissed her again, his hands running up her arms, down her back, drawing her bottom against him so that she could feel his manhood rising. He teased her with his kisses, his lips toying with hers, only to pull away a little, the softness of his lips moving to glance over her cheek, her temple, to skim over her hair. All the while his hands moved over her, drawing her skirt up, even as he pulled her down onto the rug covered with rose petals.

"Codington will not like it," Pembroke said, his clever fingers searching for her through the linen of her shift.

"Good." She laughed, her breath leaving her lungs in one long sigh as he found what he sought.

She did not lie still beneath him. This time she wanted him to fall into pleasure with her. Her fingers were clumsy but determined as she fumbled with the fastenings of his trousers. He laughed at last and helped her, freeing his erection so that she could touch it, a swelling of heat in her hand.

She laughed for joy then too as he fell silent, his breath coming in gasps as he tried to control himself. She felt him fighting her and his own desire, and this time she would not let him.

She pressed her body against him, drawing him closer. The warmth of the fire covered her, raising a sheen of sweat along her temples and along the edge of her bodice. She thought she might suffocate from the tightness of her stays, but she knew she did not want to take the time to loosen them.

She raised her legs even as she coaxed Pembroke to lie on top of her. She raised her knees, pressing her slippered feet into the small of his back, bringing him inexorably down to her.

Pembroke laughed again, still breathless, and kissed her. "If that's what you want, Arabella, you shall have it. Never let it be said that I said no to a lady."

"You cannot say no to this lady," she answered

him, slipping her hand between them, drawing his erection to her sheath.

He took her hands and raised them above her head, sliding home in one stroke that left her gasping. Her body stretched to welcome him, and she laughed again, this time with a joy she never could have imagined even a week before.

He began to move inside her, but this time she could not bring him to do as she wished. She wanted him to move faster, to draw her deeper and deeper into pleasure, but he would not. He rose over her, her hands still clasped in his above her head, her breasts rising before him.

He kept her wrists pinned in one hand as he drew down the front of her gown with the other. He did not bother to unbind her laces but pulled down the front of her bodice so that her breasts were before him. He blew on one nipple and then the other until they were both rigid peaks. Arabella moaned as he took one into his mouth, laving it with the tip of his tongue, only to follow with his teeth.

He rode her even as he did this, his rhythm still slow, building a relentless pleasure within her. He feasted on her second breast then met her eyes, raising one brow. "Is that what you had in mind when you pulled me down onto this rug, Your Grace?"

She could not answer him, so she raised her hips to his, drawing him in deeper, tightening her inner muscles around him. It was his turn to lose the power of speech, and his control seemed to slip away with it. He drove into her, raising her hips to meet his, letting her hands go. She clutched his shoulders as he buried himself within her, using his body to draw out her bliss in one long spiral. She felt it then, the rising she had come to know only with him. This time, the spiral mountain rose higher, taking her with it.

She screamed his name, and he did not stifle her cries but seemed to revel in them. She did not care if Codington or anyone else heard her. She did not think of them at all, only of the man inside her, the man she loved more than her own life, the man she would give up to keep him safe from Hawthorne's madness.

It was Hawthorne who sobered her in the end. She clutched Pembroke close and listened to him gasp against her hair. They did not move for a long time but stayed before the fire, the heat of it rising.

Her new gown was likely ruined, but she did not care. She would keep it always, but she would never wear it again.

Her stolen season was over.

Twenty-four

ARABELLA SLEPT LATE THE NEXT MORNING, AND WHEN she woke, Pembroke was gone. She found a note on the bolster beside her head, saying that he had gone for a ride on Triton before heading to the village green for rehearsal. It said that he loved her.

She pressed the thick paper between her fingers, folding it carefully before slipping it into her traveling case.

The morning sun fell on the bed through the open curtains. A breeze came in from the park, carrying the scent of wisteria and roses as Arabella dressed in the blue worsted traveling gown. She had never worn clothes that she had bought with money of her own. She found the sense of freedom it gave her was almost intoxicating. Independence had its price, but it had its blessings, too.

She did not allow herself to think but took her satchel and her bag of guineas and walked downstairs. She met Codington in the hallway.

"There is a gig waiting to take you to the village, Your Grace." Codington's blue eyes rested on her bags. "It can take you no farther."

"I need borrow it only so far as that. Thank you, Codington."

"You are leaving him again," he said. This time she heard the accusation in his voice.

"I am hunted by a man he cannot stop. I will not have him killed by a madman because of me."

Codington did not seem impressed by her reasons, and they sounded weak in her own ears as she climbed into the gig, bundling her bags with her. Then she forced herself to remember Hawthorne's touch on her body and his knife in the dark. She would not bring him down on Pembroke, if she hadn't already.

She shut her mind down long enough to slip into the mail coach. It was empty save for herself and one old woman on her way to Bath. Arabella kept one bag beneath her feet and her guineas on her lap. She did not look out at Pembroke village as they passed through it, but she could hear the voices of the actors as they prepared for that day's work. She would miss the play. For some reason, this small sorrow was the thing that brought tears to her eyes.

They had not made it two miles before she heard a commotion on the seat above and felt the horses drawn to a stop. The old woman in the seat across from her woke then, blinking blearily at the light coming in from the leather tied across the window. Arabella pulled the leather flap aside to see what the matter was, only to find Pembroke outside the coach, staring back at her.

"Arabella, you are wasting these good people's time. Get out."

"I will not."

"My fiancée," Pembroke was saying to the man on the seat. "She's gotten cold feet. Women are a trial on the earth."

"Amen to that, my lord." The coachman spat for emphasis.

"I will not marry you."

Pembroke ignored her, opening the door. He took her bag of guineas first, and when she squawked in protest, he took her satchel, too.

"My Lord Pembroke!"

He did not answer her but tossed her bags into his phaeton.

"Hawthorne is coming," she said. "I must be gone."

"The duke, ma'am? He's spent the last night in Pembroke village, or so the gossip says." The coachman doffed his cap to her, accepting the gold Pembroke offered him.

"Good luck with that one, my lord. You'll need it."

The horses picked up their pace again, and Arabella was left standing in their dust with Pembroke beside her. She had never sworn an oath in her life, but she was tempted to in that moment.

"He's already there, Arabella. You can't use Hawthorne as your excuse. He's here and we'll face him together."

"He's a madman."

"So am I."

"He's a killer."

"I can claim that, too."

"In war, Raymond. But Hawthorne brought a knife into my bed. He will not let me go, and if you stand in his way, he will put that knife in you."

"He can try. He'll fail. God knows, all of the Usurper's armies couldn't kill me. I doubt one madman can."

Arabella was shaking. She gripped one gloved hand in the other, but she could not make them stop. Pembroke's touch was gentle as he took hold of her upper arms. He slid his own gloved hands down her arms as if to warm them. She felt her hands shaking even as he held them in his grip.

"I swear, Arabella, no harm will come to you as long as I draw breath."

"And when you don't?"

"Anthony will care for you."

She laughed, tears rising in her eyes. "I am not afraid for myself, Raymond. I am afraid for you."

"I think you're afraid of me," he said.

She froze, even her hands going still. He did not let go of them but looked down at her, his erstwhile lock of hair falling across his forehead and into his eyes.

"I think you fear me more than any man. More than your father. More than Hawthorne. I think you fear me because I am the only man with the power to hurt you. I'm the man who loves you."

Arabella tried to pull her hands away, but he would not let her go.

"Hear me out. You fear me because I can hurt you. Arabella, I tell you that you will not escape me by running away. The thought of me will haunt your days and all your nights until you drown yourself in a bottle. But a bottle won't soothe you. There is no place far enough away that the thought of me will not haunt you, no battlefield on earth can take the memory of me from you."

Arabella heard his own story on his lips and felt the
tears in her eyes spill onto her cheeks. She stopped
trying to pull away and listened to him.

"I love you, Arabella. And there is no doubt that love
is pain. And has the power to wound. But it also has the
power to heal. Let me heal you, Arabella. Come home."

She wept then but he did not draw her into his arms.
He did not try to cajole her with sweet touches or with
the power of his desire. He stood beside her, a friend,
the only friend she had, just as he had always been.

"I can be no man's chattel," she gasped. "Not even
for you."

"You will keep your own money. I'll sign away all
rights to it. I'll settle money on you, land, jewels, whatever you want, whatever makes you feel secure. I will
sign away my own life if it will comfort you. It belongs
to you already."

Arabella still wept, and finally he let go of her hands.
She hid her face in the cotton of her gloves, until he
offered her his handkerchief.

"Consider this, Arabella, and then I will be silent.
Have I ever given you my word and then not kept it?"

She wiped her eyes, her tears spent, the pain of
their passing like a storm that had gone. She breathed
deeply and looked up at him. His blue eyes were as
fathomless as the sea.

"No," she said. Her voice was so weak, she almost
could not hear it. But he could.

"Promise me something more," she said. "You
must leave your mistresses behind. No more gambling.
No more gaming. And no more whores."

He pressed his lips to hers once, swift and hard, as if

to seal a pact between them. He looked down at her, his own eyes red with unshed tears.

"I give you my word of honor, here and now, that I will never gamble again. I will not game, I will not whore. I will renounce my membership in the Hellfire Club. I will never touch another woman as long as I live. You are the only woman I want for the rest of my life. So help me God."

Arabella's arms went around him then, slipping beneath his coat so that she could feel all of his warmth. He clutched her hard, as if she might turn to insubstantial air and fade away. Only then did she know how much this day had cost him.

"I love you, Raymond. And our love is enough."

He kissed her, his lips lingering on her as if to seal her words between them. He drew back then and took her hand in his. He stripped away her cotton gloves and slipped his mother's ruby onto her hand. It gleamed in the summer sun like a promise, like hope.

"It's a good thing you agreed to marry me," Pembroke said. "The banns have been read already."

She laughed and dried her eyes. "You are incorrigible."

"A rogue of the first water. But your rogue, Lady Pembroke."

She kissed him. "My rogue. I like the sound of that."

"Good," he said. "You'll need the rest of your life to get used to it, I expect." He picked her up and placed her in the phaeton, as if afraid to let her move on her own. "Now let's go home."

"The duke is waiting for me," Arabella said.

Pembroke squeezed her hand. "He'll find that Anthony is waiting for him. I don't envy the bastard. He deserves whatever he gets."

❧

The players' morning without Oberon had passed in a flurry of set painting and Shakespearean language. Pembroke told her to sit at the foot of the stage and not to move without him. Lunch would soon be brought out to the tables under the trees on the village green, where the entire company would sit down together.

Arabella cast her gaze over the town square but could find no evidence of Hawthorne. She pressed her ring against her hand beneath the cotton of her glove. The weight of it was like a blessing, a promise of good things to come. She wished Hawthorne would reveal himself so that she could get the confrontation over with. He was a part of her past, and she was tired of fear. She did not know how she would escape him, or how Pembroke would. But she wanted it all to be over. She wanted to move on with her life.

She saw Angelique step out of the dressmaker's shop on the village high street, and she waved to catch her friend's eye. Arabella moved away from the stage to meet her, raising her gloved hand to shield her eyes from the noonday sun.

As Angelique approached from across the green, a shadow fell across Arabella's path. She felt a breath of the tomb on her spine, and she shuddered even before she looked up at the man who stood before her.

"Good day, Your Grace. I see that you traveled safely from London to Pembroke House. I understand that felicitations on your upcoming nuptials are in order," the Duke of Hawthorne said.

Arabella felt the ground tilt beneath her feet. She looked for Pembroke, but no one else had seen Hawthorne save for Cassie, who watched them together with a snide smile on her face.

A chill ran down the nape of her neck in spite of the warmth of the summer sun, as her mind spun in useless loops. All the plans she and Pembroke had made to face him, and her resolution to stand strong before him melted like ice in sunlight as she met his gray eyes. She stood looking up at the man who had threatened her life, unable to move or speak.

"I am sure the Earl of Pembroke is a decent match for you, though a step down from the duchy of Hawthorne."

Arabella could not find her tongue. It was as if she had swallowed it down. Angelique was at her side then, her head tilted up to meet the eyes of her adversary. Though her friend was quite tall for a woman, Angelique had to crane her neck to look at Hawthorne, who stood almost a foot taller.

"Good day, Your Grace," Angelique said.

Hawthorne bowed once to Angelique, but his eyes never left Arabella's face. He watched her for signs of weakness and perhaps for some indication that he might draw her away from the crowd and take her somewhere with him, so that they could be alone. Arabella found her voice, her back straightening beneath the onslaught of Hawthorne's gaze. She had dreaded this moment, and now it was here. She could not shrink or shy away. She must face her enemy.

Arabella had been afraid all her life. She had feared first her father and then her husband. The last few weeks that she had spent with Pembroke had shown her what it meant to live without fear. She was afraid, but she would not run away. Arabella would begin her new life as she meant to go on, and no one, not even the Duke of Hawthorne, would stop her.

Her voice was strong when she spoke, so assured that it sounded to her own ears like the voice of another. "I thank you, Your Grace, both for your kind words and for your concern for my well-being. As you see, I traveled to Derbyshire without mishap. No brigands greeted me along the road. I arrived quite unharmed."

"What good fortune," the duke said. He opened his mouth, but Arabella interrupted him.

"Indeed, Your Grace. The roads from London to Derbyshire are a good deal safer than the roads in Yorkshire. I stopped here, and I will stay here for the rest of my life."

Arabella was so intent on facing her adversary that she did not see or hear Pembroke approach until he stood beside her. "Good afternoon, Hawthorne. What brings you to Derbyshire? Come to see our production, I suppose. I had no idea that you had a taste for Shakespeare."

Hawthorne smiled then, and Arabella shuddered. He turned his gray gaze on her, and she saw again his lust for her, coupled with his contempt. The sight made her flesh crawl with revulsion. She felt Angelique's hand steady on her arm, anchoring her to the ground.

Pembroke stood on her other side, his hand warm on her arm. She found herself standing close to him, almost as if his stalwart body were shelter in a storm. She found her fear rising again, this time not for herself but for Pembroke, that he had drawn this man's ire. She wondered if she could bring it back onto herself.

"Hawthorne, it was good of you to come," she said, addressing the duke as a man would, as an equal. "But once you have signed over my property, our business together is done."

"But you have no property rights on the Duchy of Hawthorne," he said. "As soon as you marry another man—this Sunday the banns said"—Hawthorne looked to Pembroke then, raising one inquiring eyebrow— "the Hawthorne lands revert back to the estate."

"You will turn over my money to me directly. And then you will go back to London, and I will never see you again."

Hawthorne smiled. "What a charming story. You sound almost as if you believe it. But I will not let you go."

The air was as electric as before a fierce summer storm. Arabella shook with fear and mingled fury. If she held a pistol, Hawthorne would be dead. As it was, she feared that she would not be able to swallow the bile that had risen in her throat.

Lord Ravensbrook crossed the green, leaving his carriage drawn up before the inn. He strode out to meet the duke, and Caroline followed a step behind, bringing baby Freddie in her arms. Arabella wanted to call out to tell her to take her baby away from the poison of Hawthorne's gaze, but she returned her eyes to the man who wanted to wrest her freedom from her.

Freddie, like his father, seemed not at all intimidated by the foreboding duke. He took one look at the man before dismissing him, turning to lay his head on his mother's shoulder where he promptly fell asleep.

Anthony Carrington did not smile, nor did he speak, but stepped between her and the Duke of Hawthorne, staring the man down as if he were a member of the French cavalry, as if Hawthorne were a man he meant to kill. Caroline stood at her husband's back, cradling Freddie, flanking Arabella. Arabella saw an equally cold assessment going on behind her eyes, as if the Countess Ravensbrook might draw a dagger from her reticule and make short work of the duke herself.

"As charming as it is to see you, Hawthorne, I know that you will not be at liberty to attend the performance tomorrow night," Ravensbrook said. "I do hope you managed to bring the paperwork we spoke of when I was last in London. The papers that the duchess needs to sign in order to accept a lump sum in lieu of her widow's portion before she marries."

Dark spots swam before her eyes. Angelique's grip stayed firm on her arm, holding her up. Pembroke flanked her other side, drawing close as if to shield her from the piercing dagger of Hawthorne's gaze.

"Indeed, Ravensbrook. It is kind of you to mention our last meeting. I have the papers with me. I will send them up to Pembroke House with my man as soon as it is convenient."

Arabella almost laughed out loud. She did not play

chess, nor did she play at cards, but she knew a bluff when she heard one. She knew better than to think that Hawthorne would give her up so easily.

Lord Ravensbrook did not seem concerned. "Later this afternoon would do," Anthony said. "I will be happy to escort your man to the house myself."

Hawthorne's gray eyes hardened. "That will not be necessary."

He turned his gaze on Arabella as if the rest of the company did not exist, as if the Carringtons, Angelique, and Pembroke had vanished from the earth. She felt his eyes move over her body, leaving slime in their wake. His voice was cool, but his eyes glowed with fire. She wondered that no one else could see it. "It was lovely to see you again, Your Grace. I hope we meet again soon."

Angelique's hand tightened on her arm. At least one person had.

Arabella did not speak but watched him as warily as she would have watched a mad dog. She felt herself begin to shake. The duke showed no sign of anger or displeasure but bowed once to the whole company before striding in the direction of the public house.

Angelique's palm cupped her elbow, offering support. Only then did Arabella realize that her knees had given way. Pembroke wrapped one arm about her waist to hold her up. "We will take luncheon at the house," he said. "I have had quite enough of playacting for one day."

He nodded to Titania, and she waved him on. The actress had been watching the exchange as the rest of the acting company and the village had. There was speculation in her eyes as Pembroke led Arabella to his carriage. Titania's outspokenness was refreshing, but Arabella knew that for once she would not be able to bear the actress's pointed questions.

The party returned to Pembroke House, Angelique riding with Pembroke and Arabella in stony silence while Freddie returned to the house with his parents in his father's barouche. The baby continued to nap on his mother's shoulder, completely disinterested in the drama played out before him on the village green. They ate their luncheon in the rose garden, and in spite of the beauty of the day, Arabella could not shake the sense of foreboding that her meeting with Hawthorne had brought.

Early in the afternoon, a courier arrived with the legal documents from the Duke of Hawthorne, just as Ravensbrook had said it would. Arabella could not believe that it would be so simple. She looked past the courier, waiting to see Hawthorne step out from behind him.

Adjourning to the library, Lord Ravensbrook and Pembroke studied the papers for the rest of the afternoon, and neither could find a flaw. She sat at Pembroke's desk and signed them with the courier as witness. He was a clerk and a notary public from Oxford, come to Derbyshire for this sole purpose. The papers stated that she was entitled to fifty thousand pounds as well as a dower property in Shropshire and her father's estate, Swanson House, all the property that Pembroke had already agreed she could keep.

She stared at the thick document that held her signature as Pembroke sanded and sealed it for the courier to return to the duke. She could not quite believe that with the stroke of a pen she was free from Hawthorne. There still seemed to be a shadow over the day.

With her signature on that document, she was transformed from a woman with only a sack of gold to her name to an heiress.

Angelique wished her joy on her upcoming wedding but only after she perused the property agreement that Arabella and Pembroke had signed, which left her money and land in her own hands. Angelique smiled at Pembroke as she finished reading the document, a look of respect coming into her eyes. She did not stay for supper but left for the cottage she had rented in the village, the little house that Arabella had fallen in love with.

There was no formal dinner that evening, as Anthony and Caroline retired early, electing to take their dinner in their rooms. Arabella watched them as they climbed the staircase, hand in hand. Married for almost three years, they still seemed like newlyweds.

Pembroke sat with Arabella on a bench in his mother's rose garden as the quarter moon began to rise above the trees. He drew her close, his arm around her shoulders, his lips on her hair.

"This has been a bigger day than you bargained for when you woke this morning, Lady Pembroke."

Arabella laughed, relaxing against him, leaning on his shoulder. He shifted on the rosewood bench, lifting her into his lap. She wrapped her arms around his neck, pressing her lips to his cheek. "I am not your lady yet," she said.

"Indeed you are. I have your oath on it. Don't try to wriggle out of it now just because the curate hasn't blessed us."

Arabella laughed, but she felt almost as if Hawthorne watched them even then, the gray chill of his eyes touching her spine, making her shiver. She huddled closer to Pembroke, trying to shake the feeling off. Though they had signed legal documents setting her free, she knew that she had not seen the last of that hateful man.

She lay her head back against Pembroke's shoulder and looked up into the night sky filled with stars. She saw Cassiopeia and Andromeda wheel above their heads, and she thought of the day when she might show those stars to their children and teach them their names.

Raymond kissed her but did not devour her lips with his own, drawing back to look into her eyes. "You do not deserve a rogue like me, Arabella. But you have me. I am yours, for the rest of my life."

"And I am yours," she said.

"God help me," he quipped.

Arabella laughed, shoving her elbow in his side. He laughed with her, his lips playing over hers until all else was forgotten.

Twenty-five

MIDSUMMER'S EVE CAME AT LAST, THE SUN RIDING high for the longest day of the year. Dressed in a gown of robin's egg blue with a dark blue pelisse, Arabella rode to the village in the Carrington's barouche with Caroline and baby Freddie. The child had taken a long nap and was ready to greet the village ladies, all of whom loved to fawn over him.

Angelique met the carriage in front of the public house, taking Arabella's arm. Lord Ravensbrook had made inquiries and had been told by everyone he asked that the Duke of Hawthorne had left for London at first light. All the same, Angelique was not likely to leave Arabella's side that evening, and Arabella was grateful. She still felt a chill of fear, though she had faced the madman down. Caroline flanked her as well, baby Freddie on her hip.

"I have never known a woman of the *ton* to be so attentive to her child," Angelique said.

Arabella flinched, racking her brain for some innocuous comment to deflect the brusqueness of her friend's impolite observation. But Caroline did not take offense. She met Angelique's gaze, a sardonic smile lifting one corner of her beautiful mouth. "And you aren't likely ever to see such a thing. I am not a member of the *ton*. I simply married into it. I'm a Yorkshire woman. The London *ton* and I have little to do with one another."

Arabella closed her mouth and held her silence. Though she had been a duchess and had worn a coronet for ten years, she had never felt like a true member of the London elite either. She had spent all the years of her marriage separate and apart from London's balls and soirees, and now that she was marrying Pembroke, she intended to keep him far from the likes of those people. He would do better, and be happier, safe at home with her in Derbyshire.

But tonight, hearing of Pembroke's performance as Oberon in Titania's rustic production, the London *ton* had come to them.

Clusters of fashionable people stood here and there on the village green while their servants set up chairs and pavilions for them under the trees. Dressed in silks and satins as if they stood in a ballroom at Carlton House, these brightly colored birds had come to roost for the evening in Pembroke. The villagers eyed them warily, giving them a wide berth. No one wanted anything to do with the quality from London. Their own earl was enough for them.

The lords and ladies who had come all the way from the capital surveyed the village around them as if it was lower than the dirt beneath their feet. Arabella felt her anger rise at their arrogance. She wanted to send them away from the village that had been her home during the dark years of her childhood. The village had become her haven and now was her home again.

The ladies all stared at her, taking in her bright blue gown. A murmur went up through the crowd as the women discussed the fact that she was out of mourning a bare month after her husband's death. Arabella felt the sharp eyes of the *ton* on her, weighing her and finding her lacking. She felt another wave of anger rise in her breast. Where had all these people been during the bleak and friendless years of her loveless marriage? And who were they now to sit in judgment on her?

Angelique sensed her tension, pressing her arm in a show of support. She shook her head once, and Arabella reined her temper in. Her friend was right. To show her anger to these people was weakness. They may have come to watch the performance, they might sneer down their aristocratic noses at the people of Derbyshire and at her, but she did not need to stoop to their level. She would never be received in London now, and she did not care. Those people would be gone in a few days, and she would still be there, happy with Pembroke.

Arabella let Angelique lead her to their seats at the front of the makeshift theater. The play was to begin in half an hour, and Pembroke was nowhere to be seen. No doubt he was dressing in the public house with the rest of the players, donning the robes he would wear as Oberon, the Fairy King.

Caroline stiffened as a storm of whispering began to rise all around them. The members of the *ton*, who before had been busy looking down their noses at everything they saw, went from contemplating her gown to drinking in the sight of Angelique and Caroline walking with Arabella. The two women flanked her protectively, showing obvious solidarity.

The Carlton House set considered those two women to be mortal enemies, who had fought each other for the love of Lord Ravensbrook. Caroline had won that war, and the fact that she now walked casually and calmly so close to her old rival caused a great stir of gossip as the three women took their seats before the stage.

Angelique, never one to shrink in the face of gossip, reached across Arabella and took baby Freddie onto her lap. The baby cooed and cried out with joy, wrapping his fat fists in the necklace at her throat. She pried her diamonds out of his grasp, turning to smile over the assembled company as if holding her lover's child was the most natural thing in the world. The tide of whispers rose in a great wave, and Caroline laughed under her breath.

Anthony appeared in that moment, stepping out of the public house where he had been speaking with Pembroke. Like his wife, Lord Ravensbrook did not shrink from gossip, but neither did he acknowledge it. Anthony strode like Mars across the village green as if it were a field of war. He looked neither right nor left but sat down beside his wife, kissing her on the lips for all to see.

An audible gasp rose from the assembled ladies, and the local villagers applauded to see the earl greet his wife with such open affection. Anthony did not acknowledge the approbation of the locals, but Caroline smiled and waved to them.

Arabella glanced furtively at Angelique, expecting her to be mortified by the attention Anthony paid his wife. But Angelique had eyes only for the baby on her lap, who had started babbling at her in earnest. Angelique listened to Freddie very seriously, nodding her head all the while, occasionally murmuring, "Indeed!" as if the wisdom he imparted were pearls of great price.

A hulking naval man came to sit at Angelique's side, his long auburn hair tied in a queue at the nape of his neck. His Royal Navy uniform gleamed dark blue and gold in the slanting sunlight. Arabella gasped to see a perfect stranger appear beside her friend without so much as asking for permission to sit, but it seemed that the gentleman was no stranger. Angelique nodded in acknowledgement of his presence, raising one eyebrow.

"Good evening, James. I thought the tide was turning, and you needed to be gone."

"The tide is always turning, my lady. Wait twelve hours, and it will turn again."

The man's voice was deep and sweet, like mulled cider with honey mixed in it. Arabella gave her friend a questioning look, but Angelique ignored both James and herself in favor of the baby on her lap. Caroline peered down the row of seats to smile warmly at their new acquaintance, but Anthony ignored him completely.

"Forgive Countess Devonshire," the navy man said. "She is a noble savage with no manners but those used to seduce a man. Allow me to present myself. I am Captain James Montgomery, formerly of His Majesty's Navy, at your service."

"Good evening, Captain Montgomery. Any friend of Angelique's is welcome in our circle. I am Lady Arabella Hawthorne, and there you see the Earl and Countess of Ravensbrook."

Anthony had the civility to nod, though he did not spare a glance for James Montgomery. Caroline seemed of the same opinion as Arabella, that any fine-looking gentleman was worth welcoming. Caroline cut her eyes at Angelique while she greeted Captain Montgomery with a warm smile. "Good evening, Captain. What brings you to Derbyshire?"

Angelique turned her head to face him as baby Freddie made another grab for her necklace. She drew the diamonds from the baby's fat fingers once again, speaking all the while to the gentleman at her side. "Indeed, James. What brings you here?"

James Montgomery smiled at the woman beside him as if he knew her very well, far better than he would openly admit. Arabella was shocked to see a bit of color rise in Angelique's cheeks. Had Arabella not known it to be impossible, she would have thought that her best friend was blushing.

"Why, Countess Devonshire, like the rest of London, I am here to see the play."

In that moment, the music rose, the pounding of a snare drum mixed with the high notes of a fife. Anthony and James both reached for weapons at the sound of it, and Arabella remembered that drums and fifes were used in war. The play began then, and Arabella forgot the drama going on around her. She had eyes only for the makeshift stage as she waited for Pembroke to come into view.

He strode onto the boards as if he owned them, and indeed, very likely he had contributed to paying for them. His presence was as grand as any of the professional actors, his voice as strong, his deep tones carrying over the audience, villagers and nobility alike. He was dressed in blue and gold, his robes like something a Turk might wear, complete with pantaloons and a scimitar at his hip. But instead of making him look ridiculous, these clothes transformed him into a king, or perhaps it was he who transformed them.

Though she had sat through countless rehearsals and knew every line that he would speak, something about the lamps lit along the foot of the stage, the greasepaint, and the costumes transported her to another world. Arabella was drawn into Shakespeare's dream until it became her own. She watched the foolish young lovers fall under an enchantment. She watched the rustics perform their own play, tears of laughter streaming down her face. When the show ended, she rose to her feet, applauding with the rest of the audience as Pembroke and Titania took their bows at the head of the company. Pembroke looked past the footlights to find Arabella and smiled.

The sweetness of that smile in the midst of the chaos of the curtain call squeezed her heart. He was at her side in the next moment, drawing her close, pressing a kiss to her lips. His greasepaint came off on her cheek, but she found she did not care. The rest of the world faded away until there was only Pembroke.

"I love you, Arabella."

He kissed her again, and this time she heard the applause of the people around her, their voices no longer calling out to the actors onstage but to her and Pembroke. Arabella blushed but waved to the villagers, who cheered for her happiness.

The fashionable members of the *ton* did not join in, but a few scattered gentlemen clapped halfheartedly. The ladies drew their fans close to cover their mouths as they whispered together, pouring poison into each other's ears. Arabella found that she did not care what any of them thought. She would make her life here in Derbyshire among her own people, and let the *ton* of London hang.

Pembroke left her as the actors dispersed to change their clothes. She sat on her theater seat and watched as Titania's underlings from London began to tear the stage apart. Most of the troupe would leave on the morrow after her wedding. Titania said the company was heading to Leeds next and then on to Manchester in their tour of the North. Titania would not travel with them. Like Pembroke, she had performed only for this one night.

The villagers had lit the Midsummer bonfire, and Arabella walked with Caroline and Angelique to see it. Their party had grown now, with Anthony flanking the women on one side and James Montgomery on the other. Baby Freddie, still awake though the sun had almost set, was cooing at his father and at James as the mood struck him. Anthony lifted his son in his arms, gathering him up from Angelique.

James took the opportunity to draw closer to Angelique, taking her into the shadows with him. Arabella watched them go, wondering if this captain was Angelique's latest amour.

The miller drew his wife toward the bonfire to dance with him, as did the baker and the smith. Arabella turned her eyes from the darkness into which Angelique had vanished and watched as her neighbors joined in the circle around the fire. Following the tradition as old as the druids, one by one each couple leaped over the small blaze, the women gathering their skirts high in one hand and taking their husbands' hand with the other. The young courting couples began to do the same. Caroline left baby Freddie in Arabella's arms before she took Anthony's hand and jumped over the Midsummer bonfire with him.

Arabella laughed at her friends' antics, and baby Freddie shrieked with delight. Members of the *ton* stared and whispered, standing far back from the blaze while the people of Pembroke village in turn ignored the lords and ladies. Pembroke was at her side then, taking Freddie from her arms and handing him to his mother. She smiled up at the man she had loved for most of her life, the man she would marry tomorrow.

"Will you leap the fire with me, Arabella?"

"I would, even if it were high enough to burn us both."

"Well, until they put the greenwood on, it will not burn as high as that."

The heat of the blaze made the blood rise in her face, and her skin became damp as they stepped closer to it. She raised her skirts in one hand and squeezed Pembroke's hand in the other. Together, they made a running start then leaped over the flames just as the wind caught them, making the blaze rise. Arabella felt the heat of the fire on her legs, and a surge of

fear threatened to overwhelm her, but then she and
Pembroke came to rest on the other side, without a
thread of their clothes or a hair on their heads singed.

Pembroke laughed, lifting her into his arms. The
village cheered them once more as he led her into
the circle where the other villagers were dancing.
Anthony and Caroline stood outside the group of
locals, forming their own tiny circle with their little
son. But Arabella and Pembroke took their place
among the people of Pembroke, as all thoughts of the
Londoners, of Hawthorne, of the world beyond that
village vanished with the rising smoke.

Twenty-six

ARABELLA DID NOT RETIRE AS SOON AS SHE RETURNED to Pembroke House but sat alone in the drawing room, waiting for Raymond to come home. They would marry in the morning. She almost could not believe it. She should be panicking, thinking of some way to run and preserve her freedom. But she found that as much as she cherished her independence, she cherished her freedom to love him more. She would never be happy without him. So she would stay, and marry him, and take what came.

She stood in the open door to the garden, breathing in the scent of the roses his mother had planted so many years before. Most of the candles were already put out, but one branch burned by the door, ready to light her way to her bedroom with Pembroke beside her.

Caroline and baby Freddie had returned with her in Anthony's barouche, and both now slept, tucked away in their suite. Pembroke and Anthony had stayed in the village, drinking with the miller and the mayor, discussing plans for a new thoroughfare through the town to be built sometime next year.

Angelique had left the Midsummer festival with her sea captain. Arabella would see her in the morning at the church, for Angelique was standing up with her, just as Anthony was standing up as witness for Pembroke. She hoped she had half a moment to inquire who James Montgomery was and who he was to Angelique.

As Arabella was musing on Angelique's penchant for taking inappropriate lovers, she heard a crunch of gravel in the rose garden beyond the window. She could not see him in the dark, but she was sure Pembroke had come home at last. She moved back into the room, sitting down by the hearth though no fire burned there. She waited patiently, her hands folded in her lap, for the man she loved to step into the room.

A figure stepped through the French doors that led to the garden. The man who stood there for one long moment was tall and thin. Though his face was in shadow, she knew him at once.

"Hawthorne," she said.

Her enemy stepped into the circle of feeble light. "I prefer the title 'Your Grace.' I believe I have earned it."

The signing of her new inheritance agreement had been a farce. It was too good to be true, that he would simply let her leave him, simply let her go.

Hawthorne carried no bouquet of poisoned flowers with him this night. His gloved hands were empty, their clear white kidskin glowing against his evening clothes of midnight black. All Arabella could see of him were those hands in their dyed leather and his face.

"You have defied me for the last time, Arabella. I have been more than reasonable, but my patience has come to an end."

"What man of reason comes to rape a woman in her own bed and threatens her with a knife?"

Arabella still had not moved from the settee. She could not believe the words that kept rising to her tongue and falling from her mouth, unbidden.

To agitate a man who was potentially violent was foolhardy. The rules of survival had been drummed into her by her childhood. Hide your feelings. Wait for the man to leave. If he will not leave, run away. If you cannot run away, brace yourself as best you can for the blows that you know are coming.

But now she did none of these things. Instead, she rose to her feet and faced him, smoothing the silk skirt of her gown.

"I do not make threats," Hawthorne said. "You left me in your husband's bed, alone. Did you think I would require no recompense for that? You will leave your lover behind, and you will come with me."

"I will not."

"Then I will have you here."

Arabella moved quickly, not toward the light and the hallway as he expected, but toward the darkness of the rose garden. She was quick, but he was quicker. Hawthorne's long fingers wrapped around her arm, drawing her close to his body, so that she could smell the cedar his clothes had been pressed in. She raised her hands to strike at his face with her nails, trying desperately to pull away, but he was too strong for her.

He drew her close, his breath on her cheek. She

could feel his arousal beneath his trousers through the thin silk of her gown. She also felt the sheath of his knife tucked away in the breast pocket of his coat. She reached for it, fumbling against his chest, until he caught her hand in his and bent her arm behind her.

The pain shot up from her elbow to her shoulder, and she cried out as he bore her down on the hearthrug where she and Pembroke had once made love. He used her body to trap her arm behind her, leaving both of his hands free. She felt his fingers tearing at the bodice of her gown. She heard the silk rip even as she felt the night air on her breast. He drew the knife from his pocket slowly then and ran the edge of the blade over her.

She screamed, and he slapped her, the knife nicking her skin so that a well of blood rose on the curve of her breast. She held her tongue then, knowing that he would kill her before help came.

He reached down to draw her skirts up, and she lay quiet under him as if he had conquered her. She waited until his vigilance had waned, as he began to unfasten his trousers. She reached for his hand then, the one that held the knife. She kissed it, running her tongue over his thumb. His eyes met hers and he shuddered with pleasure, fumbling at his clothes so that he might enter her faster.

She bit him then, digging her teeth into his hand until she drew blood. And in the same moment, she turned the knife away from her breast, toward his heart.

She missed and caught his shoulder instead.

He howled with pain and backhanded her once,

but then he was lifted off and away from her, his weight gone as suddenly as it had fallen on her. She sat up, drawing the ruined bodice of her gown over her breasts as she watched Pembroke drag the duke by the throat to the settee.

Pembroke's large hand cut off Hawthorne's air. He used his body to weigh the duke down, taking the handle of the knife and driving it deeper into Hawthorne's shoulder. The duke made a strangled sound of pain with what little air he had left.

"If I ever see you again, in London, or in the country, by the seaside, or by the Thames, I will kill you. I will not be merciful as I would have been tonight. I will make it slow. You will beg for death before the end. I will not use some puny blade meant to menace women. I will bring my own. Be warned. This is the only warning you will ever get."

Pembroke got to his feet, and the duke lay gasping on the cushions. Ravensbrook stepped into the room, circling Pembroke carefully, moving between his friend and the duke.

He need not have bothered with his caution though, for Pembroke turned to Arabella, taking off his coat to cover her with it, pressing his handkerchief to the blood on her breast.

"Dear God, he cut you."

Pembroke sprang across the room, and Hawthorne flinched away from the death he saw in his eyes. Ravensbrook caught his friend around the middle and held him back.

"You can't kill him here. Wait until later. There are too many people in the village. There will be talk, and not even the Prince Regent will be able to save you. You have to let him go."

Pembroke did not answer. For one horrible moment, Arabella was afraid he had forgotten how to speak. Then he drew a ragged breath and shook Ravensbrook off.

"All right. I'll kill him later. But get him out of my sight."

Caroline stepped out of the shadows then, a knife in her hand. She watched Hawthorne as Ravensbrook came to take him up. When the duke tried to remove his own knife from his shoulder, Caroline said, her voice laden with contempt, "No, *Your Grace*. Leave it where it is, unless you want the next one lodged in your throat."

Hawthorne did not speak but blinked at her, the reflection of his pain mirrored on his face, blood welling between his hand, pressed to the open wound. His knife stood out from his shoulder, its steel handle glinting in the candlelight.

Ravensbrook took him by his good arm and dragged him out through the front door, careful to catch the blood in Hawthorne's coat so that it would not stain the rug in the front hall.

Pembroke cradled Arabella close to his heart, making sure that she had room to breathe. "I will go after them and kill him now, if you wish it."

"No," Arabella said, reaching out to touch Raymond's face. "Let him go. It's our wedding day."

The clock struck midnight in the hallway. Pembroke pressed his lips to hers gently, keeping his great body between her and the rest of the world.

Pembroke lifted her, holding her against his chest. He moved to carry her from the room, to take her upstairs where he would place her in their soft bed, but Arabella stopped him with a touch.

"Thank you for your help," she said to Caroline.

The Countess of Ravensbrook smiled, lifting the skirt of her evening gown so that she might sheath her long knife in her boot. Her weapon secured, she met Arabella's eyes. "I wish I had gotten here sooner. But what little I did was my pleasure."

ACT IV

"One turf shall serve as pillow for us both,
One heart, one bed, two bosoms, and one troth."

A Midsummer Night's Dream
Act 2, Scene 2

Epilogue

ARABELLA SLEPT WELL IN PEMBROKE'S ARMS, BUT WHEN she woke just before dawn, he was already gone. A rose from his mother's garden lay beside her on his pillow, the first thing she saw as she woke on their wedding day. The horrors of the night before had followed her into her dreams, but Raymond's touch had comforted her when she thrashed in her sleep. He would be there all the nights to come.

Rose, newly promoted to lady's maid, came in with tea and toast and helped her bathe. Her wedding gown lay on the bed ready to draw on, a light blue silk the same color as her eyes, fashioned by Mrs. Bonner, and a white bonnet trimmed with lace, white roses, and cornflowers. Arabella stood looking at herself in the full-length mirror. A patch of morning sun fell across the carpet, catching the sheen of silver thread woven into the embroidery on her slippers.

Her cheeks were not pale this morning but glowed pink, and her eyes shone with joy. She touched the pearl choker around her neck, the something borrowed that Angelique had given her to wear that day.

The strands of pearls bound with a diamond clasp had once belonged to Angelique's mother, and the pearls were so white and fine that Arabella was almost afraid to wear them. They were also her something old, for they had been strung during the Old Regime, long before Napoleon had ever shown his face.

Angelique waited for her at the door of the parish church. All the village had come to welcome the bride, waving bright ribbons strung on slender branches shorn of leaves. Arabella waved back at them, and Caroline smiled as she kissed her before she went to sit with baby Freddie and his nurse at the front of the church. Only Angelique walked before her down the aisle.

Pembroke was dressed in midnight blue superfine, a coat so tight that every muscle of his upper arms was bared to the eyes of the crowd. His cravat was snow white, his waistcoat silver and dark blue. His hair was trimmed for the occasion, but the long lock was there as it always was, falling in a shadow of dark blond across his forehead so that he had to push it out of his eyes. As Arabella took her place beside him at the altar, she raised one gloved hand and pushed that errant lock of hair back, only to watch it fall again.

She laughed, and then he kissed her before they turned to the scandalized curate to hear the service read over them, to exchange their vows. Titania and a few of her actors had decided to stay as well, though most of the troupe had moved on to Leeds early that morning, Cassie included.

Captain Montgomery sat in the front of the church, his eyes never wavering from Angelique. Arabella was far gone in her contemplation of the man she loved, of the joy of marrying him at last, but she was not so far gone that she did not see the auburn-haired man watching her friend as if she were the answer he had been seeking to the only question worth asking.

Angelique for her part ignored him, just as she ignored Anthony where he stood beside Pembroke. But Arabella knew her friend well and saw a blush rising in her cheeks, a sparkle in her eyes that looked suspiciously like hope.

Their vows made and blessed, Pembroke defied convention and propriety and kissed her. Baby Freddie cooed, then squealed so loudly that Caroline and his nurse offered sweetmeats to shush him. He ignored them both, waving his fat fists in triumph as Pembroke and Arabella walked past him down the aisle, out into the warmth of the midsummer day.

Their wedding breakfast was not in the formal dining room but was held on the lawn of Pembroke House. All the villagers came to celebrate the wedding, which became almost an extension of the Midsummer festivities of the night before. There was wine and mead for all who wanted it, though after one glass of champagne, Arabella stuck to cider.

Angelique stayed at the party until mid-afternoon, Captain Montgomery never far from her side. Her friend left, saying that she had pressing business in Shropshire that she must attend to.

"Keep the pearls for the moment," Angelique said. "They will give me an excuse to return to Derbyshire to see you."

"You need no excuse," Arabella said. "You are

always welcome in my home. You need not even send
word. Just come."

Arabella watched her friend and her sea captain
drive away, feeling bereft for a moment.

"I hope he is good to her," she said.

Pembroke drew her close, pressing a kiss to the top
of her head. She had long since taken her bonnet off,
and the sun had begun to freckle her nose. She was a
country woman now indeed, since she did not notice
or care.

"I hope she leaves him his manhood intact," he said.

They climbed the staircase to the sanctuary that was
her bedroom, done in soft blond woods and ice blue
silk. They were going to sleep in that room for the
rest of their lives, for Pembroke was abandoning the
master suite down the hall. Blueprints lay on the table
by the fireplace, plans for the expansion of her room
that would soon begin.

Arabella entered their room to find a bed of
cambric laid before the fire. Rose petals were strewn
on the soft nest, and there was a small fire in the
hearth, giving off light and warmth.

"I know it is summer," Pembroke said. "But I
wanted to make love to you as my wife for the first
time by this fire."

Arabella did not speak but drew him close, her arms
rising to circle his neck, her fingers delving into the
silky softness of his hair. His mouth was on hers then as
he drew her gown from her body, laying the delicate
silk aside, draping it carefully over an armchair. He
took off his own clothes, and she watched him wearing
just her stockings and Angelique's pearls. Pembroke

stood looking at her for a long moment before he took the pearls off and laid them aside as well.

He moved naked across the room to a box he had set by the bed. He brought the box closer and laid it in her hands.

A deep ruby pendant sat nestled in velvet, already strung on her mother's gold chain. The ruby was as large as a robin's egg and shone in the firelight like the heart's blood of some mythical dragon, like the one St. George had slain so long ago.

"It was my mother's," Pembroke said.

Arabella raised her hand and the ruby on her finger flashed in the light of the fire. The two stones were perfectly matched and had been part of a set. "There are earrings, too," Pembroke said, "and a bracelet. But I wanted you to have this first tonight."

Arabella could not speak for the tears in her eyes, so Pembroke fastened the necklace around her throat before laying her down on the bed of soft cambric. They lay naked together in the firelight, and Pembroke did not tarry with love play but pressed himself into her as if to seal their vows again.

Arabella gasped at the onslaught of his body on hers, of his body in hers, but she was ready to receive him. Her own desire rose like an incantation out of thin air to slide along her skin, to bury itself in her innermost parts just as Pembroke buried himself in her. She moaned and rose with him as his body pounded into hers, feeling as if she were a wave of the sea, being pressed again and again against the shore.

Pleasure uncoiled within her, raising her up only to cast her down once more, breathless, with Pembroke's body over hers, lying heavy against her. His breath was harsh in her ears, his body a great weight on her limbs. She smiled and stretched beneath him, feeling the delicious lassitude that would soon turn once again to desire. The fire warmed her where Pembroke did not, and she lay back against the soft carpet and bedding, contentment filling every curve of her body and every limb, overflowing in her heart.

"I am sorry I was rough with you," Pembroke said when he could speak again.

Arabella laughed, pressing her lips to his jaw. His stubble had begun to grow back, and in his ardor, he had forgotten to shave before coming to her. He had carried her into the house and up the stairs to their room. He had not stopped for anything, and Arabella knew that she would have had their wedding night no other way.

"I like you rough," she said. "I want you any way you'll have me, Pembroke. I am yours, now and forever."

He smiled at her, tears in the blue of his eyes. He raised himself on one elbow, fingering the ruby that lay nestled between her breasts. "Forever is a long time," he said.

He lifted her in his arms and carried her toward the soft feathered mattress of their marriage bed. "Our love will last at least that long," she said.

He kissed her, his lips lingering over hers. "Longer."

Acknowledgments

As always, in the creation of a novel, there are many people to thank. I must begin with the amazing editing team at Sourcebooks Casablanca, Leah Hultenschmidt, Aubrey Poole, Kimberly Manley, the marketing team, the publicity team, especially Beth Pehlke. To say that these people made the book infinitely better is utterly true, and yet the words fall short.

I also thank Margaret O'Connor, who has been with me since the beginning of this journey, when she took *The Queen's Pawn* in hand and helped me make it what it became. Here's to more storytelling, in more foreign lands, and to telling the best stories we know how to tell.

And as always, I must thank my family, my mother, Karen, my father, Carl, my brother, Barry, for their unending and unwavering support. Language falls short once again, and I can only hope that the inadequate words "thank you" are enough.

My early readers are also my friends… many thanks to Laura Creasy and LaDonna Bollinger, who give their time and their attention to all my novels in their early stages and who help make them shine. Thank you to my beloved friends who stand behind me and put up with me, even when I am delving into yet another rewrite. Marianne Nubel, Amy Pierce, Troy Pierce, Vena Miller, Heather Wilson, Susan Randall, may you be blessed a thousandfold, as much as you have blessed me.

And thank you to my Facebook and Twitter friends, and to all the people who read this book. Without you, I would be nowhere, telling stories in the dark.

About the Author

After years of acting in Shakespeare's plays, Christy English is excited to bring the Bard to Regency England. When she isn't acting, roller skating, or chasing the Muse, Christy writes romantic novels (*How To Tame A Willful Wife*, *The Queen's Pawn*, *To Be Queen*) from her home in North Carolina. Please visit her at www.ChristyEnglish.com.